THE CRIMSON HORSESHOE

Jim Allard rode into Antelope Valley with what looked like a good job ahead—a peaceful job. Allard was tired of guns and killing. But a deadly range war was brewing. Both sides tried to hire Allard's gun. Then they ambushed his only friend and pinned it on him. Jim Allard had to fight back...

THE CRIMSON HORSESHOE

Peter Dawson

First published in the United States 1941
By Dodd, Mead & Company, Inc
And in the British Commonwealth 1941
By Collins

This hardback edition 1997
By Chivers Press
By arrangement with
Golden West Literary Agency

ISBN 0 7540 8001 3

British Library Cataloguing in Publication Data available

Printed and bound in Great Britain by
Redwood Books, Trowbridge, Wiltshire

1

FROM this high pass at aspen level, the foothills of the La Bajadas made an uneven but majestic downward sweep from the peaks in three directions, to the west, the south and east. Some were smooth and rounded and stippled by the emerald green of open pasture and the darker shade of pine; others, a jagged and barren maze of chimney-rock, steep-walled canyon and butte until finally, belted by an unheaved mass of crumbling rock and sand, the smaller undulations reluctantly gave way to the sparse-grass flats that edge the desert.

Around the long finger of these abrupt heights, the right of way of the Sierra and Western made a long desert-level sweep to the southward. Except for this tight two-hundred-and-forty-mile loop, the rails crossed horizon-to-flat-horizon in one uninterrupted string-straight line. At the foot of the poorer eastern slope, the way station of Cody marked the beginnings of the long detour. To the west, the town of Sands lay at its ending. Thus, for most of one day, passengers in the hot stuffy coaches found a pleasant change from the endless sage-studded monotony of the middle Arizona landscape and scanned the cool heights enviously, a few wondering why the rails couldn't have gone straight on and up and through these hills to give a welcome, if but temporary, relief from the desert's blistering heat.

The rider on the claybank, who had before dawn broken camp in the low eastern foothills, looked down from the pass this late afternoon and idly noticed, among other things, that long break in the railroad's straight line.

It reminded him of a slender fragile horseshoe—a horseshoe heated rosy-red by the forge. For the rails caught the sun's late glare and reflected it brightly in a crimson line circling the hills. He judged, accurately, that a mind with foresight and imagination could have seen that the laying of perhaps fifty miles of rail, the throwing up of some trestles and the gouging out of a few abrupt slopes could have saved much in time and money. Then, because he was engrossed in other things, he forgot the railroad.

What took his attention and held it the longest was the faint dark blotch against the lighter shade of the flats flanking the railroad before it made its gradual swing into the west at the heel of the shoe. A less experienced eye could not have defined that shadow at this distance as being a town. He scanned the maze of foothills that lay between him and the town and concluded finally that he would have another camp to make before he reached his goal, which was Sands.

He had taken his look at the country below from behind a high finger outcropping. The shadows were cool at this height and it would have been more comfortable to rein his stallion out into the fading sunlight. But he didn't. And when he went on down across the boulder field he took advantage of each bit of cover and put the claybank quickly and precisely across the open ground, wasting no time getting into the concealment of the aspen trees immediately below the pass.

It was also significant that, farther on, he kept to the timber whenever possible, making long detours to avoid exposing himself. His high-built frame was erect, almost tense, in the saddle. And his eyes, shaded by the wide brim of his Stetson, kept a ceaseless shifting vigil ahead and to either side.

With dusk beginning to thicken about him, he crossed a trail that would have taken him directly down out of the hills. Ignoring it, even being careful not to cross it until bare rock blanked out his claybank's sign, he struck into the beginnings of a twisting gorge that grew more steep-walled as he went on. He followed the gorge for three miles, until it was nearly dark, and finally halted.

Habit made him careful about his camp, for this was strange country. He off-saddled in a narrowing of the gorge where a thicket of scrub oak and cedar would hide his fire from sight below. A quarter mile along his back trail there had been ample feed for the claybank; it was scanty here. But even the fact that the animal had carried him a hundred and forty miles in the last thirty-six hours, and could use good graze, didn't outweigh the need for his own concealment. He staked out the stallion barely seventy feet back from the oak thicket.

It was habit again that made him light his fire of tinder-dry, smokeless cedar with a yellow dog-eared telegram and thus destroy the last physical evidence that would identify him or explain his devious way into this country. And, after hungrily wolfing his meal, it was his capacity for anticipating trouble that made him uncinch the two sagging shell belts from his waist, remove the pair of cedar-handled .38 Colts from holsters and take down first one and then the other. He was meticulous in the manner in which he set about cleaning and oiling them.

While he worked on the second gun, its empty frame in his hand, a thick cedar branch that held up one edge of his frying pan burned through and dumped part of his coffee into the hot coals. He came up out of his crouch at the sound of the hissing liquid spilling; a step took him to the fire.

He was stooping over, reaching for the pan, when the brittle snap of a twig in the brush below sounded into the night's utter stillness. On the heel of that sound he cocked his long body for the backward step that would take him within reach of his second weapon, lying loaded on his saddle blanket behind him.

He turned his head as he took that step and saw instantly that he was too late. Ten yards away, his shadowy outline imprinted against the blacker screen of cedar, stood a squat-shaped man with a leveled gun in his hand. Details were blurred by the darkness, yet he knew that the weapon lined at him was cocked and that a finger touched its trigger.

For a brief interval he stood turned rigid by the futility of holding a useless gunframe. At length, he drawled evenly. "Howdy."

He saw his one word visibly strike this intruder, for the man straightened a trifle from his stooped posture. Then, strangely enough, the lined weapon dropped and hung straight down and the man said in a voice hushed by sheer amazement, "Money says I'm seein' wrong! Is it you, Jim?"

It took Jim two seconds to place that long-unheard voice. And in that brief space of time all the tautness went out of him and a smile broke the severe lines of his lean, weathered face.

"Your eyes were always good, Billy," he said. "Come on up."

Billy holstered his weapon and took three slow steps that put him barely into the light. There he hesitated.

This involuntary gesture of wariness made Jim say quickly, "Come ahead."

"Your fire," Billy said. "You better come down out of the light."

The harsh, strained quality in the man's voice prompted Jim to roll the cylinder of his Colt into its frame and thrust home the pin. He leaned down and scooped into his palm the five cartridges lying on his blanket; and as he walked out of the light toward his visitor he dropped the shells through the gun's loading gate in a practiced quickness.

Billy didn't offer to shake hands. He backed farther into the shadows. The lack of a greeting, the furtiveness of those backward steps, made Jim say, "Last time I saw you, four years ago, you claimed you were through with a diet of night air, Billy. Who's followin' you?"

"I don't know . . . yet." Billy stood there motionless for an interval, head cocked to one side, listening. His forehead under under his Stetson brim was beaded with perspiration; his brown eyes were dilated in obvious fear. He went on: "I saw you cut across that bench above about sundown. Didn't know but what you'd be forted up here waitin' to stop me. So I left my jughead below and legged it."

"Didn't you remember the claybank?"

"Thought I did. But it was hard to believe it was you. And I ain't takin' chances tonight, Jim."

"So I see," Jim said.

"I had to come through here tonight," Billy went on, his words spilling out in a relieved rush. "It's the only safe way through the pass. If I ain't in Cody by sunup, hoppin' a freight, they'll soon nail my hide out to tan."

Jim took this in soberly. At length, he asked, "Feel like tellin' me about it?"

Billy swore, softly, feelingly. "Why not?" Abruptly he hesitated, regarding Jim with a higher quality of alarm edging his glance. "You ain't headed down there, Jim?"

Jim nodded and waited.

The other asked warily, "Any special reason?"

What Jim remembered of Billy made him answer, truthfully, "Hugh Allard wired me to be in Sands today. I'm late."

Billy breathed almost inaudibly, "Goddlemighty!" From far below, muted by the distance, came the eerie hoot of an owl. The small man's square features stiffened and shaped a mirthless grin. "Hear that? It might be the real thing, then again it might not. They're headed this way and I've got to get the hell out of here!" His attention was once more directed to his friend, severely, as he said, "I've often wondered if you were kin of Hugh Allard's. Some would claim you ought to be proud of it. I don't agree."

"I'm obliged for the warnin'. Never laid eyes on him. My father was his cousin." By way of explanation, Jim added, "He offers good money."

"Sure! He's got it to offer. But take my word for it and let him stay a stranger! Throw your hull on that claybank and ride out of here with me. Today, down there, they lit the fuse for a war their kids won't finish! It's my hard luck I saw it done."

"Let's have it, Billy. What's wrong?"

Once again Billy stiffened into a listening attitude. Once again the night's utter stillness seemed finally to reassure him. At length he queried, "Then you're stayin'?"

Jim Allard's wide shoulders lifted in a shrug. "I'm broke, Billy, flat broke. A poor man can't choose."

Billy seemed to sense the futility of carrying his point. He knew this Jim Allard as well as any man would ever know him; what he remembered of Jim brought a wry, thinly etched smile to his lips. "You're still the same," he said. "Damned if I wouldn't like to be here to see how you go about it!"

"Go about what?"

"First, Spade drifted in a while back. Him and some of the boys."

Jim Allard's brows lifted in a quizzical expression. "Which might mean anything," he intoned. "I thought you were finished with Spade Deshay."

"I've seen him—once. We had our understandin' and he's let me alone. I told you before I was all through with that, the same as you."

"I'll take your word for it, Billy. What else?"

Billy hesitated for a moment, then exploded, soft-voiced, "You can have it all—all I know. Damned if I'll see a friend of mine ride into this thing blind!" He paused to reach a hand up to his vest pocket.

He was that way, arm across his barrel-like chest and mouth open to speak, when his whole frame jerked convulsively. Jim Allard, watching, saw a blue hole suddenly appear on the back of Billy's outspread hand as his body went rigid. And as Billy fell, stumbling backward and with his broken hand groping wildly for something to break his fall, the brittle crack of a rifleshot shuttled down from a point high above along the gulch's climbing wall.

What Jim Allard did then was prompted by sheer instinct. He lunged for the oak thicket ten feet away, throwing himself flat to the ground beneath the cover of the screening branches. And when he lay prone, his glance directed above, his gun was cocked, ready.

He wasn't a split second too soon, for as his glance whipped above it was in time to see a blossoming wink of powder flame in the darkness up there. The second bullet slammed into Billy's frame and made it jerk loosely, as though a powerful hand had suddenly started to roll him over and then as quickly stopped.

Jim Allard dropped his sights onto that now blacked-out target and thumbed three thought-quick shots. The low-pitched, pulsating explosions of his weapon drowned out the sound of the rifle's third explosion and set up a racket between the gorge's walls that ripped its way flatly down across the corridor below. Before the echoes had died out Jim Allard had moved deeper into the thicket, at a crouch now and punching the empties from the loading gate of the Colt. All at once a scream, high-pitched, awful, cut clearly into the stillness and died as quickly as it began.

The next ten seconds would have weighed on any man. They held Jim Allard's unblinking gaze riveted to the spot above. To one side of him he heard Billy gasp thickly, with a rattle to his breathing that could be brought on by nothing but a constriction deep in his lungs. He wanted to look at Billy, couldn't, as his senses strained their attention to make out any hint of a movement above.

Finally it came, a sound only. It might have been a pebble sliding downward—or the scrape of a branch along a man's bullhide chaps. Still Jim Allard waited. Suddenly his attention was rewarded—the wispy branches of a *chamiza* bush far above bent to one side and stirred as though moved by a stiff breeze. Then a black, shapeless shadow slid out from behind the bush and rolled downward, loosing sand and pebbles in its fall and leaving in its wake a faint cloud of dust turned gray in the starlight.

The shadow took on a man's shape. His loose, broken roll ended within twenty feet of where Jim Allard crouched. The gnarled trunk of a low-growing cedar a few feet up the slope stopped his fall at last and he lay jack-knifed across it, legs lined down one side of its trunk, arms and torso and head limply motionless and downhanging from the other.

He was dead, from a bullet that had torn away one side of his face and driven upward into his brain. Jim, stepping over to take that in at a glance, left the body untouched and strode quickly to where Billy lay.

The bullet that had broken his friend's hand had left a neat hole through the left pocket of his brown vest—a hole now rimmed by a stain darker than the color of the cloth. Jim knelt beside him, throwing open the vest. Billy opened his eyes and stared upward, unseeingly.

"Easy, partner," Jim drawled. He tore open the shirt—and one look made him take his hands slowly away.

Billy turned his head and must have caught the bleakness that came to Jim's gray eyes. "Finished, eh?" he whispered, and the effort of speaking left his lips bloodflecked. The trace of a smile wiped away some of the lines of pain from his face as he read his answer in Jim's eyes and inscrutable set of countenance. He tried to raise his right hand from where it lay at his side, but the pain made him drop it again and use his left to reach into the vest pocket below the one with the bullet hole through it.

He brought his hand away and opened it. In his palm lay two round pellets of lead. "Take 'em, Jim," he said, speaking aloud this time. "You'll need 'em for what you're headed into."

Jim caught them as they fell from Billy's shaking hand. He looked at then closely, saw that the were marked darkly with a brown stain against their grayish hue; and when he rolled them between thumb and third fingers they felt sticky.

"Buckshot," he said. "What'll I do with them, Billy?"

It was a long quarter minute before the other answered. All this time he was trying to speak, couldn't. Finally he coughed, clearing his lungs momentarily; but then he gasped the words, "They . . . rolled out of . . . of a dead man's throat . . . this . . . this afternoon. Judge . . ."

A lancing of pain all at once stiffened his body to rigidity. His hands clawed into the dirt, one brokenly. He died that way, without a sound, with a leering smile graven grotesquely on his blunt features—a smile that didn't relax until his chest settled from its last vain effort at dragging breath into his choked lungs.

Jim Allard didn't go near his fire for the next half hour. He sat hidden in the deep shadow of the oak thicket, ten feet from where Billy Walls' body lay so stiffly, not quite that far from the other dead man. Time and again he put down a hunger for the taste of tobacco. But the grisly evidence of that other loosely sprawled body warned him against lighting a match. If one man had been on Billy's trail, there might be others.

When that long half-hour interval had run itself out, when the fire's coals gave only a feeble light, he came to his feet and stepped over to stare down into Billy Walls' face, now obscure in the blackness. He stood there realizing that trouble had queer ways of patterning itself to his life, dogged ways that seemed to follow him as insistently as his shadow. In five minutes' time tonight he had learned of trouble in the making, had killed a man and watched a friend die. He had been given mute evidence of murder, been warned against a relative he knew was boss of all the range he had this afternoon surveyed from the pass. He had been told to ride out before it was too late.

As he stood there, a tall man lacking the awkwardness of most tall men, lean face set inscrutably and a bleak look in his deep-socketed gray eyes, he dismissed the idea of riding out of here. He dismissed it with the fatality of a man whose experience has never encompassed running from anything. He was thinking of the Billy Walls he had known three years ago, a man forced by circumstance into the life of the outlaw, a man so good-natured and honest and undeviating in his code of friendship that his loss was like losing something clean and fine that would never again be experienced. And he was thinking of Spade Deshay, that unpredictable outlaw whose purposes were as obscure as Billy's had been plain.

Last of all, he was thinking of his own past in relation to these two men. They had lived together for a time, all three of them—lived recklessly and wholly for the moment. Their parting had been casual, unemotional, a quick breaking off of ties each of them had known could not be enduring.

Now circumstance had thrown them together again. In what relationship, Jim Allard had no way of knowing. Billy was already gone, leaving behind him two bloodsticky pellets of lead and the ominous words, *They . . . rolled out of . . . of a dead man's throat . . . this . . . this afternoon. Judge . . .*

As he belted on his guns once more, those words were graven firmly in his memory. And the lines of his aquiline face became harder and cleaner for the knowledge that he would someday have to know the meaning behind them.

2

SHERIFF Fred Blythe reined in at the crest of the rise that flanked Hugh Allard's Pitchfork layout and took his time about filling his cob pipe and lighting it.

The flare of the match blinded him for long seconds, for his brown eyes had for two hours peered into an unrelieved darkness. He kept the flame alight, unshielded by his hands, until it burned close to his fingers and he snuffed it out.

There was a purpose behind that open and unguarded burning of the match. That purpose became evident when

Blythe didn't immediately rein on down the slope toward the winking lights of the house and bunkhouse below, but sat listening. Soon his attention was rewarded. From close to his left came the unrhythmic muffled thud of a pony's four hoofs striking against the soft sandy ground. In another ten seconds the lawman could make out the shape of a rider off there. That shape turned at once and faded from sight, the sound of its going dying out so quickly a less vigilant man couldn't have been sure what he had heard.

The sheriff smiled thinly, spoke his paint gelding into motion and rode on down the slope with pipestem clenched hard between his teeth. He had wondered how much truth lay behind the two-week-old rumor that Hugh Allard was keeping a night guard about his place. Now he knew.

He had long ago lost his awe of Pitchfork, its maze of outbuildings and corrals scattered beneath the cotton-woods, its huge and sprawling adobe house fronted by two neat rows of majestic poplars lined out from an immaculately smooth sandy-clay yard. And now he rode straight for the hitch rail of the 'dobe's nearest wing and swung out of the saddle. Coming in, he hadn't overlooked signs of activity at the bunkhouse down beyond the cotton-wood grove, where time and again wide-hatted figures passed before the lighted rectangle of the open door; nor did he miss the fact that as he rode in four riders set out at a stiff trot from the big corral that flanked the barn.

He read his own meaning into these clear signs of restlessness, yet to all appearances he was a man intent only on the immediate work of tying his paint and beating the dust of a long ride from his faded Levis.

A low adobe wall with an arched gate at its center joined the two front wings of the H-shaped house to enclose a pleasing patio. Blythe went through the gate, stooping low beyond it to avoid the downhanging branches of a willow that centered the enclosure.

A paneled door midway the length of a broad center *portal* opened to let out an elongated rectangle of orange light. The figure of a man stepped into the opening.

"Evenin', Hugh," Fred Blythe said as he crossed the flagstones. "You're mighty careless about showin' yourself." He had the feeling that he'd been expected.

"Oh, it's you, Fred." Hugh Allard's voice was pitched to the level it rarely broke from, its smooth unruffled quality giving as clear an indication of the man's calculating nature as anything about him. He ignored the sheriff's pointed remark about showing himself against the light. "Come in."

Blythe would have stepped in through the doorway but for the fact that he looked into the room just then and saw the girl who sat in a rawhide-backed chair before the huge stone fireplace on the opposite wall. Ann Allard was always a welcome sight to him. She was now, with the firelight edging her chestnut hair with burnished cooper, softening the strong outline of her half-turned profile in a way that invariably made him pause to admire its outright beauty.

But the thing that had brought him here made him say, low-voiced. "Let's chew the fat out here."

Hugh Allard hesitated a moment before closing the door behind him. A slight raising of his thick black brows was the only indication he gave of his curiosity. He didn't speak.

Blythe's pipe was dead. He took the time to light it once more, the deliberate gesture a true sign of his character—for he had a lot on his mind and, where another man would have hurried to tell it, he took his time.

At length he asked Allard, "Anyone come by to see you this afternoon, Hugh?"

"Cattle buyer from Fort Apache." Again Allard let his thin face break from its inscrutable set, this time in the him of a frown. His physical make-up, average—since he was slight-framed and no taller than Blythe—was made insignificant by a face all angles and bearing the flinty graven quality of rimrock. But it was the focal point of the face, black eyes bright and alive, that bore the unmistakable quality of an inner strength and an iron will kept always in hand. Hugh Allard had never been called a weakling.

"Anyone else?" Blythe sucked at his pipe patiently, drawing the smoke deep into his lungs, this being the only sign of his inward tension; he didn't inhale by habit.

"Don't circle the thing," Hugh said quietly, in his sometimes surprising directness. "What's eatin'you, Fred?"

"Did Kurt Locheim drop in here this afternoon?"

In the darkness, Blythe couldn't be sure that he caught a change in Allard's expression, a tightening of that already tight face.

Hugh Allard said, "Why would the judge be riding twelve miles to see me?"

"I wouldn't know why, wouldn't much care. But it'd help if I knew whether or not he got here." Blythe sighed, realizing that he already had as much of an answer to that question as he would get. He knocked the bright red dottle from his pipe and watched it throw out a small shower of sparks at it hit the flagstone. "At any rate, he did leave town at three, on his way out here to see you. Three hours ago that damned stallion of his hit town at a run, luggin' the saddle under his belly and dragging broken reins. His hind hoofs were all bloody. Half a dozen of us got lanterns and started out here. We found Kurt . . . dead."

"Dead?"

The one word and the hushed voice that uttered it more clearly conveyed Hugh Allard's surprise than a host of words from another man.

Blythe's face showed pale even in the scant light that shone from a far window. He took out a bandana, shoved his Stetson onto the back of his head and mopped his brow with a hand that wasn't too steady. Then, bitterly: "It must have been hell for him. The stallion kicked in his chest, his face. You wouldn't know him from a fresh butchered beef. He was thrown and dragged half a hundred rods along the trail, until his boot heel tore off and let him free. We found him on that stretch of *malpais* by the rim below."

It was at times like this that Hugh Allard reacted typically and in the manner that had built his reputation for wisdom on this range. He didn't say anything, and in so doing showed himself a sensitive man. After all, there was nothing he could say except that he was sorry, and that was understood.

"I come right on up here," Blythe went on, "thinking you might spare me a couple men to get on north and spread the news. We're having the inquest at ten in the mornin'."

"There'll be a few you can't reach," Hugh Allard observed. "They won't like being left out."

"I know. But with the mess Kurt's in it's best to get him underground as soon as we can." Blythe paused, and a thin smile creased his old, weathered visage. "I'll swing over to Kittering's place on the way back to town and save you the trouble of getting a man shot, Hugh."

The muscles along Hugh Allard's jaw went firmer. He said evenly, "That's not my fault, Fred. Four nights ago I lost fifty head out of my feeder pasture. When my men went through the fence, following sign, someone took a shot at them from the timber up there."

"That's why your bunkhouse light's on this late, why I come across one of your crew ridin' lookout on the ridge?"

"Why else? Anything might happen. Kittering might get it into his head to burn me out." Allard glanced back at the closed door and Blythe knew that the rancher was thinking of the girl inside. "Fred, this can go only so far. My patience is about gone."

"Any proof this time?"

Allard shook his head.

"You're sure it's Kittering? Somehow, I've got it in my craw Miles wouldn't go about it this way . . . if he really wants to make trouble."

"I'm not sure of a damned thing! Only I'm going to put a stop to it if you don't."

It was rarely that Hugh Allard put anything so plainly, so bluntly. It alarmed Fred Blythe more than another man's outright raving, for he had so far been helpless against the happenings here at Pitchfork and the bitter feeling that was growing between Hugh Allard and his neighbor to the south, Miles Kittering.

Because he was uncertain and half afraid of what was to come, the sheriff said, "It'll take another month or so for them to appoint a new judge. If he'd lived, Kurt would have settled this once and for all, legally. But now that he's gone it's up to you to see it isn't settled the other way."

"Not up to me. It's up to Kittering."

"Find me proof and I'll arrest Kittering."

"Proof be damned!" Hugh Allard breathed, in as violent a reaction as Fred Blythe remembered ever seeing him give way to. "How can there be proof when a thousand head of beef can be lost in these hills in half a day's drive? There no proof of who shot at my men yesterday. Yet I know."

Blythe had an idea that made him ask abruptly. "Ever hear of Spade Deshay?"

For a fraction of a second, Hugh Allard's face broke from its gravity. But his voice was as even-toned as ever when he answered. "Who hasn't? But I'm talkin' about Miles Kittering."

"Ever heard that Deshay once worked this country?" came Blythe's insistent query.

"They've had Deshay working every hill country from the Pecos to the Snake these last few years. What's that got to do with this?"

"I had it pretty straight yesterday that Deshay's here with his wild bunch."

The rancher shrugged his bony shoulders in a casualness Fred Blythe thought too pronounced. "That's your lookout. But right now let's tend our own knittin'. That, or by all that's holy you'll have trouble on your hands!"

"Meanin' you'll go after Kittering yourself?"

"I didn't say so, did I?"

It was as though Allard had caught himself overstepping a previously set margin. He now retired behind his habitual reserve so definitely that Blythe knew the interview was ended.

The sheriff stepped off the *portal* and into the patio. "We'll see, Hugh," he said. "I've got to be gettin' on to Kittering's. Then I'm goin' back to town and kill that damned stallion." He snorted, raised a hand feebly in what was mean to be a parting salute. "Who'd ever think a horse would bust this thing wide open?"

"It had to bust sooner or later," Allard said as the lawman went out the gate. "Remember what I said, Fred. Get this thing licked!"

Blythe didn't answer. He was already too engrossed in several things he'd discovered tonight. Chief among them was the certainty that Hugh Allard had known Spade Deshay was in the country. Strangely enough, as he climbed stiff-jointed into the saddle and headed out across the yard, his thoughts turned to the girl he had seen back there ten minutes ago. "Maybe she ought to go visit her relatives in St. Louis," he muttered, half aloud. "This'll be a poor place for a woman if things shape up the way they're headed."

Blythe didn't find Miles Kittering at his cabin that night. The lawman gave his news to a Block K rider, Ed Beeson, not wasting much time and taking the trail down through the timber directly for town less than five minutes after he had arrived.

The reason he didn't find the rancher at home was that Kittering was twelve miles to the northeast, out of his saddle and standing deep beneath the shadow of a towering gray-barked pine, his fingers closed over the nostrils of his nervously standing bay mare. He made an erect, thick shape in the darkness, a full head and a half shorter than Fats Holden, his foreman, who stood beside him. Holden in turn gripped the muzzle of a black gelding.

A hundred yards out from the margin of the trees, cutting a dust-fogged and weaving line across the lighter shade of the cedar-studded sandy ground beyond, crawled a thin and swaying line of cattle, their hoofs setting up a dull rumble that blended with their bawling to drown out the hoof stomp of Kittering's bay as it shifted restlessly and tried to back out of reach of the rancher's restraining hand.

This pair stood in silence as a rider's dim shape suddenly loomed out of the dust below and set his horse at a swinging lope up toward them to cut off the flight of an unruly steer.

The man's falsetto, yipping yell mounted for an instant above the monotonous sound of the herd; a moment later he swung down and out of sight in the dust.

Holden, tall and gaunt, said without looking at Kittering. "I never saw that gent before, or the horse."

Kittering made no comment. He stood with legs spread apart, as though his thick shoulders and barrel-like upper body would overbalance him. He was somber-looking, outfitted darkly, trousers, vest and coat black against a dark gray shirt. He wore a short-clipped but nevertheless bushy black beard. His eyes, a dark brown, seemed to possess a hint of brightness even in this thick shadow; they were wide-spaced above prominent high cheekbones that didn't rob the impression of roundness from his face. That countenance didn't change in expression as Holden spoke; nor had it betrayed any emotion for the past three minutes, since they'd climbed out of their saddles to witness what was going on below.

"We could go back after Ed and Johnny and Mule and swing up to the peaks in time to head 'em off," Holden went on.

"They're Allard's critters, not mine." Kittering's voice was edged with a faint scorn.

Holden nodded jerkily. "His, and he'll be sayin' tomorrow we drove 'em off! There's all of three hundred head down there, Miles—too many to be got away with unless . . ."

"Unless they were supposed to be got away with." Kittering spoke the words so soft-voiced that they were barely audible against the onrush of sound. The drag was crawling past below, the main body far ahead now. "We'll wait and see what comes of it. This is Hugh Allard's game and I want to know how he's playing it."

An hour later, as they swung out of the trees and across the pasture that backed Kittering's hill layout, Fats Holden finally spoke his mund: "Miles, you've got your neck out! Sure, you've been fightin'—up until now. But you've got the sense to know what Judge Locheim's decision will be. He'll let Allard throw up that dam and take all your creek water. If you appeal, Allard will tie you up in the courts for ten years with writs, injunctions, postponements. Ten years will see you and every small rancher on this slope ruined! You can't get along without that water."

"I know what I'm doin', Fats."

"You may think you do. But why sit back and part your whiskers while your throat's cut? Tonight you missed your chance. We could have rounded up the jaspers workin' that herd and found out who's behind this."

"Someone else, too. I know every Pitchfork rider. That jasper we saw wasn't one."

Kittering held his silence, a gloomy one that was typical of his mood these past few weeks. And Fats Holden, for the hundredth time since the beginning of the trouble he knew instinctively was now gathering to entangle them all, held himself back from voicing any more of his own thoughts, knowing that Kittering wouldn't welcome them.

He watched Kittering's wide shape as it crossed the yard and took the back way around the cabin; then, cursing softly, he gathered up the reins of the two ponies and took them down to the corral. Lately he'd been keyed to an unaccustomed wariness. Now he found himself eying the shadows beyond the corral, where a low sandy hog's-back ran in a crescent-shaped rim that rose half the height of the wagon shed and petered out into the gentle slope of the pasture. There was enough cover to hide a man out there, he was thinking.

With a crisp oath, he crowded that thought from his mind and turned the horses into the corral as quickly as he could. Ordinarily he'd have lugged the saddles the fifty yards across to the wagon shed; but tonight, taking a brief look at the stars and out toward the horizon to the east where massed clouds blanketed the sky, he heaved the saddles into an empty feed bin alongside the corral. That would have to do until morning; it was late and he was too tired to waste any more energy than need be.

For all Holden's hurry, the light that shone through the cabin's two back windows didn't go out for another hour and a half, which meant that he, as well as the rest, didn't immediately hit the blankets.

A full fifty minutes after the light did go out, a rider walked his tired horse in toward the layout. Once near the corral he swung his animal aside and skirted a smooth stretch of ground where a shelf of rock lay exposed, thus avoiding any clatter his pony's shoes might have made. It was plain he didn't want to be heard.

Although his movement in off-saddling were hurried, he took the pains to carry his saddle to the wagon shed before he went to the cabin, skirting it in the shadows and making for the back door which let into the bunkroom. He was a small-bodied, almost frail-looking, man and even in the faint light of the stars his face looked exceedingly pale.

It was a young face stamped with a premature gravity and wickedness that might have been explained in the way he wore the holstered gun at his right thigh. In this country a decade of law and peaceful living had made the carrying of a weapon a whim few men indulged in. The fact that this man's open holster was worn awkwardly low, tied to his thigh by a rawhide thong, became at once the thing that dubbed him for what he was—a gunman.

Ten feet short of the cabin's roofless back stoop, he leaned against the wall and took off his boots, carefully, making no sound. He had taken two steps toward the door, walking on his toes, when a voice shuttled suddenly out of the darkness at the back of the yard, from the direction of the lean-to.

"You needn't bother being so damned quiet about it, Mule!"

Mule Evans, at the first hint of unexpected sound, dropped his boots and lanced his right hand toward his thigh. But he stayed the motion as he recognized Fats Holden's voice. He peered hard into the lean-to's shadow but couldn't make out the tall man's shape.

Letting his breath out in a gusty sigh that might have been one of relief or anger, Mule drawled, "I was tryin' to get in without wakin' the bunch."

"Been to town to see Mary again?" Holden's tone was crisp with sarcasm.

Mule Evans didn't answer immediately, as though not trusting himself to make the first reply that came to his mind. At length: "Sure, if it's any of your business." He knew how Holden felt about Mary Quinn.

"Any news from town?" Holden put the question casually, avoiding further mention of the girl.

His query put Mule on the spot, for Mule knew immediately that something had happened. It could have been one of a number of things; yet he didn't trust himself to voice a guess, so he said, "The town's still there."

"You don't say!"

For a full quarter-minute after Holden's softly drawled words, Mule Evans stood there not knowing what to do, sensing helplessly that by his answer he had in some way exposed the lie of his whereabouts tonight. Then, because he hated Holden with a live and deep-running passion and yet respected him for a shrewdness he himself couldn't match, he turned without a word, picked up his boots and went in through the door.

Holden watched the door and both far corners of the

cabin's back wall for a good fifteen minutes. It was possible he'd prodded Mule too hard tonight, for he knew the kid's surly temper. Finally, stepping around to the back of the lean-to, where the shadow was thicker, he hunkered down on his heels and rolled a smoke and lit it, snuffing the match quickly and shielding the burning tip of the cigarette in his cupped hand.

He was thinking about Mule Evans and about Judge Locheim mainly, although there was some thought of Mary Quinn. He had liked the judge, had given him the respect he gave all honest and strong men. Tonight's news, brought out by the sheriff, had brought a definite shock to Holden. What was to happen now that the judge was dead was something he hated to think of but couldn't help.

He didn't like Mule Evans, didn't care that Mule knew it. Although Mule had minded his own business these past six months since hiring on, although he was a capable hand, there were things about him Fats didn't trust. First there was the gun, which was as much a part of Mule's outfit as his boots. Then there were his surly silences, his too quick temper and, lately, these too frequent absences from the layout Miles Kittering hadn't yet begun to notice. There was a mystery about Mule and Fats didn't like it.

Of course, Mule had the right to go to Sands any time he chose and see Mary Quinn; any man had. Fats admitted now that he was slightly jealous, then asked himself what right he had to feel this way. None, of course. He was nothing more than a friend to Mary and had never thought of overstepping that line. But Mary was a fine girl, too good for Mule. The trouble was, he was a different man around her, a pleasing youngster making his intentions of courting her plain enough for anyone who wanted to see.

"So the town's still there, eh?" Holden mused as he ground the cigarette under his heel. His bony shoulders lifted in a meager shrug. He was stumped. It was a cinch Mule hadn't come from Sands tonight, for the town would be in an uproar over the judge's death. If he hadn't been in town, then where had his night ride taken him?

3

SANDS' single street was more attractive this morning than on the average day. Last night's rain had settled the dust along it, darkened the drab light brown of the adobes that flanked both its far ends; and the wind that accompanied the storm had swept the wide thoroughfare clean of some of the usual litter.

All this was lost on Jim Allard, who had no previous acquaintance with Sands as a comparison. He saw a town that was outwardly like a hundred others he knew, and inwardly different only in detail. The reason for Sands being where it was, on this waterless, treeless flat that edged the desert, was obvious. The two-acre maze of cattle pens flanking the railroad at the south edge of town was that reason. Because the railroad had scorned the close green hills, so had the town. All the cattle shipped out of this hundred-mile strech of hill-graze doubtless used those corrals. The community had grown up around them, for they represented the one big business that had drawn men to this country in preference to a greener and more outwardly prosperous one.

Nothing about Sands was mellowed with age, yet nothing about it was new. The groupings of adobe buildings at each end of the street looked weathered after the scant rains of the past few years. Some were abandoned, their yards littered, windows broken, deserted by their Mexican owners who had gone on when the railroad was completed. Others were neat, window and door frames whitewashed and hard-packed grassless yards swept clean with a broom. Farther in along the street were painted frame houses, a few of brick. Some attempt had been made to grow trees—poplar, locust, cottonwood and tamarisk. But only a few of these had attained any large size, for water wasn't plentiful here; the rest, stunted and thin, made man's effort of fighting the sun's pitiless bright glare seem ineffectual and only temporary.

The two rows of stores at the center of the street were replicas of the stores in every other town in the West. Gray-weathered boards, tin or tar-paper roofs, false fronts and garish faded signs added the final touch of ugliness to a scene where little effort at architectural beauty had been attempted. To the eye of a man of western breeding, Sands was satisfying bcause it was typical. It was satisfying to Jim Allard without his being conscious of it.

He took in each detail along the street purposely, for later he might want to know it well. His eyes were squinted against the early reflected sun-glare from the tin roofs. He passed the only crosslane, the cinder road that led to the red-painted railway station beyond the back boundaries of the lots on the street's west side. The tracks ran close in to the rear of the stores, he saw, leaving a scant alleyway behind them. He passed the first wooden awning that shaded the walks and became aware of something that hadn't at first seemed odd but was now clearly so.

It was a few minutes short of eight o'clock. Yet the street was crowded. A thickening stream of traffic moved in under the awnings and he had a hard time finding a place at the tie rail in front of Quinn's Elite, where he hoped to get his breakfast. Rigs of all sorts lined the street—buckboards, spring wagons, a few buggies. The saddle horses outnumbered the vehicles many times over. Crossing the walk to the door of the restaurant, he broke his stride twice to avoid colliding with passers-by.

As he took a stool midway the length of the restaurant's crowded counter, his right hand automatically ran along his empty thigh. He missed the weight of the guns at his waist and felt somehow incomplete without them. But he had thought it wise to ride in here without carrying them today, so as to be less conspicuous. Hugh Allard's telegram had specifically requested him to arrive as unobtrusively as possible.

He ordered an ample meal from a blonde clean-aproned girl, putting down the impulse to ask her the reasons for the early crowd on the street. But in the twenty minutes he spent eating, the conversation of other customers told him all he needed to know. An inquest was being held this morning.

As he paid for his meal, the girl was being kidded by a 'puncher who had just come in. The 'puncher called her Mary. Her face was flushed, half in embarrassment, half in pleasure; and as she handed Jim his change she gave him a smile that made him really see her for the first time. When she smiled her face lost its plain look and she became rather pretty. Leaving, he envied the men at the counter their easy familiarity, yet respectfulness, toward the girl. This striking down of roots, getting to know people more than casually, was a thing he hungered for and one that had been so far denied him.

Hugh Allard's telegram had mentioned the hotel as a meeting place. The Prairie House was four doors down the street. Starting toward it, Jim remembered the claybank's short rations of last night and took the animal across to the feed barn. He was flattered by the admiring glance the young hostler gave the stallion. He paid for a day's stabling and feed, then went over and up the steps to the hotel veranda, his spurs setting up a metallic jingle of sound. He took a chair at the end of the veranda, cocked his feet on the rail and watched the crowd moving along the walks. He'd wait a while before asking for Allard inside. Maybe it wouldn't be necessary, since the other loungers greeted most newcomers by name.

Presently, he noticed the arrival of half a dozen riders forking ponies jaw-branded with a crude pitchfork. The animals were all above the scrubby standard grade of cow horses and his approving eye studied the riders carefully. They were a trifle aloof, not paying much attention to what was going on. He decided that the slight-bodied man on the sleek chestnut must own the brand. This individual wore a broadcloth suit, expensive-looking, but plain boots and a straight-brimmed black Stetson set squarely on his head. He swung aside from the others a few doors short of the hotel and came down out of the saddle and tied his horse before a small adobe building on the railroad side of the street. The legend "Sheriff" was lettered on the window of the building.

The other five riders came on, four of them heading for the hotel tie rail. He almost failed to identify the sixth rider, on a buckskin, going on down the street. If she hadn't turned and lifted a hand to someone on the veranda near him, he wouldn't have known that the man's outfit was worn by a girl.

That brief glance he had of her face and her smile startled him into sudden interest. Her face was golden-tan, proclaiming acquaintance with the sun. As she turned he saw that her wide-brimmed hat hid burnished chestnut hair gathered in a braided knot at the nape of a slim and graceful neck. He had a glimpse of smiling deep hazel eyes, a wide mouth that gave strong character to the face; then he was looking at the sure erectness of her slim back, seeing the proud tilt of her head as she went away down the street.

He asked involuntarily of a man in the chair alongside him, "Who's that? That girl?" And the man smiled broadly and said, "Hugh Allard's kid. She's an eyeful, ain't she?"

Jim was so intent on watching her that he didn't reply.

Beyond the general store across the way she reined in toward the walk. An oldster with the glint of a metal badge showing on his vest pocket came out from the walk to stand at her stirrup.

Across there, Ann Allard was telling Fred Blythe, "I'm on my way to see Vera." Vera Locheim, the judge's widow, was one of her best friends despite the great difference in their ages. She added, "Hugh's at your office. He wants to see you."

Blythe sighed audibly. "I saw him comin'. That's why I ducked out the back away. What's on his mind?" He looked up at her sharply, seeing that the events of the past twelve hours had taken a great deal out of her. The judge's death had been a blow, of course; it looked like she was taking it hard.

She said, "Another bunch was driven off last night. From that fence near the breaks. The rain and the rock up there took care of the sign. There's nothing we can do about it." Her level glance met his a brief instant before something akin to panic touched her eyes. "Fred, what's going to happen? Is Miles Kittering really . . ."

Blythe shook his head solemnly as her voice broke and let her thought die. "You know better than to think that," he said reprovingly, "even if Hugh don't. As soon as this other's out of the way, I'll come out and look things over. But this mornin' I can't spend the time arguin' with Hugh. It's after nine and Tom Oldham wants me to round up a jury for him. You get on up to Vera's and forget the inquest. See that she isn't there."

"You'll help, Fred?" she asked, and the strange lines of care that showed on her forehead made him answer immediately, " 'Course I will. This'll all blow away and in a year we'll have forgotten it. Don't you worry." He gave her a reassuring wink, adding, "Gosh, you're somethin' to look at today, girl!" and slapped the buckskin, sending the animal on.

When she had ridden away, he set about finding men for Tom Oldham's jury. He went over to the hotel, knowing that it was the best place to have his pick. He chose eight of his acquaintances, men whose judgment he accepted without question, all of whom had known Kurt Locheim. He completed the dozen by selecting four strangers. Two of these complained bitterly of having urgent business. Blythe, who had been up all night, who had taken on the distasteful task of shooting Locheim's killer-horse early this morning, was impatient and curt with the strangers and put them in charge of his deputy, Sid Bailey, to take to the inquest hall.

At ten the warehouse room over Len Glidden's hardware store was packed, the benches crowded, the aisles each side and at the front windows jammed to capacity. Blythe and Tom Oldham had seated the audience facing the rear of the barnlike room. To the left of the small open space at the rear was a table, occupied by Oldham, Blythe and Sid Bailey, Deputy Sheriff; across from it the twelve jurors sat in chairs placed at right angles to the spectators' benches.

As Bailey stood up to motion the room to quiet, Fred Blythe's glance ran toward the high windows that faced the street. He knew most of the people here, and in identifying them saw that the places they had taken had assumed a somewhat ominous arrangement. Sands' prominent citizens were in the first few rows. Farther back he recognized Bill Blazer and most of his crew, Sid Olney and his wife and two boys, the Semples and old Hickory Wood—all of these being plains ranchers whose outfits lay south of town, well out from the hills.

But near the stairway door Hugh Allard's slight frame stood almost out of sight. At his elbow were grouped Trent Harms, his foreman, and two other Pitchfork men. As though this segregation must be balanced, across the room in a corner by the far window stood Miles Kittering, topped by Fats Holden's high gaunt shape. They were the only two Block K men present. But near them were Hawley, of the Circle H, and two of his men. Crippen with his kid brother beside him; Tooley, alone, the absence of his ever-present wife an ominous sign, as though Tooley had come to town half expecting trouble. Kittering's expression was one of watchfulness and uneasiness; for these men who stood near him were his neighbors, uninvited. All of them would see their futures made precarious if Judge Locheim's successor ruled that Hugh Allard could dam Antelope Creek.

Worriedly, Blythe wondered how many guns were back there. He'd seen all of Pitchfork's men but Allard carrying weapons openly this morning as they rode into town. He'd also noticed that neither Kittering nor Fats Holden was armed. What made his worry deeper than usual was that he knew the news of Allard's herd, stolen last night, had spread around town. He was wishing now he'd told Kittering and Holden not to attend the inquest.

As though reading his mind, Tom Oldham leaned over and said in a hushed voice, "Wouldn't hurt to close the saloons, Fred. This crowd's liable to develop a powerful thirst."

"I already thought of that," Blythe answered irritably. "They won't open until either Kittering or Allard takes his outfit home. Let's get this over with."

Oldham got to his feet, smoothing his black cutaway over his ample paunch in a gesture familiar in half a dozen of this country's courtrooms.

He knocked on the table for order, cleared his throat and began: "In order to hasten these proceedings, in fitting respect to our departed friend, I will briefly mention the events of yesterday afternoon in the order of their happening." . . . People strained their attention to take in every word, a little awed by the formality of speech of a man who had for twenty years been the outstanding member of Antelope County's bar. . . . "Kurt Locheim, at shortly before three o'clock yesterday afternoon, stopped at the Cattleman's Bank to have a word with his son, Franklin Locheim. At the time he mentioned he was riding west from town to Hugh Allard's ranch. Last night, at eight-twenty-seven, Fred Blythe and three other men who were sitting on the hotel porch saw Locheim's . . ."

At the back of the room, as Oldham's voice droned on, Trent Harms nudged Hugh Allard. Hugh frowned at the distraction; but looking sideward and catching the expression on Harms' saddle-colored visage, he cocked his head to listen.

Harms' pale blue eyes shifted their look to the back of the room, and he said in a voice barely above a whisper, "There's your man, boss. Fourth chair from this end in the back row of the jury."

Hugh looked back there, examining the jurors. The man Trent mentioned didn't appear to be paying much attention to what Tom Oldham was saying. He sat peering down at his Stetson, running its wide brim around between his fingers. Hugh judged his age to be close to thirty. His face was distinctly aquiline, the eyes gray, and but for the broadness of a mouth that narrowly missed being thin-lipped he would have been called handsome. A denim shirt clung damply to his wide shoulders, revealing flat muscles that Hugh sensed must be hard and saddle-toughened.

Allard's inspection was a close one, not because he yet knew the point of Trent Harms' remark, but because the object of his foreman's interest was a man who took the eye. Finally he said, "Never saw him before."

"It's Jim Allard. I remember his face on the reward notices." Immediately the rancher's glance became sharper. "You sure?" Harms nodded, the movement of his head barely perceptible. His lined, sun-blackened face was now set in a quizzical look as he studied Jim Allard. All at once he breathed, "It could have been him."

His tone, his expression, brought a narrower look to Hugh Allard's sharp-featured countenance. Allard said, "What could?"

"Up the canyon last night. It was too dark to see well. But let me have a look at his horse and I'll know for sure. The man that shot Elder rode a claybank. I was where I could see the jughead."

Hugh said, "Keep your mouth shut, man!" and his glance went to the faces of those nearest him. But if anyone had heard Trent Harms, he didn't show it. Tom Oldham had just called on Frank Locheim to testify, and everyone was looking at the judge's son.

For the next twenty minutes, while Locheim, Blythe, and Tate Olson—feed-barn owner—testified, Hugh Allard's glance never strayed from the man in the jury box.

Tom Oldham, finished with his witnesses, ended by addressing his jury: "You are instructed to bring in a verdict based on the facts you have heard. Everything points to Kurt Locheim having met accidental death, the immediate cause being blows inflicted by the hind shoes of his horse." He paused to blot his perspiring bald scalp with a handkerchief. "Are there any questions?"

"I have a couple." It was the juryman in the fourth chair of the back row who had spoken.

Jim Allard had five minutes ago been jerked from the boredom of listening to all this testimony. Confronted by the sheriff at the hotel, he had been unwillingly compelled to serve on the jury. At first he'd listened to the details of how this total stranger, Locheim, had met his death in being thrown and kicked by his horse. The testimony, lengthy and uninteresting, he'd endured as stoically as he did the oppressive heat of this loft.

But when the sheriff, five minutes ago, had referred to the dead man as "Judge" Locheim, there flashed into Jim's memory the sound of Billy Wall's voice speaking the same word last night; and from then on he had listened with a growing conviction that Billy would have mentioned the name Locheim had he been spared another breath.

Now, having spoken, he felt a little foolish and angry with himself. He had come into the country secretly, in a roundabout way, so that whatever happened with Hugh Allard would leave his back trail obscure and hard to trace.

But here was something more important than his business with Allard and now he threw aside all caution. Nervous as he was, when he thrust his hands in his pockets and eased back into his chair, his fingers closing on the two pellets of lead told him he must go through with it.

The feel of the buckshot steadied him, and when Tom Oldham spoke he had made his decision. What Oldham said was, "You have a question? I thought we'd made everything clear."

"Nearly everything. But I'm new here and didn't know the Judge. How long had he owned that stallion?"

Oldham shot Fred Blythe a perplexed look. It was Blythe who answered, "Four years."

"Was he a good rider? Ever have an accident like this before?"

"A man can die only once," was the sheriff's sarcastic rejoinder.

Jim Allard smiled, the ease of his manner strangely enough increasing the tension of the watchers; a keen hostility had crept into the glances of more than a few men in the audience, although Jim Allard didn't see this because he was watching the sheriff.

"What I meant was, did he ever have trouble stickin' his hull?"

Tom Oldham said curtly, "See here, stranger! The rest of us didn't come here to enjoy ourselves. If you've got anything to say, get it said!"

"A verdict of accidental death can't be given unless the jury's unanimous, can it?"

Oldham shook his head. "No. You must be in complete agreement."

"Then you'd better recess and round up a new jury."

Jim Allard started to say something else, but the angry mutter of the crowd cut him off. Here and there the length of the room men came to their feet, calling loudly words that were lost in the confused blending of many excited voices all trying to make themselves heard at once.

Oldham looked helpless. But for a moment only; he banged his fist on the table and shouted for order. It came, gradually, but only after Fred Blythe stood up and raised both hands.

When Oldham could make himself heard, he shouted, "Quiet, or we'll clear the room! Sit down, all of you!"

He waited out a short interval, until he had comparative silence. Then, turning to face this rebellious juror, he asked harshly, "You mean you don't agree that Kurt Locheim met his death accidentally? You never knew the man."

"No, but I know horses," Jim answered. "They're pretty much the same no matter where you go. I've never yet seen a killer-horse that could stay four years under the saddle of a good rider and not give it away he was dangerous."

When Tom Oldham started to protest, Fred Blythe held up his hand again. The room was ominously quiet now, and the sheriff, sensing the suppressed violence that held these tempers in check, was trying to focus thoughts he hadn't been able to grasp since early this morning when he'd destroyed the stallion.

This stranger's reasoning made a little sense to the sheriff; that was why he now said, "Hold on, Tom. Let's hear him out." He glanced across at Jim. "Go ahead and finish what you started to say."

"I reckon I've already finished. But if I were you folks and thought as much as you say you do of this Judge Locheim, I'd look for a better reason to his gettin' killed than a horse turnin' against nature."

The silence that held on after his words was prompted by pure awe and a blending of mute anger.

Tom Oldham was the first to find his voice, saying curtly from where he sat, "The judge didn't have enemies. Stranger, you're speaking out of turn!"

Jim Allard lifted his wide shoulders in a shrug. "Then you've got my apology. But you can't have my vote on accidental death."

Oldham said harshly, "This is a court of law. You can be held for contempt. I'll have you . . ." The lawyer felt a tug at his coat sleeve. He leaned over to hear what the sheriff had to say, every eye in the room on him.

After a quarter-minute in which the silence was acute enough to make the jingle of harness of a passing wagon on the street clearly audible, Oldham stood up, smoothed his coat back into place across his stomach and looked out over the audience.

"Is Doctor Swain present?" he queried in stentorian tones.

There was a scraping of boot soles near the street windows and a thin small man wearing spectacles started down the crowded side aisle. He gained the cleared space before the coroner's table and stepped up to Tom Oldham, and the two of them conversed in undertones for a few seconds.

Then Oldham faced the jury and cleared his throat officiously, speaking to the rebellious juror, "Stranger, would a doctor's testimony convince you?"

Jim took a long time answering. And when he spoke, it was deliberately: "Yes."

Oldham looked down at Blythe to catch the lawman's sober nod. "There'll be a short recess," he finally announced. "Doctor Swain and the sheriff are going across to the undertaker's."

A long sigh escaped the crowd, the sound going out along the room like a fitful breeze sweeping the top of a stand of pines. Heads turned slowly to follow the progress of Swain and Blythe to the side stairway door. The closing of the door behind their backs loosed a restless, hushed undertone of whispers and low talk. The stubborn juror occasioned some interest, but now that interest lacked hostility and was tinged with a certain respectful curiosity.

Hugh Allard, studying Jim's impassive set of countenance, once lifted his head and said to Trent Harms, "He'll do."

Across the crowded room from Allard, Fats Holden had been restless these last few minutes. The thin man was usually bothered little by the heat, but now perspiration trickled down off his bony forehead so that he had to wipe his face with his neckpiece.

He finally muttered to Kittering, "I'm goin' out for air," and abruptly elbowed his way along the packed aisle by the windows and then past Hugh Allard and Trent Harms and the Pitchfork crew, going toward the stairway door. There was a grudging respect in the way the Pitchfork men made way for him—all but Hugh Allard, who stood his ground and made Holden move around him.

Outside, at the bottom of the stairway, Holden leaned against the front corner of the building and rolled a smoke. When he heard the storeroom door at the head of the stairway open and close again he didn't at once turn around to look, even though a keen urgency to be on the move was in him.

But when he did turn, to see the head of the stairway empty, he flicked the cigarette away, cut at a quick stride across the street and took a narrow passageway between two stores. Forty seconds later, Stetson in hand, he was edging close in to the alley window of Hill's drugstore. The back room of the store served as Sands' undertaking establishment.

Inside, Fats heard the scrape of a boot, then heard Swain mutter something unintelligible. Shortly, Fred Blythe's voice came clearly out to him: "Hurry it, Doc. My stomach can't stand this much longer."

Swain said, "You don't have to watch," and Blythe replied, "I know, but I'm goin' to," and there was a longer silence.

Fats, crouched under the window, kept looking up and down the alley, making sure he wasn't seen. Sweat stood out again on his forehead, dampening his matted hair; his long bony face was set in a tense, tight-lipped expression.

Suddenly Fred Blythe's voice was sounding out through the window above Fats' head. "Good God! Buckshot!" and Swain was clearing his throat, adding explosively, "Damn it, why did we have to run into this?"

Every muscle along Fats Holden's bony frame went tight. He heard Blythe say, "I hope he was dead before the stallion dragged him," and didn't wait for more.

Going back along the passageway to the street, Fats mopped his face and tried to take in the full significance of the information his eavesdropping had netted him. Kurt Locheim murdered! That meant that hell might break loose when the sheriff returned to make his announcement.

He took the stairs up the side of the hardware store two steps at a time, wanting to be out of sight before the sheriff and the doctor came along the walk. He stifled his quick breathing as he edged in through the door. He closed it behind him and leaned back against the wall, about to go get Kittering when he heard steps on the stairway outside.

Now it was too late to warn Miles. He eased his frame once more against the wall and waited. His hands came up and hooked in the belt of his waist-overalls. When he pressed his left forearm against his body he could feel the reassuring bulk of a short-barreled .44 Smith and Wesson he had that morning thrust beneath his shirt.

He was thinking out the best way to get his right hand inside his shirt when the door opened close by. Fred Blythe was the first in, followed closely by Swain.

Blythe stopped just inside the door, his look running over the room. Then he went along the aisle at the side and to the table before the jury. He sat down. Fats waited until Swain was approaching the table before he looked away, back toward Hugh Allard and Trent Harms; he was deciding the best way to get to them when Tom Oldham spoke.

"Doctor, will you give your report to the jury?"

Holden didn't look that way. His muscles were cocked. He had forefinger and thumb of his right hand already inside his shirt.

Swain's quiet voice said, "It is my opinion that Kurt Locheim died in the manner already described. He was kicked to death by his horse."

Fats Holden, bewildered, let out his breath in a near sob.

He had to stand with boots spread apart to support himself, for in his relief his knees had suddenly refused to stiffen and hold up his slight weight.

4

FRED BLYTHE took the chair before his deal desk in the jail office and tried to make his face assume an unnaturally severe expression. He had just watched Miles Kittering and Fats Holden ride out the street. He was relieved and thankful for having the danger of an immediate flare-up between Allard and Kittering removed. There were important matters awaiting his attention: the judge's funeral, scheduled for eleven and already late; he had to see Hugh Allard about his trouble last night; Bailey, alone, was keeping order on the street as the inquest crowd broke up. But before all these Blythe had to satisfy himself on one thing—his curiosity over the juror who had sent him out to discover the truth of Locheim's death.

He had brought the stranger to the office, where they could talk uninterrupted. Now the man stood waiting to take the chair along the side wall by the desk. Blythe waited out a proper interval, one intended to impress subtly upon this stranger the law's authority. Then he said, a trifle curtly, "Have a seat."

Jim Allard sat. His lean mahogany-brown face was without expression and for a moment Blythe thought him awed. But then Jim let his long frame slouch easily into the chair and tilted back against the wall and reached to shirt pocket for tobacco. It was a casual gesture that all too clearly conveyed nothing but patience and a certain tolerance for Blythe's highhanded manner. He obviously wasn't impressed.

Blythe scowled against this knowledge. "About that idea of yours, stranger," he said gruffly. "You satisfied now?"

Jim nodded.

"What was in back of it?"

"In back of what?"

"Your hunch that the stallion didn't kill the judge."

"Plain horse sense. It seems I was wrong." Jim's attention was concentrated on his long-fingered hands that built his smoke. He added abruptly, "Next you'll want to know my name and my business here. Anything wrong with a man holding an opinion?"

The bluntness of his words, the lack of respect toward Blythe's authority, made the sheriff at first angry, then wary. A train pulling out of the station shook the building as it passed along the right of way barely twenty feet out along the alley behind the jail. The sound jarred against Blythe's nerves, wouldn't let him think. He had wondered many times why they couldn't have built the jail on the other side of the street; now he was wondering again, not able to put his mind to this other business.

Debating what to do next, he studied this stranger more closely, seeing things he hadn't seen before. One was the mark of holster thongs low along the man's thighs. Blythe decided for no reason at all that the generously proportioned hands so smoothly rolling a cigarette would be uncommonly adept at the use of a weapon. He grudgingly approved of the man's looks, the faded work-worn Levis, the gray Stetson soiled enough to look as comfortable as the dusty boots. Blond bleached hair showed above a high wide forehead beneath the pushed-back hatbrim. When Jim's gray eyes lifted to regard him steadily, the lawman decided he knew all he was going to know of the stranger's shrewd guess at the inquest.

That was the reason for his meager smile and his saying mildly, "It's my job to be curious, that's all. You had us worried."

Jim's wide shoulders lifted in a shrug. "It had me worried."

"Driftin' on through?" Blythe abruptly changed the subject.

"Maybe; maybe not. I'd take a job."

"What kind?"

"Any kind."

Glancing once again at Jim's empty waist, Blythe was thinking of two possibilities. The first he dismissed because he hadn't yet quite made up his mind about this man. He voiced the second, trying a shot in the dark: "You might hire on to Hugh Allard. He's taking men who're handy with their irons. He . . ."

He straightened in his chair all at once, looking out the window onto the street. He frowned, muttered a low oath irritably and his face plainly showed his disappointment at the interruption that was coming. Hugh Allard was on his way across the street, the jail his unmistakable destination.

On the spur of the moment, the lawman got up and went

to the back of the room to push open the heavy steelfaced door of the jail. He motioned to Jim: "Step in here and wait. The man I just mentioned, Allard, is on his way across here. You can listen to what he has to say."

"Anything wrong with my listenin' from where I am?"

"Hugh's as tight-lipped as a mute around strangers. He wouldn't talk with you here."

Jim gave a meager smile at the sheriff's lame explanation. He got up out of the chair and went in through the jail door. As he passed the sheriff, he drawled, "You may know what you're doin'. I don't."

Blythe pulled the door nearly shut. No, he didn't quite know what he was doing. Because things were so confused in his own mind, he'd had the sudden desire to want the stranger to hear what Hugh Allard was going to say: a man who had already made one shrewd guess this morning might be able to make another. Blythe wanted help, wanted it badly. Yet as soon as the jail door was shut on the stranger he wondered angrily why he'd chosen this man he didn't know for that help.

He was easing back in his swivel chair as Allard came in through the door. "Sorry to make you wait, Hugh," he said, "but I've had a hell of a lot to attend to this mornin'."

Allard came on into the little room, stopping a stride from the desk, so that he looked down at Blythe. "You heard what happened last night, Fred?"

Blythe nodded. "Ann told me."

"Going to do anything about it?"

"She said the sign was washed out. Anything else I could work on?"

Hugh Allard slowly shook his head.

"Then what do you want me to do?"

"Swear out a warrant on Kittering! Keep him locked up until this is settled once and for all." There was no anger in Allard's tone. He was merely stating what he wanted done.

"And have every rancher north of your ridge in here howlin' for me to let him out?" Fred Blythe gave a low, mirthless laugh. "Can't do it, Hugh. It wouldn't stick."

"Then I'm to take it your hands are tied? That I can go about it my own way?"

Blythe sobered instantly, his narrow-lidded gaze studying the rancher's face. "That depends, Hugh. I'm not playing favorites. If you want my view on the matter, I don't think Kittering is your man."

"I know he is."

There was no answer to that. Blythe didn't attempt any,

feeling once more a return of his helplessness of last night in reasoning with Allard.

The rancher went on: "Another thing. Two of my men disappeared last night."

Blythe's eyes widened in unfeigned surprise. "How?"

"I don't know yet. But they're gone, Walls and Elder. They've been ridin' my south fence for the past two days, since that last breakout."

"Where'd they be?" Blythe asked, plainly at a loss in face of this sudden unexpected development.

Hugh Allard shook his head solemnly. "Your guess is as good as mine. But if anything's happened to them . . ." He left his thought unfinished, allowing it to convey an unmistakable meaning.

Blythe fought against his helplessness. "See here, Hugh. You know Kittering as well as I do. He's been hounded plenty and he's swallowed it and gone about his business. He came in here and took land no one wanted—"

"Land I'd used for graze ever since I came here," Allard reminded him.

Blythe waved aside the interruption, almost irritably. "Sure. But it was all there was to take within fifty miles, government land. He was within his rights. You let him stay there six years. Now you make a play to take all his water away by damming Antelope and turning it into your upper meadows. He's sore, sore as hell. But before he'd do a thing like this he'd come to you and try and talk it out. Has he been to see you yet?"

Allard smiled thinly. "You know Miles would never do that."

"But he's made his fight in court. He's tried to stop Locheim from giving that ruling in your favor. Folks say he had a chance. And I say he wouldn't start anything until he lost that chance."

"Maybe he did lose it."

"You're wrong, Hugh. I've talked to Frank Locheim. He seems to think the judge was going to give the ruling against you, not against Miles. Whoever's appointed may decide the same."

A subtle change rode over Hugh Allard's face, making its expression harder. All he said was, "The new judge will decide that."

"And I still say that Kittering will wait for the new judge to decide before he does anything. You should do the same."

"And meantime have my range bled white of stock?" Allard gave a laugh that was more like a racking cough from out of his flat chest. It carried no amusement and his eyes didn't lose their faint smoldering anger. "No, Fred. Something has to be done now. It boils down to this. Kittering has to leave, to get out of the country. I've offered to buy him out. He refuses to sell. What's the next move?"

Blythe was about to answer that when a rising undertone of excited voices out on the street distracted his attention. Men hurried along the walk, more voices joining the others. Abruptly the screen door swung open and a ruddy-faced oldster stuck his head in and said urgently, "Better get out here, sheriff."

His tone brought Blythe up out of his chair. He crossed to the door and stepped out onto the walk in time to see a rider swing in toward the rack immediately beyond. The rider held the rope of a lead pony in his free hand; the lead pony, a sorrel wearing a Pitchfork jaw blaze, was almost surrounded by men walking alongside. The animal bore a packsaddle across which were slung two bulky tarpaulin-wrapped bundles looking like two oversized bedrolls.

Fred Blythe's face went pale as he stepped out across the walk. He'd forgotten his impatience with Allard. He ducked under the tie rail and approached the stirrup of the rider, a man whose legs curved nicely to fit the barrel of his horse.

"What you got here, Jerry?"

"Better look for yourself, Blythe," the 'puncher drawled. "Found 'em up a gulch below the pass trail."

Blythe, already knowing what was beneath the tarpaulins, turned and curtly nodded to Allard, who was standing in the office doorway. "Lend me a hand, Hugh." He added in louder tones to the gathering crowd around the lead horse, "Clear out. Everybody!"

The crowd moved away, melting both ways out of the street toward the walks.

The unyielding weight of the burdens they lugged into the jail office with Jerry's help made it all too plain to Blythe. He wasn't surprised when he pulled the dirty canvas off Billy Walls' grimacing dead face. After one quick look at the other, he let the tarp fall back into place, saying hoarsely, "It's Bob Elder's hair. There isn't much else left to tell by, Hugh."

The rancher's face was set bleakly. It had lost some color. He turned and asked Jerry, "How did you find them?"

"I was workin' the brush up there for strays. . . ."

"Not that," Allard cut in. "How were they lying?"

"Billy, there, was near the ashes of a fire, on his back. Elder was down a ways in the brush. Billy's got a hole in his chest, another in his side. I found a Winchester half-way up toward the rim above where Elder lay. Billy's gun carries two empties. It's there in the tarp with him."

"Any sign?" the sheriff asked.

Jerry shook his head. "That rain last night about washed us out south of here. I found the sorrel tied to a tree a quarter-mile down the wash. So I went back home and got the pack-saddle and brought 'em in. That's all I know."

For the space of a quarter-minute, the grim silence was broken only by the muted voices of the crowd gathering once more on the walk outside. Finally Fred Blythe ventured to comment, "They must have shot it out."

Hugh Allard wheeled on him abruptly, his eyes betraying real anger. "Hell, man, they were friends!"

"Then what's the answer?"

"I know the answer; so do you!" Allard glanced down at the two bodies again, said brusquely, "I'll send a wagon along to take them off your hands," and went out the door. His manner of leaving made it all too plain that he had come to Blythe for the last time for help.

For the space of a long ten seconds there was silence in the room. All at once Blythe said with surprising intentness, "Jerry, you're handiest. Get a fresh horse and make tracks for Kittering's place. Go like blazes! Tell him what's happened and what's likely to happen."

"I'll have to know what it is before I can tell him," the 'puncher drawled cautiously.

"Elder and Walls were riding Allard's fence last night at the spot where a herd went through. It looks now like they might have seen too much and were taken along. You heard Allard say they were friends and wouldn't have shot it out. That makes it pretty plain. He thinks they were murdered, left there so it would look like they'd gone at each other. Tell Kittering that. He'll know what to do."

Jerry didn't move at once. "Something damn' queer's goin' on here. I don't want to be mixed up in it."

"You won't be," Blythe assured him, impatiently pushing him toward the door. "Hurry!"

When he faced back into the room once more, it was to find Jim Allard standing in the open doorway leading to the jail. Blythe had forgotten the stranger. Jim's glance went to the two covered bodies, then met the sheriff's. "And what *is* likely to happen?" he queried.

"You heard Allard. You're good at guesses. Try this one!" Blythe was angered once more by his helplessness. All at once he remembered his reason for sending the stranger into the jail. He said caustically, "This makes three in the last twelve hours."

"But only two murders," Jim drawled in thinly veiled sarcasm, and smiled.

Blythe looked sharply at this man whose words had a way of taking on a double meaning. Once again he was asking himself whether the stranger was only remarkably shrewd in his guesses or actually knew more than he was telling. He knew for a certainty, then, that he couldn't afford to let the man go until he was sure how much he knew.

He remembered that first possibility that had come to him when Jim spoke of wanting a job—the possibility he hadn't mentioned. He said, "This means I've got my hands full. Either I'm a fool or Kittering is as innocent as you are of that rustling and these murders. I'm going to need help. Will you take a deputy's badge?"

Jim Allard's eyes widened. It took him a long moment to say, "You've got a deputy, haven't you?"

"A man with a skull too thick to have many brains," Blythe scoffed. "You seem to have some, although they work the wrong way sometimes. Will you take a badge?"

Jim slowly shook his head, his ready smile taking away the sting of his refusal. "Not for any money you could name. I know when I'm well off."

Blythe sat down in his chair. "I don't have much luck," he sighed wearily, having half anticipated the answer. Then he glanced up and said shrewdly, "But you're lookin' for work."

Jim nodded. "I may see Allard."

Blythe's lined face settled into a frown. "So it's like that, eh?" His shoulders gave an irritable lift. "A little advice, stranger. If I was you, I'd stay as far from Allard's place as horseflesh would let me."

"Advice, or a warnin', sheriff?"

Blythe seemed about to give an explosive answer. But finally all he did was wave a gesture of dismissal: "I've got some thinkin' to do and I can do it best alone."

"As good a habit as I know." Jim cast one last glance at the two canvas-wrapped bodies and went out the door.

5

JIM tilted his Stetson down to shade his eyes against the sun's midday glare, shouldered his way through the curious onlookers on the walk and sauntered obliquely across the street to the Melodian saloon.

Over a glass of bourbon at the bar, he lost the last cool excitement the presence of Billy Walls' body across there had given him. His thoughts ran clearly over all he had learned since spilling his coffee into his fire at the camp in the gorge last night.

The first few pelting drops of rain had given him the idea of leaving Billy and the other dead man as they lay, so that it would look as though they had fought it out. He'd put the two empties from his gun into Billy's. He'd ridden down the gorge in the beginning of the storm and put ten miles behind him before he made his second camp, without a fire, and hit the blankets with his poncho drawn up over his head to keep the rain out.

Today he had found a relative on the verge of settling a score with an old enemy. He'd found a sheriff wily enough to whitewash a murder and keep it as his hole card. He'd found a range cocked for trouble—*a war*, Billy had said, *their kids won't finish.*

Furthermore, Spade Deshay was somehow involved in this. Not openly—for a healthy reward on Spade's head, along with an obviously honest sheriff, meant he'd stay under cover. Jim wondered about Spade, what cards he held in the hand that had been dealt today.

That prompted another thought. Exactly where did he, Jim Allard, stand in this? Blythe had given him some sound advice after making that strange offer of a deputy's badge; that advice had been to get out of the country. Yet a streak of stubborn recklessness in Jim ruled out that move. Billy Walls had been a good friend, as good a one as he could remember in a life too fast-moving for the making of many strong ties. Billy was dead from a bushwhacker's bullet. There was small satisfaction in thinking he'd killed the man who had cut Billy down. What he wanted was to find the man who'd put Elder on Billy's trail.

He owed Billy a little effort in squaring that account. And the thing that had brought him here, Hugh Allard's telegram promising *something interesting if you get here in a hurry*, reminded him that his pockets were nearly empty and that he hadn't yet heard Hugh's proposition.

"Better stick around," he decided, speaking half-aloud. When the apron brought him his change for his drink, he said on impulse, "I'll have another," and excused this extravagance in the surety that shortly he would be relieved of his temporary financial embarrassment. Hugh Allard had seemed to be a man who knew what he was doing.

Over that second drink, Jim justified his reasons for keeping his mouth shut at the inquest this morning, after the doctor had announced the judge's death as accidental. It didn't matter to him how Locheim had died. But it did matter that someone—someone other than Elder—had had good reason for silencing Billy because of what he knew about that murder. If Billy had lived, Jim might have gotten the whole story out of him. But, since he didn't have that story, keeping to himself what he knew about the judge's death might give him an advantage. Just as the sheriff had kept mum about it for the same reason.

Leaving the saloon, he was remembering the conversation he'd overheard in the sheriff's office. Here was another advantage he had: he wondered how differently Hugh Allard would have talked had he known that the man he had called in so mysteriously was receiving information firsthand.

Two hours later, one of Mary Quinn's meals under his belt, he went to the feed barn for the claybank. He saddled and asked the youngster who took his money how to get to Allard's place.

"Pitchfork?" The boy scratched his head. "I could get there myself. But as for tellin' you, it's a job. You go four miles north and take the road to the right at . . ." He hesitated, looking out onto the street, then added, "The best way's to go with that girl, Allard's daughter." Before Jim could stop him he was calling, "Miss Ann!"

Jim turned. The girl on the buckskin he had noticed this morning riding in with Allard's crew was passing on the street. She answered the hostler's hail with a lift of her hand and reined the buckskin in toward the barn's ramp. She gave Jim a casual glance as she halted and he lifted his hat to her. She said, "Hello, Mark."

"Stranger here was askin' the way to your place," the boy told her.

Hazel eyes with a rare depth and a frank quality of directness examined Jim again, this time not casually. Jim said hastily, "Thanks, but I'll find it all right."

"You might and you might not." Ann Allard's voice was rich, almost husky. "You're welcome to come along with me. It'll save you time."

"I'm obliged," Jim told her, and stepped up into the saddle.

She turned back into the street and he fell in beside her, one quick glance showing him the profiled face that had stirred him so deeply this morning. Closer, her looks were even more striking. She was slim enough to look well in the tight-fitting waist-overalls. Her blue and white checked shirt, open at the throat, was tight across boyish shoulders. Yet she was a woman, having lost that gangling unrounded figure of girlhood.

It wasn't until the last 'dobe house at the edge of town lay well behind that either of them spoke. He noticed her studying the claybank intently. All at once she said, "I'll give you three hundred for that horse."

Jim laughed. "I wouldn't sell for twice that."

"All right, then! Six hundred."

He whistled softly. "Now that's temptin'. But how would I get around?"

"I'll throw in this gelding. He's a stayer."

He shook his head, his glance going approvingly to her buckskin. "Sorry, but he's not for sale."

"I didn't think so."

She smiled across at him in a way that made her face radiant and afterward dismissed the matter as though she had hoped for too much. There was no anger in her; she had tried for something, failed to get it and accepted it with an unwomanlike indifference.

As they went on, she asked pleasantly, "You're going out to see Hugh?"

He nodded. "About a job."

His reply brought a brief look of puzzlement to her eyes, and there was a new reserve in the glance she gave him. It was as though his answer somehow made her hesitate to continue the pleasant turn their conversation had taken. She looked swiftly down at his empty waist. "I thought we were through hiring."

He shrugged his shoulders and let it go at that. For the next three miles neither of them had anything to say. He noticed that she had increased the pace and was keeping it at a reaching trot, one not conducive to much talking. It made him wonder at the sudden change in her.

Until now, he had gained a lot of information by keeping his identity unknown. He was wondering what this girl's reaction would be on finding out who he was.

At the turning four miles out, when they struck into the narrow belt of broken country footing the higher hills, she pulled in to breathe the buckskin. Jim made it his chance to say, "Ever hear of your cousin Jim?"

Her head came around quickly and she gave him a direct stare. "Who hasn't? Do you know him?"

He nodded.

Her eyes widened in sudden wonderment; there was some alarm in them as she breathed, intuitively, "You're Jim Allard!"

Again he gave that slow nod of his head. It brought a surprising reaction. Brief anger flared alive in her eyes— anger as sudden and violent as the striking of a dust devil on a hot windless day—then that was gone and she seemed to draw into herself behind a shell of quiet aloofness.

Presently, curious over her reaction, he said, "You're surprised?"

She tilted her head in a brief affirmative. She didn't speak.

He began to feel a tenseness building up between them. It was clearly due to the mention of his name, and that angered him; she was evidently too reserved and polite to say what was on her mind.

He said, "Anything the matter?"

"No."

He laughed, softly, dryly, not wanting to press her for answers but his pride having its way with him. "You froze up mighty sudden. Didn't know I could do that to anyone. I'll have to remember it."

She turned on him abruptly, asking in a hushed voice, "Did . . . did Hugh send for you?"

"Wired me to come."

The color drained from her face, and the expression on it was one of acute shock. "He's hiring *you?*" she spoke barely above a whisper, seeming aghast, and the emphasis was on the last word.

A slow fury was building up in him. "Something wrong with that?"

"Please!" she said. "I'd rather not talk about it."

"About what? Me?"

"Yes. I just don't understand it."

"What? Hugh bringin' a killer in?" He said the word "killer" with a virulent scorn.

She gave him another of those direct looks. "You are one, aren't you? They put a price on your head for killing one man, didn't they, and gave you a pardon because you killed another?" Her face paled before the onrush of words she couldn't keep back. She murmured quickly, "I'm sorry I said that," and touched the buckskin with spurs and drew on ahead of him.

He let her go, misery outriding his anger. He had goaded her into saying what she had; now he was ashamed—ashamed of his outright brutality in making her speak, ashamed of his past that made such an accusation possible.

A bitter mood settled over him. He was asking himself when, if ever, he would outride the reputation these owlhoot years had saddled on him. Yes, he'd killed a man—two in fact. First was the Senator's son, an arrogant glory-hunting braggart who had tried to sleeve a card in a game of high-stake poker and then drawn a gun when Jim had called him on it. It was a clear case of self-defense, but the law, backed by Senator Rolf, hadn't chosen to regard it as such. Jim had never been in jail, but in the three years the law wanted him he had learned the ways of men on the dodge—learned them from Spade Deshay, mostly. His pardon and that second killing had come unexpectedly, after a shoot-out with one of Spade's underlings who had, single-handed, looted a bank and killed a deputy sheriff who was boyhood friend of Jim's. Jim's going after the killer had not been to gain a pardon. But it accomplished that for him, throwing him back into a society that didn't trust him and wouldn't let him get a new start.

Ann, seeming to realize his mood, had halted a hundred yards up the trail and was waiting for him in the shadow of a high rocky buttress. As he rode up on her, the pressing rock-reflected heat of this gaunt belt of badlands seemed to Jim as tortuous as the heat and confusion of his own mind. He resented this girl's opinion of him and was shamed by it even though it was the opinion of most others. Strangely enough, he wanted her to think well of him.

She dropped in alongside again without a word, her expression grave and embarrassed. She seemed to be studying the braided reins in her hands, and it was several moments before she said, low-voiced, "You're not as bad as all that, of course. I should have known. But I . . . I have nothing to go on but what I've heard about you."

"Forget it," he said gradually, feeling a fool because his voice broke from its habitual smoothness.

"No, I don't want to leave it like this." She seemed possessed of the sudden urge to talk. "You can't realize what this means to me, your coming. Things are going on here that I can't quite grasp. You aren't the first!" There was a faint surprising bitterness to her words now. "But I've overlooked these others, thinking that Hugh was merely . . . well, protecting himself. Now I know he's doing more than that. I'm worried, terribly worried!"

There was a look of pleading in her eyes when they came up to meet his. It left him helpless. "What can I do?" he asked.

"You can ride out of here! You can turn back, tell Hugh anything! But leave." She paused, struck by some inner thought. Then: "I'd even . . . pay you to leave, Jim. It wouldn't be much, but I have money."

A moment ago he had softened toward her. But her last words brought back his self-loathing, his anger. She had been talking to him as a misjudged and respected man there for a minute; then she'd offered him money, as though his loyalties, his guns, were to be had for a price.

There was an acid quality to his answer, smoothly drawled: "Not a chance. You couldn't match Hugh's offer."

That, definitely, broke the last tie of feeling that had momentarily drawn them together. She accepted the insult calmly, with no answer, as though it was deserved for the one she'd given him. They rode on steadily, each engrossed by thoughts too deep for wording. They traveled the bed of a shallow-walked canyon, coming presently to a branching in the trails.

"That's the way to Kittering's," she told him, lifelessly, and indicated the branching to the right that led south and east. She took the one to the left, striking northeast. It led them immediately up out of this arid land to the first timbered foothills.

They traveled the foot of a high ridge, mounting it gradually. Jim, awakened to the full realization of what his coming here might mean to this girl, went on stripped of his cloak of habitual wariness, hardly seeing the trail that unfolded before him.

He was jerked from his morose thoughts when she said suddenly, "What's he doing up here?"

He looked at her and followed her glance, which had gone on up the trail. He saw a rider on a buckskin horse shades darker than hers cutting off through the trees three hundred yards above on a higher turning of the trail.

"Is he out of bounds?" he asked, matching her casual interruption of the silence.

Ann was frowning worriedly. She didn't answer at once. When she did speak, there was real concern in her tone: "He's a Kittering man. But that wouldn't mean much to you."

"No," Jim said, and let it go like that. He, like she, wondered what a rider of Kittering's was doing here on Pitchfork's trail, for he was well aware of the feeling between the two outfits.

Their way abruptly climbed the face of the rim and over it. Jim saw that it marked a definite dividing line between the badlands and the sparsely grassed flats below and a broad lush-grassed mesa that stretched northward for as many miles again as they'd ridden since leaving Sands. Up here it was cool, and the fragrance of pine and grass made the air good to breathe.

The girl lifted a hand to indicate what lay ahead. "There, Jim Allard, is Pitchfork. Does it look big enough?"

"All of it?"

"All of it. Thirty thousand acres. And still he hasn't enough to satisfy him."

"How come?" Jim was relieved at the absence of any feeling against him. The girl seemed to have put from her mind the subject they had discussed back there.

"Why does he want more, you mean? I wish I knew. Judge Locheim, the man whose funeral you must have seen in town today, was about to pass a ruling that would either keep Pitchfork inside its fences or move the limits to double what they are now. Hugh's fighting for that."

"Something about creek water, isn't it?"

She said, "Yes," and a weariness seemed to settle over her as she put the buckskin on along the trail.

That was the end of their conversation. Twenty more minutes of riding put them close in to the eastern edge of the mesa, and Pitchfork's headquarters were all at once in sight from behind a neck of timber coming down off the nearest wooded steep hill slope. Jim let out his breath in a soft whistle at sight of the maze of outbuildings and corrals.

Hugh Allard had laid out his place with an eye to the blending of the practical and the spectacular. Set close in to the timber to the east, toward the peaks, the spread had ample protection from the chill winter winds and was open to the prevailing southerly breezes of summer. Except for a poplar-bordered lane in front, the low-built and sprawling house commanded a broad uninterrupted view of all Pitchfork's holdings. It seemed to look down austerely and aloof on the sun-baked world, outward and below, where lesser men made mightier efforts to exist on what Hugh Allard had scorned.

Bunkhouse, sheds and cook shack were built in a well-ordered U in a grove of cottonwoods far enough south of the house to give Allard the privacy his position as lord of his vast cattle empire demanded. Then, farther out and in the open, were corrals, two barns—one newly roofed—and half a dozen lesser buildings. On the hill behind the biggest barn stood a windmill and a large galvanized water-storage tank, with a pipe line leading down the slope from it. The trail Jim and the girl now followed, along with one striking down off a hill spur to the south—the one Fred Blythe had come in on last night—were the only visible approaches to the mesa.

At the inner end of the lane, as they came into the clean-raked graveled yard in front of a low patio wall, the girl said, "You'll find Hugh in his office. First door to the right." She reined aside, starting obliquely across the yard in the direction of the corrals. She stopped abruptly and turned to him once more. "I'd like to be wishing you good luck, Jim," she said. "But I can't. So here's hoping your luck's bad!" She went on and into the cottonwoods, not looking back.

6

JIM kept the claybank at a stand at the yard's outer edge and watched Ann Allard until she had passed out of sight through the trees. He tried to put her definitely from his mind. Only then did the first small excitement of being near the goal of his long journey come to him.

He remembered his guns and reached around and took them from the pouch of his saddle, cinching the belts about his waist and thonging holsters to his thighs. Their reassuring weight did something to ease his mind and, with a lift of his shoulders that was intended to shrug off the dark brooding run of this thoughts, he looked toward the patio gate.

A man stood there, idly leaning against a post of the archway. His look was directed toward Jim watchfully. Jim had the immediate impression that he'd been observed carefully since coming in along the lane with the girl and, putting the claybank across there, his hunch was presently proved accurate.

This was Trent Harms. Jim had seen him siding Hugh Allard as Pitchfork's crew came along Sands' street this morning, and rightly concluded that he was Allard's *segundo*. Harms was medium-tall, his frame heavy without being awkward. His watery blue eyes were now fixed on Jim in a winkless, faintly hostile stare. Jim caught that hostility and wondered at it. He drew up at the tie rail near Harms, leaned over with left forearm on the horn of the saddle and asked, "Allard in?"

Harm's answer was a long moment in coming. The interval he waited was obviously intended to impress Jim with something. Then, instead of answering Jim's question, Harms put one: "You get acquainted fast, don't you?"

His glance traveled briefly in the direction the girl had taken. His tone held pointed irony, and Jim immediately understood the belligerence in the man. Harms somehow resented Jim's having come here with Allard's daughter. His manner was as transparent as it was intended to be obscure. Harms was plainly jealous; his welcome, a blunt throwing aside of range courtesy.

There was another thing in back of his curt question. Jim sensed it keenly. Harms was here and now trying to settle which of them was the better man. Why, Jim didn't know except that he suspected Harms had forgotten everything before that sight of Jim coming in the lane with the girl— their talk must have seemed somehow intimate and friendly from a distance.

He knew this breed of man. As his glance strayed coolly over Harms, he saw that here was no common 'puncher but one whose brains had lifted him above the bunkhouse ranks. Harms wore two guns, very low at his thighs. They spoke of proficiency that had nothing to do with current cattle prices, the tonnage hay would run to the section of land or the merits of cross-breeding Aberdeens with longhorns.

Understanding all this, Jim let a measure of arrogance come into his look. Then, deliberately, he swung down out of the saddle facing the man. He drawled, "Any objection to how I go about it?"

Harms' sureness left him, not visibly, for his impassive expression didn't change; but a deepening shade of color mounted to his dark face and he pushed out from the gatepost, thumbs unhooking from his belts to hang at his sides.

He said, "I'll see if Allard's busy," and turned abruptly and stepped in through the gate.

"I'll see, too!" Jim sauntered in after him.

Harms stopped and turned halfway around as the whisper of Jim's spurs followed him. Hostility edged the expression in his eyes more violently now. But something about Jim's sureness seemed to take his own away. He turned without a word and led the way to the door of the righthand wing facing the patio. Jim was a stride behind as he opened the door, stepped in through it and said in that same toneless voice, "Man to see you, boss."

Jim was in the doorway—blocked by Harms, who had a hand on the door's latch. Across the room, his back to its one window, was Hugh Allard. He gave Harms a quizzical look, seeing that he stood in Jim's way. "Ask him in, Trent."

Only then did Harms step aside and allow Jim to enter. The rancher said, "I'm Allard. You want to see me?"

Jim nodded. "Alone," he drawled bluntly, his eyes on Harms.

Sternness showed on Hugh Allard's face; it was obvious that his first impulse was to give an angry answer. But in the brief moment he hesitated he must have seen the same quality in Jim that had made Harms hold his temper at the gate. He said finally, "It's all right, Trent. Wait outside."

Sullenly Harms turned and went out the door, banging it shut. He didn't look at Jim.

Allard said, "You want to be careful of Harms. He's an unforgiving son." Then, when Jim made no comment, he indicated a chair, asking, "You're Jim Allard?"

Jim nodded, ignored the chair and glanced around the room. It was small, orderly, severe. The back of the flat-topped desk was lined with stacks of the *Stockman's Gazette,* a veterinary manual, an open wooden file crammed with letters. There was a big deal file case against one side wall, a small heavy safe opposite it on the other. A hog's back stove sat in the left outer corner. Balancing it, on the other side of the window, was a spool bed that had been cut down to a settee and covered with an indigo and black Navajo blanket. It was a man's room—lacking even the feminine touch of curtains at the window, which looked out toward the screening cottonwoods between the house and the crew quarters.

At length Jim took the proffered chair, but only after Allard had seated himself in the deep leather one in front of the desk.

Allard said bluntly, "You're a day late."

"You said to stay out of sight gettin' here. That takes time.

Does it matter?" Jim drawled, allowing the same arrogance he'd used with Harms to creep into his tone.

"No," the rancher said, and for a moment they sat openly regarding each other. It was in that measuring way that is a necessary preliminary to the meeting of two strong-minded men. Allard, finished with his inspection, added another small indictment: "You didn't waste much time making yourself known."

"That couldn't be helped. I didn't have any say in it." Jim knew that Allard referred to the inquest.

"It would have been better if you'd have drifted into things sort of easy, like I suggested."

"Into what things?"

Once again Hugh Allard let a brief silence run its course, as though passing second judgment on this man. Finally he asked cautiously, "Can you stay on here a while?"

"As long as there's anything to keep me."

"You don't have business back there—nothing to take you back?"

"No."

Allard drew in a deep breath and let it out in a long easy sigh. "I was hoping for that. We can go ahead with it."

"With what?"

Pitchfork's owner leaned forward in his chair. "Jim," he said, "I want you to hear me out. I want you to listen to what I have to say and think it over before you give your answer." He settled back in his chair again. Then, slowly, speaking so as to drive home each word, he added, "I might as well come straight out with it, Jim, I'm making you my heir!"

The "Jim" was intended to show a break, from Hugh's reserve of a moment ago, into affability. Jim sensed a lack of genuineness in it, although he didn't know why. He breathed a soft whistle, saying dryly, "Come again."

Allard raised a hand, as though anticipating objections. "I know it sounds fishy. But it isn't. You're my one surviving relative, however distant, outside the immediate family. It's time I was looking ahead, finding good hands to leave Pitchfork in."

An instant's rearranging of his ideas left Jim with disbelief and wariness. He realized in that moment that he was facing a shrewd and wily man, one whose motives were as deep-running and obscure as the swift-running waters of a muddy stream. And, because he sensed that Hugh Allard must necessarily be a tightfisted man to have gained his present position, because he himself had never gotten anything he hadn't sweat for, he laughed softly and drawled, "You've already got an heir, Allard. What's the hitch?"

"Ann hasn't the business head to take over my affairs. She doesn't know ranching. You do."

"What's the rest of it?" Jim asked.

"I'm in trouble. You can help me out of it."

Jim reached to the pocket of his vest for the tag of a Durham sack. "Trouble? What's the matter with Harms taking care of that?"

Hugh Allard gave his coughing laugh, slowly shaking his head. "Trent's about as subtle as a range bull. No good at a time like this. I need a man with a head on his shoulders, one with something at stake in this. Anyone tell you what's happening?"

"Between you and Kittering? Yes."

"What was said about us?"

"That sooner or later you'll tangle. That Kittering's mindin' his own business, while you're not. That you're trying to steal water from him and drive him out. That you're a range hog."

Hugh Allard's face colored. It wasn't customary for him to be addressed in this manner. He decided to overlook it. "Miles Kittering moved in on me six years ago," he said, "on graze I'd used since I came to this country. For six years I've held back, feeling the pinch of overcrowding. Last spring I thought I had it licked and dug a new channel from a creek in the hills to catch spring floodwater. Kittering raised hell about it. So much hell it gave me an idea. I went to the courts with it, wanting to throw up an earth dam and save snow melt for both outfits. Kittering was to get his share; I'd get mine and be able to raise enough feed in my hill pastures to make up for what he took away. But he wouldn't trust me, because the dam was to be on my land and I'd have control of his water gates. It's gone on that way, Kittering fighting me at every step."

"I'd fight, too."

Allard nodded soberly. "Naturally, for what was rightfully yours. But I'm giving Kittering what's his."

"A share of the dam? A contract that names the amount of water he's to get?"

"I don't have to do that. He's got my word, which ought to be enough. Understand, I can put this through legally without giving him a cupful of the water from Antelope. Unless things clear up, unless my herds stop straying off into the hills, that's exactly what'll happen."

"Who says Kittering's been rustlin' your beef?"

"I do. And that's where you come in. I've never bucked the law, never burned an ounce of powder that wasn't used in fighting for what's rightfully mine. I don't intend to now. But it looks like Kittering's run hog-wild on the idea he can break me. I want a man who can fight him, backed by the law. I want this thing rammed down his throat. If he gets caught, if he's driven out, then it's his own fault!"

Allard's logic was strong and Jim knew it. But there was one weak point. As he touched a match to his smoke, he drawled, "I hear friend Spade Deshay is prowlin' the country."

The change that rode over Allard was a barely perceptible tightening of the facial muscles. Yet it was there and Jim caught it.

"Who said Deshay was down here?"

"Your sheriff," Jim lied, shying away from mentioning his friendship with Billy Walls or his presence up the canyon when Billy had met his death last night.

His answer seemed to satisfy Allard, who said noncommittally, "Then it must be true. But what's that got to do with this other?"

"I know Spade, used to travel with him. He's got a peculiar likin' for anything on the hoof."

"But this is Kittering's work. Deshay, even if he is in this country, wouldn't know the tricks of losing these herds in the hills the way they've been lost."

Jim shrugged his shoulders. He had learned something, which was that Allard knew of Deshay being here. In order not to spoil his small advantage over the rancher and give his suspicions away, he quickly changed the subject. "This heir business. What does it amount to?"

Allard had his answer ready. He straightened in the chair and reached over to take a paper from a pigeonhole at the back of the desk. The paper was bulky, folded, and bore an engraved legend on one side. He held it out to Jim.

"Here's a copy of my will. Read it."

Jim's hands remained folded, thumbs hooked in the waistband of his Levis. "You tell me what it says. I get tangled up whenever I see anything a lawyer's written."

Allard tossed the paper back onto the desk. "You and Ann will have equal shares in my estate when I die."

Something was wrong here, something that didn't need even Jim's memory of the hard times for a widowed mother after his father's death to remind him that Hugh Allard wasn't noted for his generosity. This talk of Kittering being on the offensive, of trying to break Pitchfork, didn't hold water any

more than this outright gift Allard was making Jim. Now
Jim played for time to peg exactly the flaw in Allard's story.

"What's my share to amount to?" he asked.

"You'd be a rich man, one of the richest in the state.
There'd be a job for you commencing now, at wages you can
name for yourself. At present there's something like a quarter
of a million in cash in two or three banks. Then there's Pitchfork. Name your own figure on what it's worth. There are
two thousand shares of railroad stock, with a place on the
board of directors for any good man by the name of Allard.
All this, and half the business property you saw in Sands
today."

Jim let the silence drag out after the rancher had spoken,
appearing to consider what he had heard. Then, suddenly, he
put a question: "How come you want Kittering's layout?"

For a moment Hugh Allard was caught off guard. His mask
of impassivity vanished before ready anger reflected in his
black eyes. It was gone in an instant and the old inscrutability
was masking his face once more. "I don't want it. I've found
a way of getting all the feed I need without it."

"Then why do you want Kittering out of the way?"

"Who said I wanted him out of the way? I don't give a
damn what happens to him! So long as he lets me alone! It
looks like he isn't going to. I want a man here at the head
of things who isn't a gun hand, who has a legal right to fight
for Pitchfork, to take the whole crew against Kittering if
need be."

When he had spoken, another, a longer, silence settled
over the room. The rancher shifted nervously in his chair,
seeming to sense that it wasn't his position to be arguing this
stubborn relative into accepting a fortune.

Jim leaned forward in his chair, elbows on knees, and
surveyed Allard fixedly.

"See if I've got this right, Allard. You brought me in here
to put me on the spot, since I've broken pardon parole in
crossing a state line. Next, because I've got an unearned
reputation for bein' able to catch lead in my teeth and to spit
it back twice as hard as the guns that threw it. Last, because
you've heard somewhere that I don't draw the line at bushwhack!"

Allard, his face gone suddenly purple with anger, opened
his mouth to protest. Jim gave a quick lift of the hand that
silenced him.

"Then, after I've put Kittering out of the way on this
promise of yours, one of two things can happen. That will's
probably genuine, for you'd naturally expect me to check

on it. Even so, you'll act righteous about it and throw me to the wolves—which is the law. Or you'll take the easier way and sick your gun dogs on me and put me away under some nice cutbank in the hills: You'll have what you want, Kittering's layout. You won't have to be afraid of the law because you've been aboveboard in the whole thing. You won't have had any hand in it. I'll be a busted-down relative you tried to help but who turned against you."

He sat back in the chair, hooked his thumbs in his belt once more and watched the quiet fury take hold of Hugh Allard. He let it get only so far, until Allard was about to speak again, before he drawled softly, "Why not make me a fair offer? Name the price you're willing to pay to get Kittering out of the way."

The controlled rage registered on Hugh Allard's face faded slowly before a look of gradual bewilderment, so unexpected was Jim's bland statement. The bewilderment changed to shrewdness. Abruptly Allard smiled, saying, "Damned if you don't take the cake, Jim! All right, five thousand."

"Make it ten, in gold."

"Ten it is."

Jim let out his breath in a long and gusty sigh. He came up out of the chair in an indolent straightening of his tall frame, looking down at the rancher in open scorn.

"Allard," he drawled, "you've got a stink about you that'd turn a skunk's stomach! I wouldn't touch your job with a California rope!"

Hugh Allard stiffened and his face turned a sickly yellow. "You—"

"But here's what I will do!" Jim cut in. "I'll go to Kittering and—"

A loud knock at the door interrupted his words. He wheeled toward the door, said, "Careful, Allard!" and a moment later the rancher called, "Come in!"

The door swung open and Trent Harms stood there. His glance purposely ignored Jim and settled on Allard instead. Jim knew by the look on his face that he understood instantly the point the interview had reached.

Yet the ramrod said casually, "Johnson's here. Wants his money for the horses."

Allard's hand started to the inside pocket of his coat. Then some inner thought made him turn his chair to the desk, saying, "He'll have to take a check." He reached for a ledger-sized checkbook at the back edge of the desk, opened it and sat for a minute writing.

· He tore the check out and Harms came across to take it. Back at the door again, Harms paused. "Everything all right, boss?" he asked.

Allard nodded, and Harms went out. When the sound of his boot tread had faded beyond the gate, Allard looked at Jim. "Then we understand each other?"

Jim nodded.

"Better pull stakes and drift," Allard said.

"Maybe."

The rancher's glance narrowed. He was more his old self now, cold, calculating, even smiling faintly. "There are ways of framing a man," he said.

"Try one. I know a few myself."

Allard nodded. He was about to say something else but checked himself. Then, with a last look at Jim, he turned slowly and faced the desk and picked up a sheaf of letters. The interview was plainly at an end. Jim went out.

The door across the room closed so softly that Allard couldn't be sure of the exact moment Jim left the room. He didn't trust himself to look back over his shoulder and be sure until a full minute had passed. Then, as he swiveled around in his chair, a violence of raging anger lay naked on his face. He heard the staccato echo of the claybank's hoofs striking out across the gravel of the yard. They receded into the distance and finally faded altogether. But Allard's hateful look didn't ease.

Another sound came from out there, that of a man's boots slurring across the patio. With visible effort, Allard put a check on his feelings. Once more the mask of impassivity fell over his face. For a long, unguarded moment, alone, he had relaxed his eternal vigilance and made no attempt to hide his feelings. Now, hearing the approach of a man across the patio, he retired swiftly behind the sure barricade of a cool exterior.

Harms came in the door.

"Well?" Allard said, his voice suave.

Harms gave a cryptic nod. He came across and let the folded check Allard had given him a few minutes ago fall to the desk top.

"Better burn it, Trent."

Harms lit a match, opened out the check and touched the flame to one corner. The tightly scrawled words that faded into the gray ash of the burning paper read: *Put a man out to get Allard as he leaves. He's going to Kittering. Pay Johnson.*

Allard couldn't keep a little of his irritation from showing.

He asked querulously, "He was proddy from the minute he stepped in here. What happened between you two?"

"He came in with Ann."

"So?" Allard's glance narrowed as he tried to catch Harms' eye and couldn't.

Harms shifted nervously, hiking his pants up along his waist. "I didn't like it, was all."

Allard smiled wryly. "Trent, remember who you are," he drawled, referring to a private matter that lay between them. Then the rancher seemed to be thinking of his other problem and idly reached over to take a pencil from the desk, twirling it between thumb and forefinger.

After a long interval, Harms said, "Then it was no dice?"

Hugh shook his head. There was a return of his sparing smile. "No. He's pretty smart, that *hombre*. Maybe too smart!"

7

PITCHFORK'S lane behind him, Jim headed out across the mesa feeling small satisfaction over his parting with Hugh Allard. He wasn't underestimating the ability of his distant relative to carry through that last threat of framing him if he didn't leave the country. The warning from another man would have caused him some amusement and little anger. But now he was vaguely uneasy, even though he rode across open ground and had drawn well out of range of the trees butting the hill slope. He glanced off toward the crew quarters. He could see no one moving near the corrals or bunkhouse. The lifeless look of the place held a subtle menace, that same quality of hidden undercurrents that Hugh Allard's make-up seemed to carry.

He scanned the hill spur to the south and saw a faint line of lazily hanging dust marking the recent passage of a rider. But that trail angled higher into the hills at a mile's distance and he put it from his mind as a possible source of danger. All the way to the rim he was thinking back over his conversation with Hugh, and again he failed to find any assurance in the fact of having uncovered the rancher's willingness to pay big money to have a man murdered.

The trail down off the rim wound through a thin stand of jack pine. As the heat of the badlands welled up out of the bottoms, the silence grew oppressive, somehow threatening. A taut wariness rippled steadily along his nerves, cocking him to a sure keenness. He couldn't explain it nor his feeling that the stillness seemed unnatural.

All the way to the branching of the trails he rode that way, stiffly erect, watchful. He paused there at the forks and finally took the turning to the southeast, the one Ann had said led to Kittering's. He was prompted by the decision to warn Kittering.

Some of the tension went out of him as he climbed abruptly to higher ground, took the gate through Pitchfork's fence, and cut into a hilly terrain unlike that he had left. He must now be on Kittering's graze, he told himself, and he took it in with a critical eye. The hills were heavily timbered, the hollows pitched to severe slopes and thin of grass. Two miles after going through the fence, he knew that this poor graze would never have contributed much to Pitchfork's prosperity. Hugh's claim of needing this grass was pretty thin. A man couldn't run more than fifteen, at the outside twenty, head to the section here.

He thought back on his meeting with Harms, smiling meagerly at the recollection of how he had turned the man's baiting back upon him. It was an old device, learned in the years he'd traveled with Deshay. He knew it was a bluffing and brutal one; yet more times than he could remember it had served him well, that quick show of blunt arrogance that left nothing but a sultry and unforgiving anger in the man it was directed upon. Harms wouldn't soon forget.

The abrupt-climbing hills gentled out as the faint trail took him sharply east, higher toward the peaks. The meadows between them became broader but no richer. He traveled along the bed of a narrow dry wash for nearly a mile before the trail swung south and into the open again. He thought all at once of the sheriff. Blythe surely must know by now that Locheim had been murdered. Jim had caught an expression on the lawman's face, when the doctor made his announcement, that was much like that of a small boy who had been nearly caught telling an untruth. Yes, Blythe knew.

As he crossed a wide thinly grassed pasture, a rocky incline rose sharply to blot out the horizon to the south. To the east and upward lay a gradual slope, timbered, letting into a higher tier of the hills. Downward at less than a mile began the rocky breaks that edged the open flats and the desert.

His long frame was swinging loosely to the motion of the claybank's unhurried walk. The tension had gradually gone out of him as he dropped the miles behind. His thoughts were outside his immediate surroundings, engrossed in feeling for the tag ends of this knotty problem.

All at once a warning signal as definite and unmistakable as sound flashed sharply into his consciousness. Instantly it brought back the uneasiness of half an hour ago.

Without waiting to interpret it, knowing only that reflected bright light had flashed from the slope ahead, he kicked his right foot from the stirrup and bent down in a roll that started him out of the saddle.

At the precise instant he moved, a searing pain coursed across the flat muscle of his upper left arm.

As his hand hit the ground to break his roll, the sharp crack of a rifle sounded across the still air. Then he was down, his body cocked for a lunge that would bring him to his feet.

At that instant an impulse struck him so forcibly that he lay where he was, unmoving, calling softly to the claybank, "Stand, boy, stand!"

The animal's head came up and the nervousness that rippled across his sleek muscles died out. He stood utterly motionless between Jim and the hill slope that had thrown out the rifle's explosion, the sureness of a patient and light-handed training putting him instantly alert and obedient.

In the next forty seconds, Jim changed his position so slowly that it would have been imperceptible to even a close onlooker. He moved his head slightly, so that the claybank's legs and belly framed a generous brindle rectangle of the distant slope. He moved his left arm—the one he lay on—a bare four inches, aware of the smarting pain of the bullet gash, until his hand closed on the butt plates of his .38. He lay that way, unmoving, listening, for a long five minutes.

He was finally rewarded in the coming of a small sound he at first thought a fault in his hearing. It was the distant faint striking of metal on rock. Then, barely as he defined it, he saw a rider on a scrubby roan horse appear from behind a high rock buttress at the foot of the hill.

The man was all of a hundred yards distant. He sat looking out toward the claybank for long seconds, a Winchester upmuzzled and with stock plate resting on the flat of his thigh. Then he lifted the reins and brought the roan straight out toward the claybank at a slow walk.

When he was twenty yards away, still too far for Jim to be sure of his target, he swung off in a narrowing circle, evidently wanting to get a better look at the man his bullet had brought down. There was no trace of doubt in his maneuver, but it had the wariness of a hunter who uses caution in approaching all downed game that, alive, has been dangerous.

When the rider passed out of his line of vision, Jim had nothing but sound alone to guide him. His shoulder muscles, then his back muscles, crawled at the expected slam of a bullet as the roan's hoof thuds sounded in half a circle that ended at his back. There was a moment's pause that seemed an eternity. Then the animal was moving again, this time in on him.

He let the sound come nearer, almost on him. Then, with a sudden pushing of his right arm, palm flat on the ground to brace him, he rolled over quickly. He swung his sights on the target of the man's shape in a race with the Winchester's downarcing bore. He triggered his weapon by instinct. At the explosion, amazement ripped away the sudden alarm in the rider's thin face. The hands that held the Winchester clawed open, then up to the blood smear on the flat chest. The roan shied and the man's dead weight left the saddle in a loose roll. He struck hard on one shoulder; his legs bent convulsively once and straightened rigidly.

He was dead by the time Jim stood staring down into his face.

Jim's look took on a bleakness as his gray eyes roved the neighboring hills for further sign of danger. His eyes remained bleak and cold as they went down to study the outstretched figure at his feet. He had been forced to kill a man and now, considering his deed soberly, he couldn't regret it. This man had chosen his way of life and lost.

Shrugging, Jim looked off to where the roan horse stood downheaded, nibbling at the grass shoots fifty yards away. He caught the animal and led it back alongside its owner. Looping the reins over his arm, he heaved the body's loose weight belly-down across the saddle. With the rope that was looped near the horn, he bound the dead man's wrists and ankles tightly to the cinch, speaking gently to the nervous animal from time to time.

Next he unthonged the rifle's scabbard and transferred it from the roan's saddle to the claybank's. As he picked up the Winchester and took it over and thrust it into its boot, he studied again the first thing he had noticed about the weapon—the Pitchfork blaze burned in the walnut stock. Here was Hugh Allard's first act to back his advice on leaving the country. Jim decided he'd keep the weapon as tangible evidence of his luck in having come through as bad a seven minutes as he could remember.

He tied the roan's reins to the horn. His last act was to shuck a handful of .30-.30 shells from the dead man's belt.

Then he slapped the roan across the rump and stood watching it trot across to the timber to the north, nervous under its unfamiliar load, bound for its home corral. He took off his shirt and wiped clean the ugly gash along his arm, binding it with his bandanna. Then he went on. The sun was lowering now.

Barely twenty minutes later he rode a trail out of a tree margin that edged a bowl-like pasture flanked by low hills. Looking to the east and up the pasture, he spotted a blue spiral of smoke climbing out of the late afternoon's elongated shadow near the far edge of the timber. There squatted a large log cabin and a cluster of outbuildings and corrals that he knew must be Kittering's Block K.

As he rode in on the place, his critical eye approved the workmanlike spread. No beauty or ostentatiousness here. There wasn't a tree or a shrub to break the bare monotony of yard between cabin and barn; there were even stumps where tall cedars had been hewn down to open the space for utility's sake. And, unlike Pitchfork, he saw men moving openly about between corrals and sheds. He counted four of them.

He was still a good two hundred yards out from the nearest corral when two riders left it and came out the faintly marked trail toward him. He slowed the claybank's trot to a walk and let them come up on him—one solidly shaped man with a short-clipped black beard, forking a brown, and his companion, exceedingly tall and thin, striding a big-headed black that looked at first like a scrub but had the leg action of a stayer.

"Howdy," said Fats Holden as they pulled aside and reined in a few feet ahead of Jim. "Lookin' for someone, stranger?" His dark blue eyes took in the guns slung at Jim's waist, the rifle and finally the smear of blood along the shirt sleeve. He shot Miles Kittering a quick look that might have meant anything, or nothing.

"Looking for Kittering," Jim replied.

Before Kittering could speak, Holden said quickly, "He ain't over there. Reckon you'd find him on the way across to a neighbor's. I'm Holden, foreman."

Jim was disappointed. After a glance at Holden's somber-looking companion, he decided that the foreman would have to do. His judgment, mature for his years, told him at first glance that Holden was a man who would bear trusting. The long bony face with the oversized nose had an outright honesty stamped on it that was either genuine or a guileless mask behind which a dishonest man would have gone much further than the rodding of this small layout. The keenness of Holden's eyes promised a quick brain, shrewd perhaps but lacking in instinctive cunning. Fats Holden's looks—the loose-hung shirt and trousers over a gaunt and ungainly frame, sagging bony shoulders and knobby hands—approached the comical. But that somehow failed to count when a man looked squarely at his face as Jim was doing now.

On the way across here, Jim had made a decision; namely, that he would have to warn Kittering. "I've come straight from Pitchfork," he said. "Hugh Allard offered me a job. I didn't want it. I'm here lookin' for the same thing, work."

Holden's brows came up quizzically. "Particular, are you?"

"Particular enough not to take pay for bushwhack, which was all Allard had to offer."

Kittering spoke sharply in his deep, booming voice: "Bushwhack?"

Jim nodded.

Holden drawled, "You're sure you didn't take him up on it?" He was looking pointedly at the Winchester with the Pitchfork burn along the stock.

Jim decided that neither of them would believe him if he told exactly what had happened at Pitchfork. So he shook his head and said, "No. But he'll get another man to try the same thing. Better tell Kittering not to stray around alone much."

Holden's glance hardened. "What's the play, stranger? You've got a habit of spookin' people, ain't you? Like at the inquest this mornin'!"

Holden's disbelief was so plain that Jim couldn't find a ready answer. Holden evidently took his silence for confusion, for he lifted reins, about to put the black into motion, saying, "We aren't hirin', stranger. As for Kittering, he can take care of himself. He—"

Kittering said, "Hold on, Fats." Then, looking squarely at Jim: "Who are you?"

"Jim Allard. Hugh brought me in here to do a quick job for him and wind this thing up. I told him to go to hell."

"Jim Allard, from Socorro?" Holden laughed softly. "Try again, stranger. Jim Allard can't set foot outside New Mexico without havin' a reward slapped back on his head." He jerked his head to Kittering. "Let's be goin'."

Kittering hesitated a moment as Holden went on past Jim. Then, almost reluctantly, he followed his foreman.

They put a hundred yards behind them before Holden abruptly turned in the saddle and looked back to see the man on the claybank standing where they had left him. He drawled softly, "I wonder," and looked at Kittering.

"Wonder what?" Kittering queried curtly. His square face was set in a frown of worry.

"Hell, he just might be this Jim Allard. He's got a look about him. Then there was that rifle with Allard's brand on it."

Kittering's dark glance sharpened. He hadn't noticed the rifle marking.

Holden went on: "Miles, when are you gettin' next to yourself? He could have been tellin' the truth."

"Then why didn't you say who I was?"

"How'd I know but what he was there to do the job he said he turned down? Who 'gulched Elder and Billy Walls last night? Not us, but someone did. What's to keep Allard from sooner or later sendin' someone over here for a try at you? He'll have an excuse cooked up, one that'll hold in a court of law."

Kittering slowly shook his head. "Hugh Allard will never settle this by bushwhack, Fats."

"You're all-fired sure of what Allard'll do!" Holden spoke in a quick flare of anger, surprisingly, for there had been nothing on the surface of Kittering's words to occasion it.

They went on in silence, cutting sharply south at the lower end of the pasture. From there Holden looked back to see the claybank disappearing into the timber along the trail that led across to Pitchfork, and for several minutes he was thinking of the stranger and his stubbornness at the inquest this morning.

Finally he pulled in close to Kittering. "Miles, what if you knew the judge was murdered instead of kicked to death?"

Kittering's glance swung around; his dark eyes were bleak-looking, and there was a trace of real fear in them. "Don't talk that damn' nonsense, Fats!"

That answer only deepened Fats Holden's knotty thinking. Late yesterday afternoon, at the time Judge Locheim would have been riding for Pitchfork, Miles Kittering had been away from Block K, riding alone. And last night when Holden had casually asked him his whereabouts during the afternoon, Kittering's reply had been a little too vague to suit him.

This along with Kittering's look just now and his strange reluctance to fight back at Allard when it was obvious that he was being crowded into either fighting or running were things Fats Holden couldn't understand. He couldn't even get Kittering to talk about it. On top of this was the knowledge he'd gained in listening this morning at the back window of the drugstore. Kurt Locheim had been murdered, with buckshot. Did the stranger know that or was he a stubborn man who had been playing a hunch? Was he really this Jim Allard that legend had made a Robin Hood of outlaws, or was he a saddle bum trying to talk his way into some free grub and a clean bed for the coming winter layoff?

Holden was impatient with Kittering. They were on their way to see a neighbor about the now seemingly trivial business of a broken fence.

Holden said abruptly, "You go talk to Corbett. I'm on my way to town."

"Something the matter?" Kittering asked, his frowning regard on his foreman.

"Nothing you could savvy." Holden was curt as he swung aside, striking west and north. He went on without another glance at Kittering.

He was suddenly hungry for the companionship of someone who could understand and not ask questions. Invariably, when he felt this way, he'd go to town to see Mary Quinn. Maybe he'd only stop in at the restaurant for a cup of coffee, to be bolstered merely by her presence. Or, if things went better, they'd get to talking and pretty soon he'd have told her what was worrying him and she would have either straightened it out or given him her generous sympathy.

She didn't know how he felt about her, he was thinking— probably never would. But tonight he wanted to get away from Kittering and his trouble. There was a dance in town, unless it had been postponed out of respect for the judge's death. If Mule didn't get there first, and if there was to be a dance, maybe Mary would go with him.

The clang of the cook's triangle broke late afternoon's drowsy stillness that lay over Pitchfork. Men drifted in from the corrals and barns and lined up at the bench and washbasins by the well house, their shadows long streamers thrown out across the yard. Trent Harms sauntered over there and said to one of the crew, "Lay off Louie for one night, Shorty."

Shorty Adams, one of the oldest hands and chief complainant on the demerits of the cook's coffee, grinned and drawled, "He'll be hurt if I don't say somethin'."

"Forget the clownin'. Mind what I told you!"

Adams sobered, nodded gravely and set about lathering his hairy forearms. When Harms was in this mood it paid not to argue or even pretend to argue with him.

"Anyone seen Eaton?" one of the men asked. He got no reply.

Harms waited until they'd filed into the cook shack at the summons of the cook. It was a little too early yet for supper at the house, where Ann and Hugh and Trent ate. He went to the cook-shack door and stood idly leaning there, listening to the sparse run of words as his men packed the food away. Ordinarily he kept pretty much aloof from the crew; but this evening he was restless, a little worried. He was wondering why Eaton hadn't come back.

A horse at the big corral whinnied and was answered by another from the direction of the pasture. Harms, curious, turned and looked over there. He saw the roan walking in off the pasture and he saw the burden roped to its saddle. Eaton had ridden a roan away from here this afternoon as Jim Allard left. A small excitement hit Harms for a moment, then left him cool and already resigned to what he knew was coming.

He looked back toward the table and the crew. "Daniels, come on out here a minute," he said casually. "You, too, Utah."

He waited until the two came out the door; then led the way to the big corral, which seemed to be the point for which the roan was headed.

Behind him, he heard Daniels catch his breath and say explosively, "Hell, give a look at that, Harms! It's Eaton!"

Harms drawled, "That's why I got you too. I want him out of the way before the rest find out. We'll bury him after it's dark. Turn his jughead out onto grass. And if anyone asks where he is, he asked for his time and hit for town."

He stayed with them long enough to see the roan led behind the corral and out of sight—long enough, too, to make sure that Eaton was dead, as he'd suspected he would be. He had little feeling for the dead man; his thoughts concentrated mostly on Jim Allard in a cold dry anger.

Presently, he left Daniels and Utah and walked in through the cottonwoods to the house. It was a few minutes past the usual supper hour. He'd have to think of some excuse to give Hugh if the girl was there, for Pitchfork's owner demanded punctuality at mealtime.

Ann was standing, straight and slim, with her back to the big fireplace in the living room's long wall. Her face held a tight, wide-eyed expression that at once warned him something unusual had happened.

He said, "Sorry I'm late."

For a moment she made no reply, standing there staring at him in obvious alarm. Then, in a hushed voice: "Trent, what happened to Eaton?"

The question caught him off guard. He hesitated, his slow brain trying to think of a story to give her once he realized she'd seen what had happened down by the corrals.

She said, "He's dead, isn't he?"

All Trent could do was nod, and his answer widened the alarm in her hazel eyes.

"How, Trent?"

"You've got me." He shrugged his heavy shoulders. To cover his confusion, he queried, "Where's Hugh?"

"He left for town an hour ago. Trent, why was Eaton shot?"

He could see something deep in her eyes that had never been there before, something that disturbed him more than the question. He sensed that he'd have to be very careful about his answer.

"Why does anything happen around here?" he said gruffly.

An interruption came as the hall door opened. Hugh Allard's Chinese cook appeared to announce, "Supper ready, Missy," and closed the door again.

"You're trying to say he was killed by Kittering's men?" the girl asked, hardly aware of the interruption.

"That'd be my guess." He spoke without thinking, on the defensive.

"But, Trent! That isn't Kittering's way!"

He knew how she felt about Kittering and knew he'd made a mistake in agreeing with her guess. Now there was a live suspicion in her eyes. It angered him and he told her, irritably, "Your supper's ready. I'll be along in a minute."

She made no move. "Aren't you going to tell me, Trent?" she asked.

"Tell you what?"

"What you know about this."

"Should I know anything but that Eaton's dead?"

"Where was he when he was killed?"

"Along the south fence."

"What makes you so sure he was there?"

"I put him out yesterday, when Billy Walls didn't show up."

"But I saw him down by the barn this afternoon."

A flush darkened his face. He had been caught in his lie. He couldn't think of anything better to say than, "He must've come in for grub." Then, all at once feeling an imagined accusation in the glance she held on him, he turned to the door leading out onto the patio.

"Trent." Her calling his name stopped him. "I don't think we'd better go in to the dance tonight."

"Why not?" he said sharply.

"Don't you know? Because of Vera Locheim."

He was disappointed and showed it. "You're takin' that too hard, Ann."

She gave him a long level look, said simply, "I'm fond of Vera," and left him, going through the hall door that led to the dining room. He stood a long moment looking after her and his face was slack before the knowledge that this girl didn't quite trust him. He'd been very particular in everything he did and said around her. Lately she'd seemed to favor him. But something unworded that was building up between them now changed all that.

8

JIM ALLARD made the branching in the trails below Pitchfork's high mesa as the brief dusk was thickening into total darkness. He was headed back for Sands, reluctantly, faced with the knowledge that neither side would have him, that Hugh Allard could and would wreck his last chance of staying on here and serving as Fred Blythe's deputy. Allard would simply let the sheriff know who Jim was and that would be an end of it.

Passing this point in the trail this afternoon, he'd been keenly wary after the direct threat Hugh had made. That wariness had paid him a good dividend when the threat was made good. Now he felt let down, uncertain and vaguely helpless after Holden's flat refusal to hire him. At first he'd resented Holden's manner; now he saw that Kittering's foreman had acted shrewdly.

A shadow passed close over his head, etched plainly against the deep cobalt of the night sky. He jerked in the saddle and his glance whipped up there. It was a big owl, gliding silently and low over this treeless waste of land on his night hunt. Jim smiled at the touchiness of his nerves. The smarting of the bullet crease on his arm didn't help this feeling of frustration and defeat. Nor did the heat, which hadn't slacked off with the coming of darkness; it was heat stored up by naked rock under a full day's baking by the sun and down here, out of reach of any breeze, it would last well into the night.

He put his mind to the problem at hand, the possibility of staying on here. He wanted to; in fact, he told himself nothing would make him pull out. First, there was Billy Walls and the matter of exacting his small vengeance for Billy's bushwhack. Then there was Hugh Allard, his blunt offer, his warning and finally the killer he had put out after Jim. That had taken on the cloak of a challenge, one Jim wouldn't let pass. He could stay here, of course, wait out his time and chance to meet Hugh alone. He would have absolutely no feeling about prodding Hugh into a shoot-out and killing him. The man had made an attempt against his life and a return of that favor was part of the code that ruled men's lives.

But was this what he wanted? No, he told himself, it wasn't. Giving the law one more excuse, this time a sure one, for wanting him was a foolish act. Slim though his chances were for the future, he didn't want to undermine them.

What he did want was to throw in with Kittering against Hugh. As far as he could see it, Kittering was in the right and would, if he lived through this, come out with the law on his side. But Kittering was obviously refusing to fight Allard. Neither was Kittering, or Holden, rather, disposed to hire a man who came to Block K nursing a grudge against Pitchfork. Was there any way of making Kittering hire him?

He gave this last a lot of thought, considering and throwing aside half a dozen ideas until finally one seemed workable. Kittering was evidently a stolid and stubborn man. But there were limits to which a man's patience could be tried. Exceed that limit and even Kittering would strike back with the same stubbornness that had held him aloof until now.

Jim reached down and let his palm run over the smooth walnut stock of the Winchester nudging his right leg. Then, his plan taking on its final shape, he left the trail along a stretch of rock that would hide his pony's sign.

He was at the east upper end of Kittering's meadow as the wheeling stars overhead told him the time to be just short of nine. He left the trees and came in toward the layout with the claybank at a slow walk, his senses attuned to all the night sounds, interpreting them, wary of any foreign sound that might mean danger.

Dismounting a good quarter-mile short of the cabin, he tied the stallion's reins to the branch of a low-growing cedar. This far away, there was little danger of the stallion whickering and giving away his presence. He fished into a saddle pouch and brought out a dog-eared envelope and the stub of a pencil. He tore the back from the envelope. Using the hard smooth surface of the saddle skirt, he carefully printed out a brief crudely penciled message on the scrap of paper.

It read: *Hire Jim Allard and it's war.*

He started down in the direction of the cabin. Just short of the low sandy hog's-back he stopped long enough to remove his boots, hanging them from the left side of his belt by their straps. He went on, being careful to cross the hog's-back behind the barn along a shallow cross wash that put him close in to the corral. He worked around the barn and then in toward the cabin, keeping the roofed well house between him and the one lighted window along the cabin's side wall. From behind the well house he waited two minutes in the faint hope that the light would go out. Then, knowing he was increasing his risk each moment he remained here, he came erect and stepped soundlessly toward the obscure rectangle of the cabin's side door.

His breathing came shallowly as he hugged the wall alongside the door, then stooped to pick up a rock and place it on top of the scrap of paper which he laid close in to the door's sill. He left the cabin and crossed the thirty-foot stretch of open yard as soundlessly as he had come. Beyond the well house his pulse settled to its usual slow beat and the nerve tension left him. He was pulling on his boots beyond the hog's-back before the end of another ninety seconds.

The quarter-mile walk back to the claybank tried his patience. But in the end, as he climbed into leather once more, he was glad for having taken this precaution. He reined immediately north toward the shadowed dark line of the timber. Once in among the trees he turned toward the layout again.

Seven minutes of careful going put him within sight of the cabin, this time looking down on it from the north. He dismounted and drew the Winchester from its boot. He filled the magazine with some of the shells he'd taken that afternoon from the belt of Hugh Allard's dead crewman. Then he walked a few paces that put him out of line with the stallion and went belly-down on the sloping ground, the rifle cradled across a rotting windfall.

His first shot ripped away the night's silence with a suddenness that startled him. Before its flat echo had slapped back from the far hill across the pasture, he had levered a fresh shell into his weapon and sent it speeding after the first. His target was the faintly outlined bucket hanging from the pulley of the well-house roof. Into the sharp explosion of that second shot he heard his lead whang into the metal, saw the bucket pitch and swing.

What he had expected immediately happened. The light in the window died. The door's shadow became blacker and he knew that it was standing open. He drew a careful bead to a point well above the door and squeezed the Winchester's trigger a third time. Into the echoes of his shot the solid slamming of the door shuttled clearly up to him.

He moved away from his position with a knowing quickness. He had taken three steps to one side when a gun answered from below. The *whunk* of the striking lead sounded from the pulpy windfall behind which he had been lying a few seconds ago. His lips drew out into a thin half-amused line.

Twenty yards to the left of his first position, he took up another. He picked it purposely so that the trees blocked out all but a narrow windowless rectangle of the cabin's side. The length of stovepipe atop the stone chimney was centered in that slit. He threw four bullets down at it, his firing quick-timed, sure. The fourth shot knocked the pipe from its mounting and it clattered down along the slope of the shake-roof and hit the ground in a staccato metallic banging.

Again a gun spoke from down there. A second joined it. He distinctly heard the air-whine of the bullets a few feet out from him. But he was well protected here, the trunks of two pines directly in line with the window, so that as he stepped backward deeper into the trees the threat of further replies from the cabin didn't interest him. He walked far up the hill slope before he cut across to where the claybank stood. He climbed into the saddle and walked the animal on up and away through the trees. Minutes later, he crossed the trial at right angles and continued west until he had descended well into the breaks.

He went through Pitchfork's fence the way he had come. An hour and fifty minutes after riding out of sight of Kittering's cabin, he was crawling in between thin blankets in his room at the Prairie House in Sands, too dog-tired to take off anything but shell belts and boots.

Sands' street lay deserted and asleep at this late hour. The lights in the Melodian went out at midnight and the last man out through the swing doors, the barkeep, closed the shutters and went down the empty walk and straight home to bed. As was the case almost every night, his echoing footsteps were the last to pass along the street.

Starlight laid an edge of deeper shadow in under the awnings. The faint glow of lamplight came through the glass side panels of the door to the hotel lobby. In there, the old clerk on night duty stirred on his cot in the cubbyhole room behind the counter and rolled over restlessly, his snoring breaking to a steady deep breathing. A black cat, tail gently swaying, walked the length of the veranda rail and jumped soundlessly to the top step and settled there, licking a paw and then sitting motionless, gleaming eyes scanning the shadows at the foot of the steps.

Somewhere to the south a rooster sent a restless call into the night and far out on the flats a coyote's yipping complaint went unanswered. For two hours after the echoing stride of the saloon's barkeep had faded down the plank walk, the street seemed to be resting peacefully under the night's cool blanket of starlight. It was as though Sands were taking these hours of darkness to gather strength for the coming day of hot sunlight and dust; the town seemed ghostly and deserted, the winking green light of the semaphore tower near the station the only visible evidence that life still went on. The silence was acute, so complete that it seemed tangible —something that shrouded the long wide street like a curtain.

A muted sound like the far-off slamming of a heavy door stirred that curtain of silence.

That sound, thinly muffled in the hotel's upper story, jerked Jim Allard to abrupt wakefulness. He stared into the total darkness of his room. He heard faint rapid steps going back along the hallway.

He came up swiftly off the bed, reached for one of his guns hanging in holster at the bedpost, and crossed to the door of his room and opened it. Looking back along the dark corridor outside, he caught a fleeting glimpse of a faint shadow against the window of the back stair well. It was gone instantly, and afterward he couldn't be sure that he had really seen it.

The first thing he noticed was a sliver of light that cut across the bare board floor from under the closed door of the adjoining room. He stepped over there, knocked. He got no answer and pushed the door open.

A hunched-over figure sat in a chair by the washstand across the room. Across the white-shirted back was slowly spreading a stain of crimson. The figure sagged limply in the chair. The head, turned sideways and resting on an arm, showed a middle-aged face, untanned, slack.

The man was dead.

Jim stepped into the room, his glance shuttling to a half-open window he knew must let out onto the roof of the neighboring store, as did his own. His attention swiveled to the made-up-bed, a suitcase lying open on it, then back to the dead man again. He saw for the first time the butt of a gun showing over the top seam of a hip pocket.

All about the man was that looseness that comes with death. Even the muscles of the face were relaxed, the lips slightly parted. The eyes were wide open, staring glassily and tinged with a look of hurt bewilderment. The suit coat hanging from the bedpost, the white shirt and string tie, clearly denoted a city-bred man.

Jim noted something else that brought him nearer so that he leaned over the washstand. The arm on the far side hung toward the floor, and on the floor lay a pen. A fresh ink splash dotted the boards near by. Jim's glance came up again. Now he could see one corner of a white sheet of paper edged out from under the arm on which the dead man's head rested. He reached over and gently lifted the arm.

He read two lines of a finely penned message across the top of the page: *Dear Art: The party I mentioned in my letter yesterday has today offered me a bribe* . . .

That was all, except that at the top of the sheet was printed in small blocked letters: *Survey Engineer's Office, Sierra and Western Railway, Denver, Colo.*

Later Jim could never be sure of the impulse that prompted him to take that sheet of paper and stuff it in his pocket. He was all at once aware that someone was mounting the stairs from the small lobby and that a moment ago a man's gruff voice had called something he hadn't caught. All he knew in that instant was that he had heard mention of a railroad today; who it was had mentioned it, he couldn't remember. But it associated itself in some way with a fragment of the puzzle he was putting together, and this was the thing that guided him now.

The steps came along the hall and stopped. Jim turned to see the watery-eyed oldster who clerked at the desk below standing there. At first there was suspicion and anger in the old man's sleepy look; then he saw the body, and fear edged into his eyes and he caught his breath. He stared down at the .38 in Jim's hand, and once more there was fear in him, this time real enough to make Jim drawl, "It wasn't me, partner. I heard the shot and came out of my room. You'd better get the sheriff."

The oldster gulped and swallowed with difficulty, as though his throat were parched. Without a word he turned and went quickly back along the hallway.

In the long minutes before Jim heard a sound in the building again, he first stood staring vacantly down at the dead man, trying to see beneath the surface signs to the motive for this killing. The letter meant almost nothing to him. The silence dragged on, oppressively, good evidence that

the Prairie House was no gold mine to its owner. Finally, he
went to his room and pulled on his boots and sloshed some
water into the basin on his washstand and bathed his face.
He was refreshed by his sleep but felt the need for more.

When he heard footsteps cross the lobby below, he dropped
his Colt into a pants pockets and went back into the adjoining
room. There was a quicker tread blended with the dragging
one of the old clerk's coming up the stairs.

It was Fred Blythe who stopped short in the doorway,
giving Jim a single cursory glance and muttering, "You
again!" before he came on into the room. His inspection
of the body was brief but thorough. Ended with it, his thin
face was pale and drawn and set bleakly in anger. He muttered,
"Didn't have a chance! Gun's loaded. Hasn't been fired for a
coon's age." He rammed the weapon in his belt and turned
to the old clerk, who had come into the room and was
standing near the door. "Charley, what do you know about
this?"

"Nothin'. The shot woke me and I clumb up here quick
as I could. Found him here with that iron in his hand." He
nodded to indicate Jim. "He sent me out to get you."

Blythe glanced obliquely across at Jim. "What about it,
Allard?"

The mention of his name came so abruptly that Jim
couldn't quite conceal an expression of surprise. Blythe smiled
wryly.

"The shot woke me. I came out my door in time to see
someone taking the back stairs. He . . ."

"Get a look at him?"

Jim shook his head. "No. There was a light on in here.
I knocked and pushed the door open. You know the rest."

Blythe's glance shuttled involuntarily to the pen lying on
the floor, to the ink spot near by. "Are you sure?" he
drawled. When he had caught Jim's nod, he added, "He
was writin' something when it happened. Where is it?"

Jim's broad shoulders moved in a shrug. He met Blythe's
level glance over an interval of silence. Then irritably, the
lawman began a search of the room. The thing he spent
the most time on was the cowhide suitcase on the bed. He
knelt there, carefully examining the clothes and other
articles inside. As the job progressed, he spoke without
turning around.

"Hm-m . . . railroad man. How long's he been here,
Charley?"

"Come in on yesterday afternoon's train."

"Anyone been here to see him?"

"Nope. He hired a rig and drove out somewheres this mornin' before the inquest. He was back about supper-time. Ain't been out of the room since he et."

"Who'd he eat with?"

"Now how the hell would I know that?" Charley growled in his old man's irascibility.

"How about you, Allard?" Blythe went on. "Ever see this man before?"

Jim's head moved in a negative. He put a question of his own, nodding to some papers Blythe had been sorting through. "Any idea what he was doing here?"

"Not much. He's a survey man for Sierra and Western. None o' this is his writin', though." He locked the suitcase and mopped his brow with his bandanna, although the air in here was chill from the open window.

"The fourth in twenty-four hours," Jim said in a low voice. Then, pointedly: "Still think you could use me over at your jail, sheriff?"

Blythe had been standing with his back to Jim, bending over the bed. At these words he straightened slowly and even more slowly turned, his right side toward the window. When he was halfway around, Jim saw his right arm moving. At the exact instant he read the lawman's purpose, Blythe was standing there with a short-barreled .45 in his fist. It was cocked and lined at Jim's belt buckle.

"Sure I can use you, Allard," the sheriff drawled. "Only it'll be in a cell, not the office! You're under arrest."

Jim said, "For shootin' this man?"

"Not yet. Right now I'll say I'm holdin' you for extradition. Tomorrow a wire goes to the nearest New Mexico sheriff. He ought to be glad to come over here to pick you up and take you back." Blythe hefted his weapon a bare inch, signaling the clerk. "Get his iron, Charley!"

"Hold on!" Jim said sharply, taking a backward step toward the washstand that brought Blythe up tense. "Did Allard tell you the proposition he put me this afternoon? That he brought me in here to 'gulch Kittering? That I turned him down?"

Blythe's face took on a crooked smile. "He said you'd have some cock and bull story to hand me. Only it'll have to be a better one than that. Hugh has too many brains for that, Allard." Once again he moved his gun. "Hoist 'em! Charley, get in behind and dehorn him."

Jim was close to the washstand, where he wanted to be. He lifted his hands to shoulder level as the old clerk came in behind him. Then, quickly, he stepped back hard against

Charley. The oldster stumbled and sat down abruptly along-side the dead man on the marble top, knocking over the lamp.

As the chimney crashed and the room blanked out into darkness, Blythe cried stridently, "Out of the way, Charley!" and his gun exploded downward at the floor. Jim whirled, picked up the tipped-over lamp, and hurled it at the window. As the window smashed and glass clattered onto the roof outside, he ran for the open door and went through it into the hall a split second before Blythe's gun beat out its second deafening concussion.

Three long steps brought Jim even with his own door. He wheeled in through it, kicked it shut and dragged his heavy washstand in front of it. He cinched his guns to his waist. On his way past the bed he picked his Stetson from the straight-backed chair. The door panel groaned under a thrust from outside and Blythe's gun laid a sharp echo along the hallway. Jim heaved the window sash as high as it would go and stepped through the window. In the darkness he couldn't be sure of the drop to the store roof below. But Blythe shot again, his bullet knocking plaster from the wall a bare foot to one side of the window. Jim pushed himself out into space and let go.

He struck the tar-paper roof in a drive that buckled his knees and sent him in a low roll. On his feet again, he ran back along the flat roof to its alley edge. The drop into the alley was higher than the first, but he made it without losing his footing. He headed up the alley at a run, cutting in between two buildings to the street. Before he crossed diagonally toward the feed barn, he scanned the walks and made sure they were empty.

He went through the black open maw of the barn door just as the hostler was stepping, sleepy-eyed, from his office with a lantern in his hand. The youngster raised the lantern to see who it was, asking, "What's happenin' across there?"

Jim drawled, "They're after me, kid. Kill that light and lug my saddle out back!"

His tone and the guns he wore made the youngster hast-ily lever open the lantern and blow out the flaming wick. He went back along the barn's center runway to the saddle pole, where he took down Jim's saddle and started for the corral with it.

Jim whistled the claybank to him. The boy had thrown on blanket and saddle and was bending to pull tight the cinch when the sudden pounding of boots along the walk out front made him wheel toward the rear door again.

From out there came Fred Blythe's shout: "Mark! Where the hell are you, Mark?"

The boy's white face tilted up at Jim; but he made no answer, his fingers fumbling at the cinch strap. Jim said, low-voiced, "Get that gate open!" and stepped in to the claybank and tightened the cinch.

Blythe's boots were pounding down along the runway as Jim vaulted into the saddle. He swung up a gun and thumbed two shoots high in through the doorway. The claybank, nervous, reared. Jim swung him for the gate and rammed home blunt spurs. The animal lunged into a reaching run, blindly, implicitly trusting the firm hand on the reins. Twelve feet ahead, Jim saw the hostler fiddling with the lock on the low four-bar gate. It wasn't open.

In the instant his impulse was to pull in on the claybank, a shot racketed into the night from the barn's door. Jim held the claybank straight at the gate. Sure-timed, he lifted the animal's head and brought his knees in. The stallion acted on the signal, gathering steel-tough muscles under him and leaving the ground in a long, reaching jump. His hind shoes clicked a splinter from the top rail of the gate. Then his front shoes hit the ground surely and in one more stride he had put the corral out of sight in the darkness behind.

Fred Blythe had seen the stallion's dark outline rush for the gate, gather for the jump. His gun was half raised to lay that target in his sights. But as the claybank left the ground, sheer admiration held the sheriff in a tight paralysis. When he did think of his gun, it was already too late— the claybank's rhythmic hoof pound fading along the alley.

When it had gone out of hearing, Blythe called to the boy, "How high is that gate, Mark?"

"Taller'n I am. What happened, Fred?"

Blythe shook his head and pursed his lips and let his breath out in a barely audible whistle. "You saw it. He got away. Over the gate, not through it."

"I mean across at the hotel."

"Oh, that! Damned if I know!"

9

BREAKFAST at Block K was a ritual varying in detail but always of the same general pattern. It invariably ended with Fats Holden and Miles Kittering staying behind at the table to discuss the day's business. This morning that end was accomplished in something under the usual time, for Ed Beeson and Mule Evans and Johnny Dawes were well enough acquainted with Kittering to recognize the man's somber preoccupation and want to get away from it. They went outside and walked down toward the corrals, building their afterbreakfast smokes.

Holden wasted no time in coming to the point. He came out with it bluntly, as Mule Evans' boot tread faded out of hearing. "Well, Miles, what comes next?"

Kittering's scowl took in his foreman for a few seconds. But before Holden's direct glance, the rancher had to lower his eyes. He mumbled, with a lifeless quality in his deep voice, "We'll keep on mindin' our own business."

"After havin' lead thrown at us? After lettin' a man walk in here, leave a note at the door and hurrah hell out of us all at the same time?" Holden laughed mirthlessly. "Next time it won't be a warning. He could have burned you out last night!"

"We'll mind our own affairs," Kittering repeated.

Into a short silence, Holden said without rancor, "Is it the girl, Miles?"

"Leave her out of this!" Kittering flared.

"She's takin' the guts out of you, Miles! Allard knows that. He'll play it for all it's worth. This is only the beginnin'."

Anger smoldered brightly alive in Miles Kittering's eyes, making them surface-glinted, bleak. Holden disregarded that sign, went on: "Cut it off clean; forget Ann! Wait too long and you'll be run out without even your shirt on your back. That, or you won't have need for any shirt but a wooden one. Allard will—"

Miles Kittering's big solid fist smashed down onto the plank table. "Lay off!" he exploded. Then, in a sudden dying out of his anger, his solid frame eased back into his chair once more and he made a lazy gesture toward the door,

72

saying what he'd wanted to say for the past hour: "Better go in and see if you can hire this Jim Allard."

Holden went out, not because of any impulse to recognize Kittering's authority but because he knew that no amount of talking would change the man. Outside, he threw his half-finished cigarette into the dust and ground it beneath his boot heel. Then, cuffing his Stetson onto the back of his head, he stared up the slope to the west of the cabin, in the direction out of which Kittering and the others had said the rifle had spoken last night. He wished now he hadn't gone to town to see Mary Quinn, that he'd been here last night when the rifleman fired down at the cabin.

He had intentionally mentioned Hugh Allard in connection with that rifle, voicing to Kittering the thought the note had intended to convey. But, even though Kittering was positive, Holden had his doubts about the man who had delivered that note. He now sauntered on past the cabin and up the hill slope and five minutes later was carefully studying sign on the ground that gradually gave his keen eye a picture as clear as though he'd not been in town but standing here last night. Here was where the man had knelt, one knee on the ground, to fire through the lane of trees at the chimney. Here were four empties, .30-.30s, center-fired and from the chamber of a Winchester according to the pin markings.

He worked out from that spot and a few yards to the north found the imprint of a boot sole where the matting of pine needles was too thin to have erased it from the dirt. Behind a windfall he saw where the marksman had lain, the two small hollows where he had propped his elbows and scuffs in the soil farther back where the toes of his boots had rested. And, a few yards up the slope, he finally spotted horse-sign.

A quarter-hour later he was in the saddle of a bay horse and working south through the timber, following the sign of a pony with right front shoe toed in. Here and there the sign would fade in the thick carpet of needles under the trees. But Holden had a rare patience, and each time he lost the sign he cast ahead in a wide circle until it was clear once more. When it took him at right angles across the trail to Pitchfork, his eyes lost their faint look of puzzlement and a smile made his gaunt face pleasant-looking.

Shortly after crossing the trail, he lost the sign over the rocky floor of a shallow wash. But by then it was taking him sharply north, toward Pitchfork fence. Half an hour's casting at the foot of the wash failed to disclose it again, for there was plenty of rock and any man wanting to hide his back trail would have intentionally used it. So he kept the northerly direction, following the natural contours of the land and picking the easiest going for his many detours around the uptilted spurs that blocked his path. The sun, high now, was beginning its pitiless baking of this gaunt maze of badlands, and he rode in an oppressive dry heat that parched his mouth and nostrils and laid a trickle of perspiration along the channel of his spine.

Before riding down on Pitchfork's fence, he let his glance stray beyond until he was sure that no Allard rider was in sight. Then he cut east along the wire, studying it and the cedar posts with a critical eye. He rode the wire to the gate crossing of the trail. There he turned back and recovered his distance quickly and put the same careful attention to the stretch west of where he'd originally struck the fence. Half a mile below this point, he made his discovery.

Two posts showed fresh staple holes, and on one was an indentation alongside a freshly driven staple that could have been made by nothing but the sharp heel of a gun handle used as a hammer. But it wasn't this—unmistakable evidence that last night's marksman hadn't come prepared for fence breaking—that finally made his suspicions a certainty. It was three long horsehairs he found wedged in a sharp bark splinter of the post. The color of those hairs was of the exact shade he had yesterday seen in the tail of a claybank horse he had particularly admired. The claybank belonged to the stranger who had claimed relationship to Hugh Allard.

On the way in to Sands, Fats puzzled over the purpose of the stranger. At first the blunt arrogance of the man's maneuver last night brought up his anger, for Miles Kittering had been taken in by it. But Holden had a rare understanding of his fellow being and cold logic told him that this stranger's purpose was no shallow one of working off a grudge for not being hired. The note, its inference, wiped out that answer.

As he put his pony along Sands' dusty street, he had an open mind and nothing but a ready admiration for a man who would use such a devious and subtle way of accomplishing a purpose temporarily blocked. It was plain that this stranger had decided to take a hand in the fight that was building between Kittering and Allard. His reason, obscure, was the thing Holden intended discovering.

He spotted a larger than ordinary group of men on the veranda of the hotel and turned in at the hitch rail there and went on up the steps. Half a dozen of them greeted him and one said, "Hear about the shootin' last night, Fats?"

He had the whole story in five minutes—the details, he

knew, considerably amplified beyond truth. He pretended no more than a casual interest and left the veranda for Blythe's jail office soon afterward.

Fred Blythe was tilted back in his swivel chair, boots cocked up on his desk, staring glumly at the blank wall ahead of him as Fats entered. He jerked his head around, saw who it was, and didn't trouble to take his feet down, saying irritably, "Now what's botherin' you, fat man?"

"Not much," Fats told him, letting his high frame down awkwardly into the chair near the desk. He tilted back in it, took out tobacco, built a smoke and passed the makings on across to Blythe. "Thought I'd ask when Allard's going to swear out his warrant on Miles."

Blythe's glance came around sharply on him. "Suppose you let me worry about that."

"Then I can tell Miles not to go in hidin' just yet?" Fats was grinning.

Blythe lost the humor of the remark. "Tell him any damned thing you want!"

Fats took a long drag at his smoke. "They're sure pilin' up on you, ain't they, Fred? First the judge, then Elder and Walls, and now this railroad gent."

Blythe eyed the lanky man suspiciously, warily. "Why include Kurt Locheim in your list? We know what killed him."

"Sure," Fats drawled. "Sure." Then, changing the subject: "They say this feller that got away last night was Jim Allard from across in New Mexico."

Blythe nodded, his seamed face settling back into its harassed look once more.

"Goin' out after him, Fred?"

The lawman snorted. "I won't have to. He's headed back where he came from. He'll wear hell out of plenty of horse-flesh gettin' there. I've wired New Mexico to let 'em know he's on the way in. They'll pick him up for breaking parole."

"What makes you think he's headed back?"

Blythe reached down and pulled open the center drawer of the desk, taking out a crumpled piece of paper and handing it across. "This," he said.

Fats smoothed out the sheet and read: *Dearest: Today, just tonight, I have run across a man who once threatened to kill me. Tomorrow I hope to finish things here and get out before he remembers who I am. It's that old matter of helping Senator Rolf locate his son's murderer several . . .*

Fats looked up, frowning. "It's clear as ditch water."

"Jim Allard left in a hurry last night, too fast to gather up his things. That was among 'em."

"It's still ditch water, Fred."

Blythe let out a weary sigh and explained patiently, as though still wanting to convince himself of his theory: "Last night when I found Chalmers he had a pen in his hand. There were ink spots on the floor. It looked like he'd been writing when he got that slug in the back. Only whatever it was was gone. This morning Charley cleaned out Allard's room and brought me his stuff. This letter was poked down in his shavin' mug. He'd sneaked back to his room to hide it while Charley was rootin' me out of bed last night."

"Why?"

"Why! Because him and this young Rolf the letter mentions shot it out across there in Socorro a few years back. Senator Rolf had a reward slapped on Allard. This man Chalmers was mixed up in the affair some way and Allard had threatened him a long time back. He says there he was afraid Allard would make trouble for him again."

"So you think this Jim Allard would shoot a man in the back?"

Blythe said petulantly, evasively, "This letter makes it plain he held a grudge against Chalmers, don't it? And he hid the letter, didn't he?"

"You sure Chalmers wrote it?"

"I will be, soon as Charley finds his register across there with Chalmers' handwritin' in it. The old goat put it away last night and forgot where."

Fats raised his brows significantly in a look that wasn't lost on the lawman. Then he queried, "Why would Allard hang around the room and wait for you to come back and take him?"

"He wasn't expectin' I would. Thought he could bluff it through. Only I was after him anyway. Yesterday afternoon he blew in on Hugh Allard and tried to hire out to him. Seems he'd heard Hugh was havin' some trouble. Thought he saw an easy way of makin' money, so he broke his parole and came across here. He offered to pick a fight with Kittering and gun him down if Hugh's price was right. Hugh kicked him off the place and came in and told me about it. You know as well as I do how Hugh would take a thing like that."

"Yeah," Fats said in faint sarcasm. "Hugh wouldn't be that crude, would he? So Jim Allard got away after all."

Blythe nodded. "Jumped his horse over the feed barn's corral gate and high-tailed. He's halfway to the state line by now."

"What if he isn't?"

Blythe smiled wryly. "Let him show up around here again. I can take him on any one of three counts: breakin' parole and crossing a state line, conspiracy to murder and murder in the first degree. Just let him try it!" Abruptly his old impatience returned. "What the hell good's it doin' me to tell you all this! Go on; get out. I'm talked out; thought out! This thing's got me whipped!"

"Then here's something to buck you up, Fred," Fats said, rising up out of the chair and stepping across to the door. "Night before last Miles and I stood in the timber along that draw Rattlesnake Canyon and watched a bunch of strangers push that Pitchfork herd on up toward the peaks."

Blythe's boots hit the floor and he went rigid, swiveling around in his chair. "Say that again!"

Fats moved his head in a slow nod. "Thought I'd tell you, just in case you got to wonderin' what Miles and I were doin' when you called that night and found us out. I wanted to come back and get the boys and do some powder burnin'. Miles wouldn't let me."

Blythe's mouth was hanging open in sheer surprise. He snapped it shut, flared. "What's wrong with Miles! Why, won't he fight?"

"You try and guess it. I can't." Fats turned and went out the door, saying, "So long."

Out front he paused long enough to hitch up his pants and look both ways along the street, almost sure that Blythe would call him back in. But no sound came from the office, and shortly Holden went on along the walk and crossed to the tie rail in front of the hotel. He rode his bay on down to the feed barn and let Mark Dorn, Tate Olson's garrulous young helper, take him to the corral out back and tell him what had happened last night.

Here were the claybank's hoofprints where he'd taken off for the long jump over the corral gate. There, outside, was where he'd hit the ground again. The right front shoe of those prints was toed in.

"Damnedest thing I ever saw, Fats," Young Dorn told him. "There's only two horses in this country that could do it by day, that buckskin of Frank—"

"How'd he take out, down the alley?" Fats interrupted.

Mark nodded. "Like hell wouldn't have him!"

It was a little short of ten when Fats walked his bay out the street as though he didn't have a thing on his mind and wasn't in much hurry to set about doing it. But half a mile out, he swung east toward the hills from the trail and made a wide circle. Almost directly east of town he picked up the

claybank's sign, as familiar to him now as that of any horse
in the Block K string. He lifted the bay into a mile-eating
trot in toward the foothills.

The claybank's sign was easy to follow. In forty minutes
he was high in the hills beyond the strip of badlands that
edged them. He rode down into a shallow coulee and paused
briefly, openly, to study the spot where a horse had recently
been staked out to graze a circle around his picket rope. He
went on.

He was going into the first scattering of trees of a patch of
timber barely a quarter-mile beyond the coulee when a voice
spoke out sharply at his right: "Lookin' for someone,
Holden?"

The Block K foreman drew rein, turned slowly to face
the voice. Jim Allard stood leaning against a thick-stemmed
gray-bark pine, barely thirty feet away.

Holden smiled broadly and let his long frame slump out
of the tension the sound of that voice had put into him.
He drawled, "Yeah. You. This is luck."

"Whose luck?"

"Mine. I figured to come up on you sometime tomorrow."

The set of Jim's lean face was uncompromising and hard,
intended to convey a blunt hostility he didn't feel toward
the Kittering man.

It had its effect, for shortly Holden said, "You and me
have some things to talk over, Allard." He reached down
and unbuckled the shell belt he'd put on this morning, careful
to move his hands slowly. He tossed belt and gun out onto
a patch of grass and then swung down angularly from the
saddle.

He said, "That play of yours last night fooled Kittering.
He sent me in to hire you." He paused, got no reply, and
went on. "You're makin' slow tracks for a man the law
wants for murder."

Jim eyed him levelly for a moment, then said flatly, "I
didn't pack any grub away and I'm always sour before
breakfast, Holden. Forget the wise cracks. What murder?"

"That railroad man's." Holden went on to tell about the
note Blythe had that morning found among Jim's possessions,
ended by saying, "It's as sweet a frame-up as I ever saw."

"How come you think it's a frame-up?"

Holden smiled thinly. "Call it a hunch. Any man with the
guts to tell Hugh Allard off and then want to hire out to
Kittering bad enough to shoot up his place isn't going to pick
the middle of a town to work off a ten-year grudge by shootin'
a man in the back."

Without answering, Jim thrust his hand in a pocket and took out the crudely folded sheet of paper with Chalmers' even two-line scrawl upon it. He handed it across to Holden. The thin man scanned the page. He whistled softly. "No wonder the hotel register's missin'! This other didn't even come close to bein' the same handwritin'." He eyed Jim with that tight smile for a few seconds. "I reckon we've both got some things to get off our minds. Suppose I unload this first. Kurt Locheim took a load of buckshot in the chest before his stallion smashed him up. You know it. I'm here to find out how."

Jim's gray eyes took on a surface-glinted look of wariness. "Maybe you ought to answer that before I do."

"I was in the alley back of Hill's yesterday when Blythe and Swain left the inquest and examined the body."

Jim's look changed; his lean face softened a moment to show Holden that he believed what the other had said. In that interval each measured the other and in the end an unspoken understanding passed between them.

But it was an understanding Jim intended to qualify, for he said, "If you came up here with the idea of gettin' my reasons for being in this, you'd better turn around and go back again. I'm not ready to tell anyone what my reasons are. Not until I know who holds the hole card. But here's one thing you can have now. Before this is over I'm going to make Hugh Allard choke on his own guts."

Holden asked soberly, "That was the truth, yesterday—about him wanting to hire you to go after Miles?"

Jim nodded.

There was a brief silence while Holden digested this information. Presently, he noticed the brown dried stain of blood on Jim's upper left sleeve. He'd noticed it yesterday. He indicated it. "Want to tell me about that, too?"

Jim knew what he meant. He told about the man Allard had sent out to get him. When he'd finished, Holden swore softly, drawling, "A man's got to get up before breakfast to outguess Hugh Allard."

"This is before breakfast for me," Jim reminded him. "Am I in with you . . . knowin' only what you do now about me?"

Holden deliberated a long moment. "I reckon I can't be too choosy. Write your own ticket."

10

JIM nodded to Holden's gun lying on the ground. He smiled meagerly, drawling, "Better put that on before you forget it, Holden."

It was a gesture that sealed the understanding between them, vague though it was. Here was a man Jim could trust. It was already plain to him that he had Holden's trust and belief of everything he'd said.

Holden picked up the gun and cinched it about his bony hips. He said, "You'll want to know a few things. Fire away and I'll give you all the answers I can."

Jim nodded. "First, why won't Kittering fight this trouble when it's pretty plain he didn't bring it on himself? Next, I ought to know where you and Kittering were the afternoon the judge was killed and the other night when Elder and Walls cashed in."

Holden grinned. "Damned if you'd ever take a prize for bein' shy about things!" He sobered, heaved a long gusty sigh. "Two afternoons ago I was helping Johnny Dawes cold-shoe a span of mules at our corral. I don't know where Miles was. I wish to hell I did! By the way, that was Kittering with me yesterday when you rode into the layout. At the time, I didn't want you to know it. Thought you might be there to get him."

"He had the chance to meet Locheim and kill him?" Jim asked. He had already guessed that the rider with Holden in Block K's pasture yesterday afternoon had been Kittering.

Holden nodded, his face gathered in worry despite his trying to conceal it. "Yes. Only I know Miles like a book. Nothing would drive him that far. Besides, the judge was looking at things his way."

Jim filed this bit of information in the back of his mind. "How about that night?" he queried.

Fats had a ready answer, telling Jim what he and Kittering had seen in the draw below Rattlesnake the night the judge's body was found.

"What about the other?" Jim asked when Holden had finished. "What's between Kittering and Hugh Allard that keeps Kittering from fightin' this thing?"

"The girl."

"What girl?"

80

"Ann Allard. She's Miles' daughter, not Allard's."

Jim's look was a puzzled one. He waited for Holden to add to what he'd said. When the explanation didn't come, he drawled, "That doesn't make sense."

Holden slowly moved his head in a negative. "No. But I don't have the right to say more. It's Miles' business. You wanted the reason for his not havin' a backbone. There it is."

Jim hunkered down on his heels and built a smoke, passing the makings across to Holden. Finally Holden said, "What comes next? We're back where we started."

Jim shook his head. "Not quite. There's Spade Deshay."

"What about Deshay?" Fats' look sharpened.

"Didn't you know he'd drifted in?"

"The hell you say!"

Jim waited a moment. Then: "Mean anything to you?"

"It could," Holden admitted.

Jim said, "Spade's bought a hand in this or he wouldn't be here. I intend to find out what he's in it for."

"How'll you set about it?"

Jim shifted his position until his back was to the trunk of the pine. He glanced on past Holden and up along the reaching heights where the dark green of pine and cedar gave way to a lighter blanket of aspen edging the boulder fields below the gaunt peaks. "See if I've got this right, Holden. There are a hundred places up there where a bunch of men could hide as long as they wanted, aren't there?"

"Long enough to raise grandchildren."

"Years back, I traveled with Spade. I know his habits. Unless I'm 'way wrong, the man you saw with that herd the other night works for Spade."

Holden was frowning. "I see part of it, not the rest," he drawled. "Deshay has been in everything from raiding bullion shipments to rustling, hasn't he? You figure he's driving off Pitchfork's beef?"

"I think he's been hired to drive it off."

The nut-brown of Holden's thin face deepened a shade in anger. "Get this straight, friend Jim. All Kittering wants is to be let alone. There wouldn't be any point to his throwing in with Deshay against Allard."

"But there would be a point to Allard hiring his own stuff driven off so he could blame it on Kittering . . . if he wanted Kittering run out of the country."

Holden's anger left him at once. "The hell you say!" he breathed. Then a doubt came to his thin face. He shook his head. "It don't hold water. Kittering never made trouble for Allard."

"Then it must be he wants Kittering's layout."

"Why?"

Jim lifted his overwide shoulders in a shrug.

Holden went on: "Allard never needed that grass. There's something else behind it."

"And maybe Spade could help us find what it is."

Holden laughed softly. "You just agreed it'd take a man half his life to comb these hills and find a hideout. You're back where you started."

Jim frowned at the interruption, went on: "If I'm right, if Allard is working with Spade, he must have a man to keep in touch with the hideout. Give Allard a reason for wanting to send word to Spade about something, and that man will lead us up there."

"What kind of a reason?"

Jim asked, "How many men of Kittering's could be trusted to help us run off a small bunch of Pitchfork stuff and keep quiet about it afterward?"

Holden smiled at what he saw was coming. He thought a moment. "Ed Beeson and Johnny Dawes. I wouldn't trust Mule Evans on a thing like this. But, hell, Miles would never stand for it!"

"Don't tell him then."

Holden's wide mouth slowly shaped a wry grin. "It listens good, Jim. We could do it tonight. I'd have to make some excuse to send Mule away. Tomorrow the two of us could wait in that timber behind Allard's layout and spot whoever rides out . . . if anyone is goin' to. The thing I don't quite get is what good it'll do us when you do run onto Deshay."

"Throw a scare into Spade."

"How?"

"Can the station agent down at Sands be trusted to do a job for us?" Jim asked in seeming irrelevance.

Holden frowned his puzzlement at the question, finally shook his head. "Hugh Allard got him his job."

"Then where else could we go to send a wire?"

"There's a way station a few miles south. I know the operator, did him a favor once."

"Then let's get down there," Jim said, rising.

Fats, still squatting on his heels, looked up with a narrow-lidded gaze. "Why? What's this got to do with throwin' a scare into Deshay?"

"I think I know how we can do it. I'll have to get a couple of wires off first, though."

Still the thin man hesitated. There was a plain invitation here for Jim to share whatever thought was running through his mind. But Jim gave no sign of telling what it was and presently, with a meager shrug of his narrow shoulders, Fats said, "I reckon you know what you're doin'," and came erect and sauntered over to his pony. "How about that empty gut of yours?" he asked. "We've got some miles to cover if we hit that way station."

"You can pack me out some grub and a razor from Kittering's tonight," Jim answered, already in the saddle and obviously impatient to be on the move.

Holden didn't know what this was adding up to as they struck down out of the hills obliquely south and west so as to avoid Sands. But he had enough confidence in Jim after their brief talk to be willing to do almost anything his new partner suggested. He was also reluctant and a little too proud, after that first refusal of Jim's, to ask any further questions about their errand.

Later, as they worked out of the hills and onto the flats south of Sands, Fats' curiosity almost got the best of him. But a deeply ingrained patience restrained him. He decided that Jim had some good reason for keeping his mouth shut after that cryptic mention of wanting to send some wires.

Whenever the opportunity was offered, his glance would come around and study Jim. His lacking in respect for the name of Allard made him wonder at his readiness to trust it now. He saw something ironical in that and time and again the thought twisted his long face into a wry smile. Yet in Jim he had recognized qualities he envied and admired. It had taken a good brain to plan that business of hurrahing Kittering's cabin last night. That same brain was working at another idea now. Fats was willing to let it work.

In this last hour, since meeting up with Jim, the tall man had, for the first time in weeks, lost his feeling of helplessness and near despair. This waiting around for something to happen was at an end, or so his hunch told him. This Jim Allard, he realized, didn't wait for things to happen. He made them.

Only at two o'clock, when they were riding on across the bare, treeless flat toward the red and yellow painted way station of the Sierra and Western, their dust fogging around them in a following hot wind, did Holden break the silence that held during their fast ride. "What's the setup, Jim?" he asked.

"The sheriff sent us out here. I'm a friend of yours."

Holden had to be satisfied with that. They left the horses in the shade along the east wall of the shack and were approaching the door on that side when it swung open on a bald fat man wearing bib overalls and no shirt. His glance clung suspiciously to Jim for a moment, taking in the unshaven face and the brown stain of dried blood on the sleeve of Jim's shirt. Then he looked at Holden, saw who it was and grinned. "Long time no see, Fats. You ain't growed that double chin yet."

"Can't say the same for you, Joe," Fats replied. He nodded to indicate Jim. "Friend of mine wants to send some telegrams."

"Step right in," Joe said, more genial now since Jim's status had been clearly defined. Evidently any friend of Holden's was acceptable.

The shack was empty except for some packing boxes in a far corner, a cot and a table under the window that faced the tracks. On the table was a telegraph instrument and above it the levers of a semaphore. Joe found a pad of telegraph forms, wiped the dust from it on the seat of his pants and handed it and a pencil to Jim.

While Jim wrote, Fats and Joe chinned in the way of old acquaintances long separated and picking up the thread of their lives casually where it had broken off. Finished, Jim tore off the two forms he had used and said to Joe: "Fred Blythe sent us out here to get these off because he didn't want the whole town to know about it. Fats says you'll keep it under your hat."

Joe's face gathered seriously. "Fats don't say much a man can swallow without a hell of a lot o' salt, mister. But this time he's correct."

Jim nodded. "Another thing. Burn these when you're through. In a day or two someone may be along wantin' to know who wired this Pierce. You'd be doin' Fats and Fred Blythe a favor by sayin' that a Pitchfork rider sent it. Don't say what the wire was about, just say Allard's name was signed to it."

A look passed between Holden and Joe. "That right, Fats?"

"That's the way we'd like it, Joe." Fats nicely concealed his growing bewilderment.

"Then that's the way it'll be," the operator told him.

Jim held out the telegrams to Fats. "See if I've remembered everything."

Holden looked at them. The first was to the Denver office of the Sierra and Western Railway. When he'd read it, Fats looked up and nodded.

The second held his attention much longer. It was addressed to Virgil Pierce, Globe, Arizona. It read: *Jim Allard involved in killing here at Sands. Offer you personal guar-*

*antee of two thousand dollars for his capture dead or alive.
Imperative you avoid sheriff and keep business strictly to
yourself.* It was signed *Hugh Allard.*

Fats gulped and didn't raise his glance until he had enough
control of his face to hide his surprise. He didn't look at Jim
but handed the telegrams across to the agent, saying, "How
much, Joe?"

He paid for the messages after Joe had read them and
commented, "A hell of a mess Fred Blythe's in! Wish I could
help him."

"You're helpin' him now," Jim said.

They were half a mile back along the trail that followed
the glistening and heat-shimmering twin ribbons of steel
before Fats trusted himself to speak.

"Why in the name o' God bring that bounty hunter in
here to nail up your hide? Virgil Pierce. Hell, he doesn't
know what it means to quit!"

Jim answered that at some length, telling Holden how he
planned to use Pierce. His explanation failed to relieve
Holden's grave, worried expression.

"I can see that," Holden said when Jim had finished. "But
why not really get him in here after Deshay, after anyone
but you?"

"He's tackled Deshay before. Spade never traveled alone,
never gave Pierce an even chance at him. And Pierce never
crowds his luck. He wouldn't come here to hunt Deshay."

Holden swore under his breath, time and again. "You're
dealin' from a five-ace deck, Jim. Here's hoping they don't
catch you at it!"

"Here's hopin' they don't." Jim spoke solemnly, meaning
it, for he had no illusions in having sent that telegram.

11

AT dawn next morning Jim Allard was looking down on
Pitchfork's headquarters from the margin of the trees on the
hill slope behind the huge galvanized watering tank above
the barn. Ten hours of sleep, a shave and two full meals had
wiped out his weariness of yesterday and given him back his
old restless driving energy. Making the long circle that
brought him up here while it was still dark, he'd taken the

time to strip and bathe in a pool along Antelope Creek: the icy water had been a tonic that now made him restless to see the beginnings of his plan take shape.

Last night Holden and two of his men had set out late to strike at a herd in one of Pitchfork's outlying meadows. This morning, if things went according to schedule, Fats would be in town to find out if Virgil Pierce arrived on the nine-o'clock local. Jim was wishing now that he could have word of Pierce's arrival. Everything depended on the ex-marshal's being in Sands immediately.

But there was gambling blood in him, and he was willing to take the risk of assuming that Pierce would come. This was like a game of draw poker with wild cards to be drawn; he was willing to take his chances on the cards he would draw and outbet the other players.

An hour after he began his vigil above Pitchfork, the breakfast clanging of the iron triangle at the cook shanty below signaled the exact instant things began to happen. As the crew gathered for the meal, a rider ran his horse hell for leather down the hill trail to the south of Jim's lookout. Once on the flat below, the man ignored corrals and crew's quarters and streaked in through the cottonwoods toward the big sprawling house. He slid his pony to a quick stop, came down out of the saddle and ran in through the patio gate. Jim couldn't see what door of the house he entered.

A minute dragged by; another. Suddenly the man appeared beyond the gate again. Trent Harms was with him. Pitchfork's foreman hurried across to the corrals, had a man catch up and saddle a horse for him. Then he and the rider who had come in left the layout. They took the trail back up the hill. Jim gave them two minutes' start and walked back to the claybank and followed.

It was easy to keep them in sight. The hollows between the hills were open and grassy, only the hill crests timbered. Jim rode carefully but fast, for they were wasting no time. Within two miles of Pitchfork they separated, Harms keeping at a trot to the faintly marked trail that led to the higher foothills, his crewman striking off southward, fast. It was obvious that the latter's errand was urgent.

Jim chose to follow Harms. Two hours later, after keeping his quarry in sight the whole time and wondering at Harms' irritatingly slow pace, Jim saw the ramrod swing obliquely south and east. Presently, a quarter-mile ahead, Harms rode up on Pitchfork's south fence. He followed it until he came to a gate. There he came aground, tied his pony and hunkered down with his back to a fence post and lit a smoke. Jim waited from a timbered crest a quarter-mile away.

He waited there a full forty minutes. Jim was deciding he'd followed the wrong man when abruptly the rider who had been with Harms appeared from out of the trees on the other side of the fence. He had another man with him, a man on a buckskin. The buckskin was vaguely familiar to Jim; he finally remembered seeing the animal two days ago as he and Ann were climbing the trail out of the badlands to Pitchfork's mesa.

"Kittering man," he said aloud, remembering what the girl had told him that afternoon.

The two riders came on through the gate and spent a few minutes talking to Harms. Then once again Jim had to make a choice. The rider on the buckskin struck off immediately toward the higher hills to the east, while Harms and his crewman headed back the way Harms had come. Jim finally followed the man on the buckskin, for this rider was going toward the hills and it was up there somewhere that he expected to find Deshay.

Luck was with him. The buckskin's rider was in a hurry and didn't once use the precaution of climbing a high point and scanning his back trail. He covered six twisting, climbing miles the first forty minutes and finally rode out of sight into the brush-choked mouth of a canyon whose course Jim could follow high toward the peaks. A stream—the beginnings of Antelope, it looked like—struck down out of the canyon and made a snaking course across a wide rolling meadow.

Jim was wary about following the buckskin into the brush at the canyon mouth, warier still about riding on. He didn't go ahead until he had carefully studied the ground that lay ahead. But the canyon was fairly wide and he swung far aside from a faintly marked trail wherever he couldn't see what lay fifty yards ahead. The walls climbed to a surprising height in a very short distance and held their sheerness even more sharply as he went on. The stream's roaring rush down over its rocky bed served to blanket out the sound of the claybank's shoe striking the bare rock over the long grassless stretches.

Now he had to go on by feel alone, since the rider on the buckskin was well out of sight. He took his time, too, knowing that to hurry might end any chance he had of going deep in here without being discovered. The sun was obscured by the high walls, but the shadows far up along their heights told him it was already long past midday.

He judged he had covered better than ten miles of the

canyon alone when, abruptly, scanning a far climbing reach
directly ahead, he saw a moving splotch of color that made
him rein back in a tall stand of cedar and behind a high rock
shoulder close in to the left wall. From there, his hand holding
down the claybank's nose, he watched the rider on the buckskin go back down the canyon. Whatever errand Kittering's
man had come here on was evidently now finished. He wasn't
in any particular hurry now, either, holding the buckskin
down to a leisurely walk.

He passed close enough for Jim to get a brief but good
look at him. Jim caught a picture he knew he would never
forget. The man's face was young, sallow, stamped with a
rash arrogance; and the thin-lipped mouth was drawn to a
straight, somehow cruel-looking line odd in a man so young.
He wore his gun low; that, added to the light-skinned and
supple hands, gave Jim the instant impression that this youth
could be dangerous. The last fleeting glimpse he had of the
buckskin showed him a jaw brand burned in the shape of a
crude square enclosing the letter K. Block K! Here was his
proof of Holden's hunch. This must be Mule Evans, the man
Holden hadn't dared trust last night when the Pitchfork herd
was driven off.

Jim was thankful for having traveled slowly this last hour.
Evans had gone on fast, completed his errand and turned
back. This meant only one thing to Jim—that Spade Deshay's
hideout, if the hideout was where Evans had been, must lie
close ahead.

When he went on, Jim no longer made any attempt to go
quietly or unseen. He struck across to the narrow trail and
followed it openly, whistling a tune loudly enough to be heard
over the rush of water of the stream. Somewhere up here
Spade would have a guard posted. He wanted that guard to
see him. Or perhaps his guess that Spade was in hiding up
here was wrong. In that case his ride had been for nothing.

It happened a bare quarter-hour after Evans had passed
him on the way out. He was passing through a narrowing of
the canyon's deep gloom when the stallion's ears lifted and
the animal whickered. Suddenly a voice spoke from the
direction of a high outcropping: "This is as far as she goes,
stranger!"

Jim reined in. A brief silence followed. Then the voice exploded: "By God, look who's here!" There was a pause in
which Jim remembered the voice. Then: "Shuck out the irons,
Jim! Spade's going to love this!"

Jim unhesitatingly dropped his belts and guns to the

ground. Off to his left there was a rustling of the bushes front-ing the outcrop. The branches of an oak thicket parted and a short bowlegged man with a rifle hung in the crook of his arm led a sorrel horse from cover.

"Howdy, Two Card," Jim drawled, a broad smile coming to his bronzed face.

For a moment they sized each other up, these men who hadn't seen each other for several years. Two Card Bates was heavy-set, gray-haired, and his loose-jowled face fatter than Jim remembered it. Only the pale blue quick eyes gave hint of the shrewdness and cunning gathered from a past as an unsuccessful gambler. His name came from his habit of never drawing more or less than two cards in a game of draw poker. Evidently his peculiar system lacked something, for Jim had never seen him with a lot of money. He was Spade Deshay's lieutenant, loyal, unfriendly.

Two Card drawled, "You're awful damned sure of yourself!"

"Goin' to take me on in?"

"I'm sure as hell not goin' to turn you loose!" The outlaw made a motion on up the trail. "You first." He stooped and picked up Jim's guns.

Jim went on, hearing the turf-deadened footfalls of Two Card's pony close behind. The muscles along his spine crawled at the knowledge of the gun back there and the memory of an incident not calculated to make Two Card very friendly.

It wasn't a dozen rods farther along a narrow aisle of stately cedars until Jim sighted through the trees a sod-roofed shack and a pole corral squatting close to the banks of the stream in a grassy clearing. Riding into the edge of the clearing, Two Card whistled a shrill signal. The shack's door swung open and a man stepped out of it.

Three strides beyond the door the man stopped abruptly, erect. He cocked his arms slightly to bring his hands closer to his guns. Two men came to stand in the doorway behind him. Seeing his abrupt halt, and the subtle signal of his hands, they stood where they were, sensing the same thing in his attitude that struck Jim so forcibly.

The glance of he man in the yard took in Jim leisurely. He saw Jim's empty waist. He drawled, almost pleasantly, "Two Card, give him back his irons!"

Jim said, "Not until you've heard me out, Spade," and put the claybank across the open stretch toward Deshay. He came down out of the saddle barely ten feet from the outlaw, seeing the half smile on Deshay's handsome face. "I'm here to do you a favor, Spade," he went on, "in return for one you'll do me."

Deshay was mild-looking, deceptively so. Standing no taller than Jim's shoulder, his handsome dark-eyed face gave him the look of a dapper, almost effeminate man. His pants were of tan whipcord, close-fitting, and his boots and holsters were polished, fancy-stitched. He wore his guns butt foremost, high at his waist. He made a strange neat figure in this rough mountain hideout.

Jim had no illusions about Spade, particularly about his ability with his guns. Several men who had taken exception to the outlaw's looks and given way to their curiosity over the seemingly awkward way he wore his guns were now dead, brought down by those same awkwardly placed .45s. Although Jim had no fear of the man, he had long ago learned a lasting respect for him.

Just now Spade drawled, "You have a habit of doin' me favors. Such as that time in Cimarron."

One of the men in the doorway behind Spade laughed softly, mockingly.

"That's water over the dam, Spade. I tried to take your bunch away from you; you tried to frame me for it. Neither one worked. Let's bury the hatchet."

"And last night," Spade went on inscrutably.

"I had to find you. Givin' a man an excuse for coming up here so I could follow him was the surest way."

The surface coolness of the outlaw's manner broke at this bland admission of Jim's. Now his eyes for the first time reflected his inward anger. "You'll take your irons and make your try, friend!" he drawled. "Either that or I'll—"

"Damn it!" Jim cut in sharply. "Will you listen? I'm here to tell you you're being sold out, double-crossed! We'll settle this any way you like, later. But right now I need you, and you sure as hell need me!"

The intentness of his words blanked out the anger on the outlaw's face. "Go on," Spade said. "It'd better be good."

"It is. Hugh Allard's sold you down the river."

Spade smiled. "He couldn't. I've never laid eyes on him."

"Harms, then."

Spade shook his head, seeming to relish Jim's attempts. "Him either. Come again!"

"Then Mule Evans."

Wariness edged Spade's glance instantly. "What about Mule?"

Jim knew the man well enough to realize that Mule Evans'

name was the only one that meant anything to him. All at once he saw that he had so far missed a point of vital importance. He was voicing it immediately. "Spade, do you know you're workin' for Hugh Allard?"

"Am I?"

"You are. Trent Harms is Allard's right bower. He sent Evans up here this morning. I saw him do it."

Momentary unconcealed surprise showed on the outlaw's face. Then he laughed, softly. "I should worry about Mule and who pays him. If it's Allard instead of Kittering, it's all the same to me. But how do you tie into this?"

"I'm with Kittering. I'm for him because Hugh Allard brought me in here and offered me big money to bushwhack him. I'm for him because I hate Allard's gall."

"Gall seems to run in the Allard family," was Spade's casual rejoinder.

It was obvious that Spade neither knew nor cared whom he worked for, that his profits out of the stolen beef was all that interested him. For a moment Jim was at a loss and insisted stubbornly, "Allard's hirin' you, through Evans, to run off his own stuff so that he can hang it on Kittering."

"Nice setup," Spade said. "I'd like to meet this Hugh Allard. Him and me could do big things together."

Jim had a sudden inspiration that made him say, "You'll never get to meet him, Spade. Fact is, you won't be able to meet anyone in a couple of days."

"Take your guns and back that, Jim!" Spade's anger once more cut loose.

Jim ignored the invitation. "You won't be able to because of Virgil Pierce."

"Pierce!"

Spade's voice grated out that one word viciously. He eyed Jim with suspicion, his anger gone. "What about Pierce?"

"He's down in Sands. Allard sent for him. He's here to get you, Spade."

"Why me? Why not you?"

"No one knows I'm still in the country. I was framed with a murder two nights ago. Allard thinks I've high-tailed."

Spade smiled without amusement. "I heard about that." He abruptly seemed to remember the other thing and his smooth manner left him. "How the hell do I know you aren't runnin' a sandy?"

"You don't. But you can prove it. I still say you've been workin' for Allard, that he's through with you now and that he's brought Pierce in here to hunt you down. Spade, you're being double-crossed."

"Prove that and I'll . . ."

Spade didn't finish what he'd started to say, but Jim's hunch was that he had finally succeeded in centering the outlaw's anger where he wanted it, on Hugh Allard.

"Look, Spade," he said, as though explaining something extremely simple to an understanding child. "You've been in this thing how long? Six months?"

"Five."

"All right. In that time, you've helped Allard in a big way; helped him in this play he's makin' against Kittering, who wouldn't lift a hand against anyone. The thing's done now; Allard's ready for the windup. But there are certain men who've helped him. Mule Evans is one. You're another. Do you think he's going to have you around when it's over to blackmail him?"

Spade was sober now, listening intently. He said finally, "Blackmail? Who said I'd . . ." He saw the full import of Jim's words and broke off abruptly.

"See what I mean? You're dangerous to Allard once he's swung this thing his way. So he's got Pierce in here to take care of you."

"You said you could prove that! How?"

"It was two days ago that Hugh Allard made me his proposition to go after Kittering. Up until then, he had no need for Pierce. If I'd done the Kittering job, he'd have put me out after you next. But I didn't want to play his game. So he framed me, got me out of the way . . . or so he thinks. He had to think of another way of getting you. It would take a pretty good man. He thought of Pierce and probably wired him to come the night he got rid of me."

"That's a guess. It don't prove a thing."

"Go on down to Sands and see if Pierce isn't there."

"That still don't prove who he's here after."

"Then go to the telegraph office and look over the wires that have been sent the last few days. If you don't find it there, hit the way stations along the line. Allard wouldn't have had the time to send a letter. And he might be too smart to rig something like this from town."

Spade stood a moment in concentrated thought. His glance jerked up to Jim finally and he said in a barely audible voice, "You're stayin' with me until I get this thing straight, friend Jim. If what you say holds water, I reckon I'll have to pay a call on this Hugh Allard!"

He turned abruptly and jerked his head to the two men in the doorway. "Get ready to ride!" Then, glancing at Two

Card: "Keep him covered!" He disappeared inside the cabin as his men came out and headed for the corral.

They set out from the cabin minutes later with Spade in the lead, Jim followed by Two Card and the other pair of riders. It went unsaid that any attempt of Jim's to change this line-up would meet with quick suspicion, maybe a bullet in the back.

As the miles dropped behind them and the sun lowered farther along its wide arc to the western horizon, Jim wondered if he was crowding his luck too closely. Spade was unpredictable. Yet Jim knew that the outlaw, once convinced that he had been tricked into working for Allard and that Allard was about to get rid of him, would hate Pitchfork's owner for the deception he had used. Unscrupulous though he was, Spade Deshay's code was based on a few essential honesties, one of which was that he tolerated no double-dealing in a confederate. Jim, in his wilder days, had once aspired to make an understrapper of Spade, to take leadership of the wild bunch. Deshay had rebelled at that, had framed him and threatened a shoot-out if they ever met again. Now they had met. It was going to take some maneuvering to keep that shoot-out from happening.

That galling memory might even now bear enough weight with Spade to make him throw in with Allard out of sheer spite. Jim had played a long shot in bringing Virgil Pierce in here—a long shot intended to bring Spade in on Kittering's side and even the balance in men and guns.

There still remained the problem of prodding Kittering into this thing, of angering him so violently that he would thrust aside caution and decide to fight Allard tooth and nail. But winning Spade's confidence came first.

12

YEARS of incautious living had prompted in Mule Evans wary habits as strong as his never going without guns. Scanning the trails he rode had become second nature to him, as much a habit as the precaution he took of never letting a law officer get a close look at his face.

Two miles below Deshay's cabin, his unthinking scrutiny of the trail suddenly showed him something that tuned him to an instant's high-pitched tenseness. It laid his right hand low along his thigh, close to holster.

Coming in here less than an hour ago, he hadn't seen the sign now clearly imprinted in the thin topsoil that lay over the canyon's rocky bed. There had been sign, that of the coming and going of Deshay's men, but not this one of a pony with right front shoe toed in slightly in an inordinately long stride. That sign went up-canyon. It meant only one thing to Mule. He had been followed in here.

His first precaution was to ride in behind the screening branches of a tall cedar, where he could see both ways and have the solid security of the canyon's sheer-climbing wall at his back. There, held by a panic brought on by the chance of a shot echoing out any instant to slam a bullet into him, he considered what he must do.

He could go back and warn Deshay; but that, he decided, would take him directly into the hands of the man who had followed him in here. The other possibility, that of riding to Pitchfork and warning Allard, was the one he chose.

Mule was at heart a coward, one who hid behind a quick temper and an uncommon adeptness of hand to gun. The ride down the canyon, where each hundred yards held a dozen threats of ambush, was sheer torture to him. He punished the buckskin, running him recklessly over uneven steeply downpitched ground. Once clear of the canyon mouth and in the broad meadow that fronted it, he used his sharp-roweled spurs cruelly each time the animal lagged from a full-out run.

When he vaulted from the saddle at Pitchfork's patio gate, the buckskin was downheaded and badly lathered, every muscle trembling. Mule tried the office first, and was lucky. Hugh Allard and Trent Harms were there.

Allard's sharp-featured face mirrored instant anger when he saw who had opened the door. His voice intoned flatly, "I thought I told you never to come here!"

"I had to, Allard," Mule cut in quickly. "Someone followed me in to Deshay's this mornin'. I picked up his jughead's sign. Right front toed in, long stride . . ."

"That claybank! Jim Allard's!" Trent Harms breathed, barely audibly but with an insistency that brought both men's attention swinging around on him.

"Say that again, Trent," Allard drawled.

Harms nodded. "It's the claybank, all right." He smiled crookedly. "I should know. I took Eaton out there and showed him the sign before I put him out after Allard the other afternoon."

It took Hugh Allard barely two seconds to fully realize the implications behind the news Mule had brought. Coming up out of his chair, he said, "How long since you left Deshay, Evans?"

"Not over forty minutes. I damn' near killed a horse gettin' here."

"Trent, get Red and Daniels and Tellew. They're to bring rifles! Saddle Evans a fresh horse!"

"What's comin' off, boss?" Harms asked, on the way to the door.

"We're going up there and catch them on the way out. Another thing. Get Evans' horse away from the house. If Ann should see . . ." Allard left the thought unfinished. Mule and Harms left the room.

A smug smile betrayed itself on Hugh's face as he removed his coat and strapped on a pair of shoulder holsters. His thin hands deftly opened the loading gates and inspected the cylinders of a matched pair of pearl-handled guns before he thrust them into holsters. Then, coat on again, he went out the door.

"Dad!"

Ann's call stopped Hugh halfway to the patio gate. He turned toward the door of the huge big center room of the house, asking gruffly, "What is it?"

"I want to talk to you," Ann said, coming out the door and standing at the edge of the flagstones of the *portal*. She had hardly laid eyes on him in the past two days.

Hugh said impatiently, "I haven't the time now. I'm—"

"You never have the time," the girl interrupted.

A warning note in her voice made Allard control his impatience. He could see that her deep hazel eyes were examining him critically, almost in the way they would a stranger. It was a cold regard, a close one.

He walked over to her. "Sorry, Sis. These last few days have set me on edge."

"That's exactly what I want to talk about. What's happening here, Hugh?"

There were rare times when Ann called him by his given name to his face. It was always when she was angry or hurt and now he had an added warning from that. She suspected him, was judging him, and he was careful about his reply:

"I wish I knew, girl," he said in kindly tones. "Another herd gone last night. We're going out now to make a try at finding it."

"What about Eaton, the man you hired last week, Hugh?

I saw him the other evening when his horse packed him in.
He was dead. Who killed him?"

Hugh Allard's expression became pious, grave. He knew,
of course, that Jim Allard had killed Eaton. But now the
chance of planting a seed for thought in Ann's mind was too
open to be ignored. "We don't know," he said. "He was riding
the east fence that afternoon.

The girl's oval face paled a shade. "That's what Trent
said. You can't think a Kittering man shot him."

He shrugged offhandedly and reached out and took her
by the arms. "Let's don't think about it. I'll have to go now.
See you at supper." He gripped her arms tightly in what he
meant to be a reassuring way and turned and started across
the patio, stepping around the downhanging branches of the
willow.

"Hugh!"

Once again Ann's voice stopped him. This time it was she
who came out to him. She looked up into his face with a
troubled expression in her glance. "What did Jim Allard want
here the other afternoon?"

He repeated the story he'd given Fred Blythe. "Offered to
go out and pick a fight with Miles Kittering and kill him, for
a price. He'd heard I was in trouble and thought he saw a
way of making some easy money."

A hint of stronger anger, then of amusement, rode into
the girl's expression. "Is that the truth, Hugh?" she asked in
a low voice.

"Of course it's the truth," he flared, realizing instantly that
he had failed to disguise his anger as was his habit.

"He . . . this Jim Allard is the one who murdered that
railroad man in town two nights ago, isn't he?"

Hugh nodded curtly. "Shot him in the back."

"Why, Hugh?"

"How do I know why! He did it, that's all!" He was finding
these insistent questions a little disconcerting and spoke irritably again.

He caught that same shadow of a smile on her face as she
turned from him and walked back to the *portal*, saying only,
"I wanted to know what you thought, Hugh." She was gone
a moment later, the door closing behind her.

Hugh Allard would have liked to say something to stop her,
to keep her with him until he could read the meaning behind
her smile. But, for once, he was caught unprepared and
didn't speak. He turned and went out the patio gate, angry
and more than a little puzzled over Ann's strange behavior.
It was as though she hadn't believed him, what he said about

Jim Allard. What it was she hadn't believed he couldn't decide.

Within a dozen strides he'd forgotten Ann in his eagerness to get on with this job. The news Mule had brought him had seemed bad at first. Now he would put this daring play of Jim Allard's to his own use. What Jim had done was plain enough. Jim and Deshay had once traveled together. Somehow, Jim had learned that Spade was in the country. He'd seen through the thin fabric of Kittering being blamed for stealing the Pitchfork herds and rightly guessed that Spade was behind it. Last night's raid in Pitchfork's upper meadow had been only a ruse to send a man up after Spade.

Hugh saw that now and damned himself for being a gullible fool. He'd been taken in the same as the others. In fact, it was he who had ordered Harms this morning to send Mule up to Deshay's camp and find out the reasons for last night's play. He should have known that it was a trap set for him and ignored it.

But now that it was done he would take advantage of it. Jim Allard had by now seen Spade and probably told Spade a few things the outlaw wasn't aware of. Such as who he was really working for. This meant that Hugh had to act fast. These two, Spade and Jim, were dangerous to him now. He had nicely framed this thing on Miles Kittering. But Spade and Jim together would turn that against him . . . unless he could get rid of them. If he acted fast, if he'd been wise in hiring these new gun hands, neither Jim nor Spade would be alive two hours from now. With Jim and Spade out of the way, he might even use them to further his case against Kittering.

Fred Blythe might believe a story something like this: that his men had followed the stolen herd last night, caught up with it, and that there had been a shoot-out in which Jim and Deshay had been cut down. That would throw the blame clearly on Kittering. It would also necessitate getting the herd back. After that, it would be a simple matter to make things too hot for Kittering to stay in this country.

At the corrals where the others, horses saddled, were waiting for him, Allard told his foreman, "Trent, I want every man, even the cook, to get up to that break in the south fence. I don't want 'em back here until they've found that herd and pushed it inside our wire again." He was acting on the hunch that the herd wouldn't have been driven far, since the purpose of the theft was now accomplished.

Harms walked over to the bunkhouse to give his orders. He was back in two minutes. They climbed into leather and took the trail that led into the hills rising abruptly from Pitchfork's broad mesa.

The sight of Hugh Allard's grimly set face, the bulge of the guns beneath the coat he always wore even on the hottes days, caused an exchange of glances between the three new men the rancher had selected to take along. These three—Re and Daniels and Tellew—not regular members of Pitchfork' crew but men hired by Harms for a special purpose, realize that after drawing high wages and doing nothing for almos a full month they were about to be called on to earn thei pay. The trio had a certain quality in common—a set of countenance and a coldness of eye that was a tangible mark of their breed. All three wore a pair of guns and all three carried Winchesters in scabbards on their saddles.

As they topped the crest of the hill behind the layout, Allard called, "Mule, get up here and show the way." Evans, on a fresh horse, went on ahead and set the pace.

The going was hard, mostly uphill, but Pitchfork's *remuda* boasted some good horseflesh and it counted now. Hugh Allard had the firm conviction that this period of endless planning and waiting for the flare-up was over. Now that things were shaping into action, he saw the end in sight. It might come today, tonight, tomorrow, and now he drove himself with all the stored-up bodily energy that had had no outlet these past weeks. There had been a time, long ago, when endless caution and waiting stolidly to achieve his ends had been as foreign to him as to this Jim Allard, whose violence of action and words had in three days blown things wide open. The chance that today, another hour, might definitely rid him of this bothersome relative made Allard drive all the harder.

Within sight of the canyon mouth in less than forty minutes, Allard called to Mule and reined in, letting his men come alongside. Over the sounds of the blowing animals and the creak of saddle gear, he scanned the half mile of distance to the canyon mouth. He glanced upward at the sun, judging it to be close to four o'clock.

Then, crisply, he gave his orders: "Harms, you and Red and Tellew take the hill to this side of the stream. There's cover there, plenty of it. Mule and Daniels will work from these trees opposite. I'm going to make a cast across there and see if they've come out. If they have, I'll wave you down." He seemed to be thinking of something else. "I want Allard alive. Get the rest," he added.

They split up immediately, Harms and his men striking

straight in for the steep hill to the south of the canyon mouth
that climbed precipitously to form one wall farther in. Mule
and Daniels swung wide of the mouth, keeping their distance
until they were above it before they rode in toward the trees
on the far side of the stream. Allard headed straight in to
the stream.

They saw him ride carefully along it and into the tall
growth of cedar and brush that marked the beginnings of the
canyon. Before he reappeared, they were in their places, their
ponies tied far enough back to make sure they couldn't give
warning before it was too late.

Hugh Allard, coming into sight again, looked left and right.
Then he put his gelding across the stream and into the trees
to the north.

After that, for an interminable twenty minutes, the men
along the slope saw no sign of life either in the trees or along
the stream. Finally, down there, a doe jumped lightly from
cover in the brush choking the canyon mouth. She stood
poised on the stream bank, head lifted, scenting the breeze.
All at once two bounds took her back into the brush again—
not directly, for she swung to the far side before disappearing.
Then she was in sight a last time, climbing a ledge that took
her along the far talus slope and into the trees again.

"Nice shot," Tellew said to Harms, who was hunkered
down behind a stunted piñon twenty feet to one side of him.

"You'll have better," Harms told him.

Along a falling bench of bare rock outcropping, a scant
two hundred yards from the point where the canyon walls
fell away into the wide meadow below, the stream boiled
along its uneven channel with a roar amplified by the con-
fining sheer walls to either side. From here, Jim could gaze
out over the tops of the stately cedars at the canyon mouth
and scan the far reaches of near desert that lay beyond the
hills. There, straight into the west, was the line of the Sierra
and Western right of way. Almost directly below was the
gradual bend that ended the rails' long horseshoe swing
around the spur of mountains to the south.

Once again, Jim was struck by the thing that had caught
his attention that first late afternoon when he'd had his first
glimpse of this country. This rugged and lofty spur of mountains, probably mothered by the distant and greater Rockies,
had formed an obstacle man had disdained conquering in the
laying of that long line of rail. Once again he was reminded
of the waste in that far swing around the spur—waste in

material and labor that had long ago been forgotten, waste in time that might someday count in the ever-pressing rush of increasing traffic and faster schedules.

His mind was still engrossed in an idea that thought had given him when Spade led the way out of the trees and struck across the open meadow to leave the canyon behind. Jim lifted the claybank to a faster trot and came even with Spade, Two Card and his companions closing in behind.

Jim started to say, "Spade, what pass do you use crossing the peaks with the stuff you—"

Crack!

The sharp racketing explosion of a rifleshot cut in on his words. Behind, one of Two Card's partners cried hoarsely. Jim turned, instinctively raking the claybank's flanks with spurs. He was in time to see the man to Two Card's left fall loosely out of the saddle in a broken roll.

Spade bent low over his gelding's withers, putting the animal to a fast run. Jim was a scant twenty feet behind him, the claybank full out, when other rifles took up the fire of the first. The shots were ragged, untimed, and twice Jim felt the air-whip struck up by lead close to his face.

Suddenly Spade's horse went down, forefeet first, in a headlong roll that threw Spade far to one side. The claybank, drawing up on Spade, was too close to avoid hitting the downed horse. Jim pulled sharply aside. He felt the claybank's front hoofs strike into the downed horse, heard the animal's high-pitched scream of pain. Then he, too, was pitched from the saddle, unexpectedly, for he had thought the claybank clear.

He fell awkwardly, hitting hard on left shoulder and sliding along on his left side with the uneven ground tearing at his shoulder. He rolled over before his skid was complete. The momentum of his fall snapped his head back so that it hit the ground in a hard blow to blind him with pain and dull his senses.

He lay there unable to move for long seconds, dimly aware of the racket of distant gunfire, the closer explosions of answering shots, the thudding hoof pound of running horses. His senses cleared gradually. Weakly, he pushed himself up. He was in time to see Spade Deshay's spare bulk swinging up into the claybank's saddle fifty yards away. The stallion wheeled nervously, rearing and shying over toward the spot where Jim lay. But sharp spurs drove him on. Spade followed Two Card to disappear around the near bend of the hill to the south. In another ten seconds all that remained of their passing was the distance-muffled hoof drum of their fast-running horses.

Jim stood up, shaking his head to clear it and steady his vision. Barely ten feet away lay Spade's horse, dead. Farther out a second animal was down on forelegs, trying to heave himself erect. Near by lay the huddled shape of his rider, the first of the pair that had ridden with Two Card Bates. A hundred yards away, far out along the line of the stream, ran a riderless horse with trailing reins and empty swinging stirrups. Near the stream bank was a sprawled body that Jim decided must be the second rider who had sided Two Card out of the canyon.

He turned abruptly at the sound of a rifleshot that slapped out from the face of the hill. The wounded horse went down in a convulsive heave. Jim found himself staring at Trent Harms, who stood half a dozen yards away, his blunt face smiling mirthlessly, thumbs hooked over the hammers of two guns he held leveled at Jim.

"Bring a rope, Red," Harms called back over his shoulder. Then, to Jim: "Different than last time, eh, Allard?"

Jim didn't reply. By the time Harms and Red and Tellew had used a rope from one of their saddles to bind his arms securely to his sides, he was hearing the sound of horses coming up behind him. He turned and saw Allard and Mule Evans and Daniels riding up from the creek.

Allard drew rein, eyed Jim impassively a moment, then asked Harms, "Deshay got away?"

Harms nodded, indicating Jim. "Deshay and one other."

"Red, go catch up that loose horse and bring him across here. We'll attend to the burying later." Allard came aground. He strode over and took Jim's guns from the saddle of Deshay's dead horse. Then he came up to Jim and for the first time his satisfaction betrayed itself in a meager smile that took his thin face. "I told you to get out," he said tonelessly. "Now you're costing me the trouble of getting rid of you another way."

He turned and stood watching Red rope the bay horse whose rider lay near the stream bank. There was no talk while Red brought the horse up the incline toward the waiting group. Jim recognized how futile it would be to waste words now, how inevitable was the thing that he was sure was coming.

They lifted him into the saddle of the bay and roped his boots to the webbed-cotton cinch. They had started away from the stream, down across the high meadow where half a hundred sleek Pitchfork-branded steers were grazing, before Allard reined in alongside Jim to say, "Any luck with Deshay?"

"Enough," Jim replied.

His answer seemed to satisfy Allard, for the rancher went on ahead to ride alongside Harms. His silence was more condemning than any words could have been and Jim realized bitterly that now he might never know what happened to Miles Kittering, to Fats Holden and Spade—whether or not they made their fight and won or lost it. He had played a lone hand in this—a hand that showed signs of being the winning one until a few minutes ago. But all that was gone up in gunsmoke now, and ahead of him lay a pay-off he had never let himself contemplate.

They had gone a long way on their ride back to Pitchfork when Jim turned to the rider alongside. "How about a smoke?"

Hugh Allard must have heard, for his command came back sharply, "Stay away from him, Tellew!"

Spade Deshay accomplished two things in the three hours after the ambush. First, he proved wrong his suspicions that Jim had had a part in it with Hugh Allard. Four miles below the meadow where his two men lay dead, he had Two Card hold the claybank while he went down through the timber of a steep hill slope and hid close to the faint line of the trail leading back to Pitchfork's headquarters. He was there when Allard and his men filed past. He saw Jim roped to the saddle, heard him ask for a smoke and caught Hugh Allard's curt order, "Stay away from him, Tellew!" Spade could see that whoever had roped Jim to the horse hadn't been overgentle about it, for Jim's face showed pain at each uneven stride of the horse. And Allard's smug satisfied smile at Jim's request for tobacco was further proof. No, Jim and Allard hadn't planned this together.

Second, much later, Spade made another discovery. Against Two Card's better judgment, Spade went brazenly into the station at Sands. He bluntly asked the agent to see a copy of the telegram Hugh Allard had sent to Virgil Pierce either yesterday or the day before.

"Pierce?" The agent was obviously puzzled. "Where would the wire of gone? The name don't mean nothin'."

"Pierce is from Globe."

The agent shook his head positively. "It wasn't sent from here."

"Are you sure?"

The agent bridled. "I ought to know, hadn't I?"

So Spade and Two Card rode up to the way station below Sands at dusk. There, met by Joe's calm scrutiny from the doorway, Spade this time asked to see the file of telegrams.

"Hell, I never bother to keep 'em," Joe said, not at all impressed by the outlaw's looks. Then he happened to remember something and asked, "Which one you lookin' for?"

"The one Hugh Allard sent to a man by the name of Pierce," Spade told him.

Joe frowned, scratched his head and appeared to be trying to remember. All at once he seemed to, for his frown eased and he queried, "What about it?"

"When was it sent?"

"Yesterday afternoon."

"Who sent it?"

Joe remembered Fats' instructions. He shrugged off-handedly. "Couldn't tell you his name."

"Allard man?"

"He was on a Pitchfork mare."

A long slow sigh escaped Spade. He gave Two Card a look that was one of mixed relief and gravity. "Much obliged," he said to Joe, and turned back out the trail.

13

ANN recognized Miles Kittering and Fats Holden coming up along the pasture in the gathering dusk and let out a sigh of real relief, telling Johnny Dawes, who was working below her in Block K's big corral, "Here they come."

Dawes said, "I knew they'd show up. Wouldn't a kept you here two hours for nothin'."

Now that this meeting with Miles Kittering was at hand, Ann was unsure of herself. Enough had happened these past three days to unsettle her comparatively placid world. This afternoon, all at once sickened by anxiety and fear and the futility of trying to get any satisfaction from talking to Hugh or Trent, she had obeyed the impulse to leave deserted Pitchfork and ride across and see Kittering.

She climbed down off the top pole of the corral, where she'd been watching Johnny Dawes work, and walked across to her buckskin, waiting there while Holden and Kittering rode in. As always, she felt a glow of pride at sight of Miles Kittering. He had a solid and honest look about him, a purposefulness that somehow awed, almost frightened her. Now, as he took in the buckskin and then recognized her, she saw his strange impassivity settle about him like a cloak. His bearded face was unreadable, but as he came closer she caught a momentary warmth in his brown eyes.

He said solemnly, "Good evening, Ann," and swung ponderously from his saddle.

Fats Holden greeted her, "Long time no see," and reached for Kittering's reins and started leading the horses toward the corral gate.

Miles Kittering's reluctance to be alone with her was at once obvious as he said quickly, "Let Johnny turn 'em in, Fats." He waited until Holden had joined them again and nodded to the cabin. "Let's go in. Had your supper, Ann?"

The girl nodded. "With Johnny, Miles." She could never quite bring herself to call him "Father" or "Dad." "I . . . I had to come over and see you."

Kittering made no answer to that and the three of them walked silently to the cabin, Holden going on ahead and calling in to the cook to dish up two plates of food. The only formality before they set about eating was to ask Ann to have a cup of coffee with them.

She took the crude bench at the far end of the table and purposely delayed in telling Kittering what had brought her here, grimly relishing this postponement of trying for the answers to her questions Hugh Allard and Trent Harms had failed to give her. Finally, when Kittering pushed back his plate and took out his gnarled briar pipe and commenced filling it, she could stand the silence no longer.

"Miles, I heard guns in the hills on my way across here this afternoon. Hugh left earlier with half a dozen men. The rest of the crew drifted out later."

She didn't miss the significant, somewhat puzzled, look Kittering gave Holden and went on: "This morning there was another herd gone. That's where the crew is, looking for it."

Kittering nodded. Holden spoke for him: "We're just in from makin' our explanations to Fred Blythe, Ann."

"Where will this all end!" Ann breathed in sudden tenseness. "Where is it getting you, or Hugh, or any of us?"

"That's what we'd like to know," Kittering said gloomily. He felt for a match, found none, and held a burnt stub over the lamp until it glowed redly and burst into flame. He lit his pipe, waved the match out, and added, "Ann, you have my word for it that I've had no hand in this." ·

"Then who has?" she asked helplessly. She saw that neither of them intended answering that, and went on: "Things I don't understand are going on over there. Day before yesterday one of Harms' new men came in roped to his saddle, dead. Hugh claims he was riding the east fence when he was killed."

"Meanin' we shot him?" Holden smiled wryly, slowly shaking his head.

"Then there was this Jim Allard," Ann continued, her words tumbling out in a rush to rid her mind of its torment. "He broke his parole and came here to make Hugh an offer of killing you, Miles—killing you for money. Hugh turned him down, had him thrown off the place."

"No one tosses Jim Allard around," Holden put in. "And that ain't the straight of the story."

His tone brought Ann's glance around to him. She said, intuitively, "You know something about him, Fats?"

He took a long moment in giving his slow nod. "A little," he drawled. Then, turning to Miles: "You still want to hire him?"

Before Kittering could reply, the girl cut in: "You mean you'd hire Jim Allard? That killer? He murdered that man at the hotel! He . . ."

"No, Ann," Holden's voice interrupted quietly. "Jim was there, asleep in the next room. But he didn't kill Chalmers. He doesn't throw his lead at a man's back, ever. And he isn't a killer."

Strangely enough, Ann could find no reply. Deep down inside her had been a belief that this Jim Allard couldn't be the man Hugh claimed, and now a strange excitement and relief welled up in her. During these past two days Jim's image had haunted her, his warm gray eyes, the infectious smile of his lean saddle-colored face contradicting Hugh's condemnation of him as an out-and-out killer. She hadn't wanted to believe her heart, which prompted her to like the man; but now that Holden had spoken she felt a small gratitude for the assurance he gave her.

Holden went on. "We can trust you not to talk this around, Ann. Jim hasn't left the country. He's here, trying to help Miles. Right now he's up there somewhere"—he motioned vaguely in the direction of the peaks—"trying to sell Spade Deshay on the idea of slingin' in with us and whippin' this thing."

Miles Kittering boomed, "You didn't tell me that!"

"No. It was agreed I shouldn't until the proper time—until Jim and I found a way of prodding you into this whether you wanted it or not."

"You say he's seeing Deshay? Trying to bring Deshay in this?"

Holden nodded. "To help you. Now maybe those guns in the hills mean something to you." He let his words have their effect on Kittering. Then he looked at the girl, noticing that the lamplight edged her shapely chestnut head in finespun threads of copper and laid highlights across the perfect molding of her face. As always, there was a deep admiration in him for this girl. He wondered now whether or not she held the power to persuade Kittering where he himself had failed. He decided to find out. "Maybe you could talk to Miles, Ann. This thing's got him licked, has taken the fight out of him. You're responsible for that."

"*I* am?" Ann wasn't as bewildered as she tried to appear. A chill settled through her as she saw the truth of Holden's words. She looked at her father, seeing that he sat with glance lowered, studying his knotty hands clasped on the table before him, a deep flush underlying the ruddy bronze of his face. She studied his shaggy head, the frown that gathered his brows darkly over his rugged face.

He muttered, deep-toned and querulously, "Fats, you're meddling in something that isn't your affair."

"No, Miles, he isn't," Ann said impulsively, facing a decision she had made and worded before she quite knew it. "It is my fault that you haven't stood up to Hugh, denied these things, even fought them. I'm sorry for that."

"We've thrashed this out before, Ann," Miles said, still regarding his hands.

"We thought we had. Now things are changed."

Kittering looked up. "How?"

"I believed in Hugh Allard as long as I could, for Mother's sake. Today, before I came here, he lied to me. Not about one thing, but about everything! I . . . I've come to you, Miles, because I knew I'd find the truth."

A subtle change rode over Miles Kittering. His shoulders squared, the cloak of imperturbability he had been hiding behind dropped from his face like a mask removed. His eyes brightened with something akin to hope. He said, gently, "You mean you've come to stay?"

Ann's eyes were suddenly brimming with tears. All at once she came up off the bench and went around the table to him, taking his head in her hands and pressing it to her breast.

"Miles . . . I've been a fool not to see it! I've been wrong! As terribly wrong as Mother was. She knew it, too late. I won't make the mistake she did."

Fats was embarrassed and too full of a deep thankfulness to want to witness what followed. He left the room quietly— not wanting to look at the girl and her father, reunited now. It cut into a man to see the nakedness of emotion that lay in Kittering's eyes, the humbleness of the man, the strength that even now made him fight to make sure that this was no mistaken impulse that brought his daughter back to him.

Fats knew a little of Kittering's past, enough to let him see what a great moment this was in Kittering's life. Ann's mother, Kittering's wife, had left Kittering years ago and taken their only child with her. There had been a divorce; Holden knew that much—a divorce which Hugh Allard had paid for. Hugh had brought Ann's mother and Ann out here and lavished on them the bounties of his wealth. But money hadn't been able to wipe away the past for Ann's mother. Holden knew she'd regretted her choice before she died, six years ago. Kittering had appeared in Sands soon after her death, to claim his child. He'd failed in that by a ruling of the courts. He'd done the next best thing, begun a new life close to his daughter. Not once in these six years had he again tried to get Ann back. It seemed he was satisfied with the occasional glimpses he had of her. But now, through no doing of his, Ann was coming back to him. This was what lay behind their meeting tonight.

As he sauntered out across the yard, Holden's thoughts were interrupted by a call from Johnny Dawes. "Fats, better get down here and listen to this!"

Holden's glance went beyond the corral. It was still light enough for him to see Johnny Dawes standing there beside the stirrup of a pony. The rider in the saddle was Ed Beeson, who had last night helped work Pitchfork's herd into a box canyon in the hills. Ed had been left there to guard the herd through the day. It was strange that he should be here now.

"What is it, Ed?" Holden asked quickly as he strode up to them.

"I thought you ought to know about it, Fats. There was some powder burned up there in the hills today. I started down here when I heard it, thinkin' I might be needed. Then, just now as I come down off the hill, I could see a blaze over toward Pitchfork."

"A blaze?"

Ed Beeson nodded. "A hell of a big one! Something's goin' on over there."

Holden didn't wait to hear more. He said, "Get some horses saddled!" and started at a run for the cabin, calling, "Miles!"

Kittering and Ann were standing outside the door. He saw that Kittering's arm was about the girl's shoulders, and sight of that sent a renewed surge of thankfulness through him. "Miles," he said, "Ed's just in to report a blaze at Pitchfork."

Kittering frowned. Fats thought of something that made him wheel and call, "Johnny, where's Mule?"

"Gone all day," they heard Dawes call back. "Rode out this mornin', early."

Fats' look settled on Kittering and his mouth was twisted to a wry smile. "There's something else, Miles. We'll talk about it later. What's important now is that Jim Allard was to show up here before dark. He isn't here yet, which may be why Ed heard those guns up there this afternoon. Think we ought to get over to Pitchfork and take a look for ourselves?"

Kittering nodded quickly. "Ann, you'll stay here."

Ann said, "No! I'm coming with you."

"Then get down there with Dawes while I gather up a gun or two." Kittering wheeled in through the cabin's doorway.

Fats didn't move off immediately. He looked at the girl, a slow smile spreading over his gaunt face. "This is a great day, Ann," he said. It was obvious that he referred to the change in Kittering.

"For me, yes," she said, low-voiced. Abruptly she went sober. She began haltingly, "Jim Allard. Is he . . ." and left her idea unworded.

"I wish I knew," Fats said with a worried sigh. "I shouldn't have let him go up there alone."

"What kind of a man is he, Fats?"

Holden was a long moment in answering that. When he did, his voice came evenly, low: "The kind to ride the river with."

14

EVENING's light was fading into dusk as Hugh Allard and Trent Harm's left Pitchfork's office, came out the patio gate and started through the cottonwoods toward the crew quarters. Beyond the mesa's far edge the desert lay almost wholly obscured by a deepening purple blanket of shadow, while above, in the still blue sky, the evening star was taking on its pin-point brilliance. From one of the high poplars along the lane came a mockingbird's long night call. The sound served to deepen the stillness that shrouded the layout.

Trent found the absence of familiar sounds depressing; he was nervous after this talk in the office with Hugh, and now he showed it. "I don't know, Hugh. How're you sure it'll work?"

"Why won't it?" Allard snapped, the curtness of his tone indicating that he, too, was feeling a nerve strain.

Harms made no answer, knowing that when the rancher was in a mood like this the best thing to do was to sit tight and see how things worked out.

They passed through the deep gloom of the cottonwoods, crossed the yard beyond and approached the bunkhouse. A man stepped into the lighted doorway, and Allard called, "Send Evans out here, Daniels." In an undertone he added to Harms, "Not here, Trent! I don't want any witnesses to this but you and me."

"Evans?" said Daniels. "He ain't here. Left ten or fifteen minutes ago. Said he had to get in town for something."

Allard swore under his breath and his look went bleak. His lips drew out to a thin hard line as his glance came around to his foreman. "You were so damned sure he'd wait around!"

Harms shrugged and held his tongue. Allard gave a jerk of his head, said, "Come on then," disgustedly, and led the way across to the cook shanty and beyond it to the door of a root cellar set in the face of the hill slope behind. On the way, Harms breathed a slow sigh of relief. It was to have been his job to get rid of Mule—a simple task, the way Allard had planned it. He was to have shot Mule. Now Mule was gone and Harms couldn't help feeling relieved.

Pausing at the root-cellar door, Allard asked, "Everything set at the barn, or will you muff that too?"

Harms smiled thinly. "Just like you said." He took a lantern down from a peg by the door and lit it. That smile clung to his face, for he was taking a grim satisfaction in what was coming now—a great deal more satisfaction than he would have had in cold-bloodedly shooting Mule Evans.

He unlocked the heavy padlock and kicked the door open. As he stepped through, the lantern's yellow wash of light fell on Jim Allard lying in a back corner, his head pillowed on a slanting heap of sprouting potatoes. Jim's arms and legs were tightly bound by many windings of a new manila rope. His lean face was etched with pain from the numbness of arms and legs.

Hugh, at sight of him, drawled, "It'll be over soon, Allard. We'd planned to have Mule side you. But he got away."

"What'll be over soon?" Jim asked. For the last two hours he'd lain here trying to find one small hope of getting out of this. So far, nothing to bolster that hope had come to him. The pain in his arms and legs had ceased to matter; he was beyond feeling pain. Riding in here two hours ago, they had found the layout deserted—Harms reporting that even Allard's daughter wasn't at the house. Jim had no illusions about what was to happen, and the mention of Mule now was pointed enough. Hugh Allard was too shrewd a man to let Mule live, knowing what he did.

'You'll see," the rancher answered. He nodded to Harms. "Bring him along, Trent."

Harms' blunt face took on a broad grin as he bent down, took a hold on Jim's shirt front and heaved him to his feet. When Jim hunched his shoulders, trying to work the circulation back into his arms, Harms misread his move as an attempt to get free of the ropes. A sudden brutal look came to the foreman's eyes. He held Jim off at arm's length with his left hand and cocked his right. His fist slashed out and hit Jim a glancing blow on the mouth. Jim's head rocked back sickeningly and his whole body went limp in unconsciousness. He would have fallen but for Harms' tight hold.

A look of faint disdain crossed Allard's face as he looked on. "You wouldn't have done that if he'd had his hands free, Trent," he drawled, then saw the mirrored hatred on his foreman's face and added, more mildly, "Bring him along!"

He led the way, Harms following with Jim's limp weight slung over his shoulder. Allard was a little worried over Mule getting away. He had played his hand strongly today and there were many doubtful quantities in what lay ahead.

The least of these was Trent Harms. But lately Harms had grown pretty sure of himself. His hitting Jim back there a moment ago was one evidence of it; a year ago, Trent wouldn't have dared take the initiative and do a thing like that without being told to first. He needed taking down a bit.

Hearing his foreman close behind him, Allard said, without turning or slowing his pace, "Trent, I've put an envelope in my box at the bank—just in case you get any ideas."

He heard Harms' swift intake of breath. Presently, the foreman muttered in a reedy voice, "Who said I was gettin' ideas?"

"No one. But I want you to know how things stand.

You've been with me ten years now, ever since that Gold-field business. I'd hate to have you begin thinking you can demand favors. The law doesn't forget, Trent."

He was curious to see the expression on Harms' face but didn't give way to that curiosity. Any other man might have been afraid to walk in front of Harms at this moment, for the man had his guns and Allard's back offered a sure target. Allard ignored this, sure of himself. He had hired Trent ten years ago, across in Nevada, and helped the man by giving him work and a hiding place. Trent was wanted on a murder charge across in Goldfield, and Hugh knew the particulars well.

Harms had been a useful man for such things as they were doing now. Hugh had occasional need of such a man, one whose loyalty was unquestionable. But occasionally, when Harms grew too sure of himself, the rancher would find it necessary to remind him of his past.

That reminder worked now, as it had before. Harms' sullen voice said complainingly, behind Allard, "Hell, boss, there was no call for that! I know how I stand."

"Just don't let it slip your mind, Trent."

They were approaching the big new barn with the rock foundation that footed the hill to the east. Harms was breathing hard under his load. Hugh went in through the big center door that stood wide open, Harms following closely. Harms set the lantern down and rolled Jim's weight from his shoulders, not gently. Allard sniffed the air. Mixed with the sweet smell of hay and the ammonia tang of the stables was another, more pungent; it was the odor of coal oil.

The rancher was satisfied. He nodded to Trent: "Go ahead."

Harms took the lantern and went over to climb a ladder that led to the loft. Allard, looking down into the darkness at his feet where Jim lay, heard the other moving about above. Presently, looking through the loft opening, he saw a waver-ing light reflected from the underside of the high roof—a light stronger than the lantern's.

Then Harms was back again, drawling, "She's caught."

The lantern's light touched Hugh Allard's face with severe sharp-planed shadows as he glanced critically down at Jim a last time. He thought of something: "Better take the ropes off, Trent. We don't want anything like that to turn up when he's found."

Harms stooped and worked at the knots along Jim's back. From overhead a slow-mounting roar of sound was filling the roof's high dome. The light up there was stronger now.

Presently, the foreman stood erect. "All right?" he queried, and Allard, inspecting the rawhide thongs that bound Jim's wrists and ankles, nodded briefly.

"Close the door, Trent," he said, and stood outside while Harms rolled the double doors tight shut at the head of the runway. "How about the others?" he asked, when Harms had finished. "Better peg 'em." Harms made a circuit of the barn, pegging tight the hasps on the doors at each end of the stableside.

They stood a hundred feet out from the building's squat shadow, watching the rosy flicker of light coming from the cracks at the edges of the big hay door in the loft.

"Good enough," Hugh said finally, turning to the bunkhouse. "Now we'll get in to town and start things."

The bitter acrid sting of smoke in his lungs jerked Jim to full consciousness. He was first aware of the roar overhead, the roar of flames eating into dry shingles. He caught his breath sharply as he opened his eyes and looked upward. The heavy planking of the loft floor was ablaze, its underside scored with lines of licking flames along the edge of each plank. Showers of sparks were falling about him. One, on his shirt front, burned through to the skin and made him catch his breath in pain. He rolled onto his stomach to smother it out.

The stark fear that was first in him gave way to bewilderment, then cold sanity. To wake from a dreamless, almost restful sleep to an inferno like this brought a shock to his mind that almost unsettled it. But, once he saw where he was and realized what had happened, a long-trained coolness in the face of trouble returned to him.

His mouth was swollen where Harms had hit him and he could taste blood. He forgot that. Overhead, the fire was eating into the tinder-dry roof with a roar like a team and buckboard being driven across the shingles. Part of the loft must have burned through, for he could feel a cool updraft along the floor. This lower portion of the barn was lighted eerily with flickering, spreading flame from above.

He turned his head. Beyond the runway stood a new wagon and brightly varnished buggy and behind them a cultivator and hayrake. He smiled, thinking that it was like Hugh Allard to do this thing thoroughly, with no thought of the money involved. Burning a new barn and all the equipment it housed, in order to pin the guilt on an unidentified dead man who couldn't ever tell his story, was the brand of cunning Jim had known the man to possess since the first

moment he'd laid eyes on him. Hugh would accomplish one
thing for certain in destroying his barn. He'd rid himself of
an unwanted relative who'd become a potent enemy. And
he'd use the fire to add one more indictment to those already
against Kittering. Block K's owner would be blamed for the
fire.

But after that first flash of grim humor, his mind settled
gravely into an important hopelessness. He felt less pain in
his arms and legs now. He could move them. When he discovered that his feet and hands were tied only with thin but
strong thongs, he had a moment of wild hope. But the
thongs were tight, the knots secure enough to numb his fingers, and after a moment of struggling against them he lay
back breathless; and this new hope was already dying within
him.

It was plain that Hugh Allard was leading with an ace
tonight. Tomorrow's dawn would see the barn a charred mass
of ruins. In the still-hot ashes would be found the remains
of a body, probably burned beyond recognition. Allard would
have accomplished what he had wanted for months, driving
his fight with Kittering into the open. He'd probably have
the sheriff and half the townspeople out here to witness the
discovery of the body. From then on he'd have things his
own way. The finger of guilt would point to Kittering. Allard
would take the law in his own hands. There would be a
quick fierce stroke. Kittering and his outfit would be wiped
out. Perhaps tomorrow night would find everything settled
Allard's way, Kittering and Holden dead—or if not dead,
outlawed. And the Block K, threatened with ruin by the
damning of Antelope Creek, would pass into Allard's hands
because no one else wanted it.

And where was Ann Allard? Jim didn't want to think
about her, about the mystery behind her parenthood that had
been the halter to Kittering's fighting Allard. He didn't want
to think of her in relation to Harms, either. But even though
he tried to put this chestnut-haired girl from his mind, the
haunting picture of her slim straight body, her golden oval
face, kept coming back to him. Never in the years he'd been
aware of woman had Jim Allard met one who could so violently stir him. Today, yesterday, she had been much in his
thoughts. She was now, regardless of his trying to put her
from them.

Because it wasn't in him to give up easily, because all his
years of manhood had been salted with danger and fighting it,
he was fighting now. A plank overhead burned through suddenly, broke in the middle and creaked downward, pulling

loose its spikes. The near end struck the floor butt-downward, throwing out a shower of sparks. It fell in toward Jim and he threw his body in a quick roll. The end of the plank grazed his boots and its intense heat made Jim jerk his feet away. The plank lay there flaming, lighting up the runway's wide length.

That moment of danger warned Jim of more to come. He didn't have much time. His glance shuttled quickly about him. To his left, lined neatly in a row that cleared the runway, were the varnished rigs and the new-painted farm machinery. On his right side ran the long row of stalls, the double one at the front lined along the outside wall with harness, an iron watering trough and a feed bin on the runway side. The stall door leading into it stood open. Beyond, the outside door was tightly closed—locked, no doubt, as he knew the big runway doors must be. Allard wouldn't take a chance on letting his victim walk out through an unfastened door.

Back at the far end of the stables a whole section of the loft flooring suddenly gave way and fell down with a sound like the muted thunder of half a hundred guns. Out from the last two stalls rolled a billowing cloud of acrid smoke. It filtered into the air at this front end of the barn and Jim's eyes filled with tears and he coughed rackingly, no matter how shallowly he tried to breathe.

It would be over soon now, suffocation coming first, mercifully, to save him the torture of burning alive. No, it wouldn't come! All at once a blinding rage built up in him, then faded to leave him nerveless. He looked to either side once more, and what finally took his glance was the iron watering trough across there in the front stall—the trough and the two-inch pipe and valve that came out of the rock foundation above. There was a foot-long spanner on the valve.

Suddenly he was remembering the water tank on the slope behind the barn. And with that thought he turned his body in a quick roll toward the open gate to the stables.

He hunched through it on his back, boots pushing hard and his wide shoulders rubbing the ground. Half blinded by the smoke, choking as he breathed the fouled air, he had to pause twice to gather the strength to go on. Once a sudden dizziness hit him with a force that made the loft overhead spin before his eyes. From then on he worked feverishly, his will alone keeping him conscious.

He was close in to the trough, head nearest. He worked his long frame around, lifted his boots and had the presence of mind to apply the pressure to the spanner gently, so as not to kick it off the valve.

A sob choked out of his throat as a wrist-thick stem of water gushed out of the valve and into the trough. He cried out as a splinter from overhead fell on one shoulder and burned through his shirt, and his cry was lost in the howling deafening sound of the flames overhead. Now he could see only halfway the length of the stalls toward the rear, for smoke was fast fogging this whole lower floor of the structure.

Waiting for the trough to fill seemed an eternity of time. Three times he had to jerk his head aside to keep falling flaming splinters from burning his face. Then, mercifully, water dripped, then flowed in a steady curtain over the trough's edge.

He rolled under it, a long slow breath escaping his wide chest as the water ran deliciously cool onto his back. He drenched shirt and trousers and let the water stream over his face and head. What made him move finally out from that temporary relief was a prolonged low roar mounting in pitch above the others. He looked across into the wavering fog of eerily lighted smoke and saw the whole loft floor on the opposite side of the runway cave in in a solid sheet of flame. The roar held on, deafeningly. The barn couldn't last much longer. Next would come the loft floor on this side, then the roof, and finally the walls would cave inward in one last magnificent inferno.

He struggled to his knees, then erect. He stooped a little, bringing his wrists in against the trough's rough cast-iron edge. He began sawing at the thongs on his wrists, standing unsteadily, coughing with each breath, eyes squinted shut to keep them from watering. Panic hit him like a blow—a panic he downed with a force of will that he knew couldn't last.

The jagged rough edge of the iron all at once bit into the flesh of his wrists. He moved his arms to a new position. His hands came apart!

He fell to the floor, rolling under the curtain of water falling from the trough's edge. The bare dirt floor was muddy now. He lifted his face from the mud and let the water soak him again. Then he sat up and awkwardly put his numbed fingers to the knots in the thongs about his ankles.

A creaking overhead warned him that the loft floor was going. He kicked out savagely and broke the last strand of rawhide. He rolled onto his feet, choking, gasping, his senses reeling. He saw the stable door six feet away. He lunged against it, but it was solid. He stepped back and this time picked the exact spot where he would hit with his shoulder —the spot where the bent nail ends that secured the hasp showed.

He heard the snapping of joists above his head, sensed rather than saw the whole loft falling in on him. In three lunging strides his long frame gathered momentum. Then his shoulder was crashing into the sheathing of the door. The hasp snapped and the door burst outward and he fell face downward, hearing behind him the muffled thud of the loft planking as it struck the stable floor.

He lay there gasping for breath, the air tasting cool and sweet as it drove the smoke from his lungs. He pushed up onto hands and knees and looked out across the yard.

There, running in toward him, came a man's high shape. The runner held one arm across his face. Jim realized without being aware of it that it must be hot here, that the relief he felt came in contrast to the intense heat inside the barn.

Quick wariness hit him. He had fought his way out of a fiery grave and now a Pitchfork rider was headed for him, probably to finish the job that had so narrowly miscarried. He stood up unsteadily, hands automatically reaching for his guns. They weren't there, of course. Then, boots spread wide, he lunged at the man, now within two strides of him. He struck out with both arms, wildly.

15

THE change in Miles Kittering was an amazing one, even to Fats Holden who had known him before this trouble with Allard. It was on Kittering's order that they cut directly across country, ignoring the roundabout badlands trail and riding point for Pitchfork. It was Kittering who cut Pitchfork's fence and led them through it with no thought of repairing the break. He was a new man, the beacon of Pitchfork's blazing barn seeming to summon him out of his inaction of these past weeks.

They rode in on the layout from the ridge to the south. At a quarter-mile's distance, with the glowing framework of the barn's roof a huge pyre that cut the shadows even at this distance, Ann drew alongside her father and called, "I'm going ahead. You can't go rushing in there! You'll be shot!" She pushed her pony on ahead of the others.

Kittering drew rein and let Holden and Dawes and Beeson come up with him. For a long moment they sat there, watching the girl swing down on the corrals and crew's quarters. Then Kittering breathed. "We'll go on, slow. God, what a blaze!"

The roof of the barn was now a skeletal mass of red-tongued glowing timbers, with a geyser of sparks whirled aloft a hundred feet from its high center cupola. Smoke fingers curled out of every crack of the lower siding and from around the doors, and as they rode down off the slope they could see the first long tongues of flames licking out from the planking of the huge double doors in front.

Holden swore solemnly, in a voice hard and bitter, saying, "It was set to burn from the loft down. Miles, they'll hang this on you!"

Ann appeared around the near corner of the wagon shed, the closest building, riding toward them. She called up to them, "There's no one here!"

They lifted their ponies to a trot and went down to her. Kittering and Dawes and Beeson angled off toward the barn, circling toward its far north side. Fats stayed behind with Ann, and followed her as she slowly rode in on the side of the barn opposite the one her father was approaching. She said to Holden as he closed in beside her, "Fats, what does it mean? Is this something else Hugh will blame on Miles?"

"Hell, yes!" Holden's profanity was caustic.

"But this time I can prove that it wasn't Miles, can't I?" Her tone was worried, awed at the implications she saw behind the burning of the barn.

"I reckon . . . only maybe it's gone too far for us to need that."

They were close in now. As Holden spoke, a shifting current of air brought them a wave of sudden dry heat. Ann's head came around and she eyed Holden in alarm. "What do you mean, Fats? It's gone too far for what?"

He didn't answer, for his bony frame was abruptly standing in the stirrups and his eyes were squinted into the glare of light. A moment ago the stable door had bellied open in a gust of flame. Now he thought he saw a vague shape stagger out into the open, enveloped in those flames.

Without waiting to be sure, he rammed spurs into his gelding's flanks and quirted the animal with rein ends. The gelding lunged nervously in toward the barn for half a dozen mincing steps, then fought the bit and shied aside.

Fats leaped from the saddle and struck the ground at a dead run. He ignored Ann's strident cry behind him. He stooped low in his run as he neared the barn's wall, and put an arm up to shield his face. The strange apparition of the man who had come out the door a moment ago staggered toward him and struck out clumsily with both fists.

In that instant Fats recognized Jim Allard. The next, Jim's high-built frame slumped forward and Fats caught him in his arms.

Ann, looking on, saw Fats catch Jim. She quirted the buckskin and gouged the animal with her spurs, trying to make him go in toward Holden. That failed and she slid out of the saddle and waited there for Fats. When he was beside her, breathing heavily, he told her, "It's Jim! See if you can find some whiskey. He's in bad shape." He lifted Jim face-down into her saddle and steadied him, leading the animal away as Ann ran off toward the cook shanty.

"Kittering!" he bellowed, once he was beyond the steady roar of the barn.

Presently, Miles and Johnny Dawes came into sight far on the other side of the barn. Holden called again and his hail brought them across. Ann came out of the cook-shanty door and ran toward him. She and her father arrived at the same time.

Kittering saw the shape across the buckskin's saddle, asking hastily, "Who is it?"

"Jim Allard. We saw him break out that stable door down at the barn. He was on his feet then but he keeled over tryin' to hit me. Must have thought I was one of the crew."

"He was in there!" came Kittering's hushed words. "Why?"

"How the hell do I know?" Holden said gruffly, lifting Jim down and laying him on the ground. He reached up for the bottle of whisky in the girl's hand, uncorked it and tipped it to Jim's mouth.

Jim gagged as the raw bite of the liquour went down his throat. He reached up and struck the bottle aside. Then his eyes opened. Pain and rage were mirrored on his face for a brief instant. Then, as the light of the fire struck the faces of those standing above him, that expression died and a broad smile came to his face.

He drawled, "This is more like it."

"Take it easy, Jim," Fats said. But Jim sat up.

Kittering wheeled around and said crisply to Ed Beeson, "Go find Johnny. We're gettin' out of here!"

Ann had been looking down at Jim intently, her face gone pale. Now she knelt beside him. "Jim!" she said suddenly, tensely. "Did they put you in there to . . ." She couldn't finish what she'd started to say.

He nodded gravely and took the bottle of whisky from Holden and downed a big swallow.

She sensed that there was something he didn't want to tell her. "I want to know, Jim. Tell me what happened."

He looked up at Kittering, then at Holden. Fats said, "Maybe you'd better. She has a right to know."

Jim understood only a little of what had happened between Kittering and his daughter tonight. But Holden's word gave him enough to go on to say, "Guess I knew too much. They fired the barn and left me there to be sure it caught."

"Hugh did?" Ann asked in a low voice, her face drained of all color now.

He nodded. "And Harms."

Beeson and Dawes rode up and Kittering said quickly, "Ann, loan us that buckskin. We're shy a horse."

The girl stood op. "I'm coming with you."

"You're not!"

"But I can't stay here, Miles! I can't! Hugh did this, left him there to die!" She looked out toward the flame-engulfed barn and her gaze held as though fascinated. "They wanted to murder him!"

Kittering was uncertain now, and didn't reply at once. Finally he turned to Ed Beeson. "You and Johnny double up. Give Jim your—"

"She's not going." Holden cut in sharply. "You want her sleepin' in the hills, dodgin' lead with us? Use your head, Miles! Leave her here. She—"

"I say she goes if she wants!" Kittering flared in a quick reversal of decision. The danger of leaving Ann within reach of Hugh had struck him as forcibly as the girl having to remind him of it.

Jim's quiet drawl broke the tension between them. "You could stay here until things get squared away," he said, speaking to Ann. "Kittering could use someone who'd keep him posted on what's going on."

They were all silent before this new suggestion. At length, the girl gave a slow nod. "I'll stay if it'll help. But how can I keep from letting them know how I feel?"

Jim said, "You'll have to."

His tone decided Ann. She turned to her father. "It would be better that way," she said. Kittering gave her a searching glance; then motioned Jim across to the girl's buckskin, impatiently.

Ann's glance came around and followed Jim. Then, on sudden impulse, she went across to him and stood at his stirrup. She said in a hushed voice, "I want you to know

I'm sorry this happened. Sorry for what I said the other afternoon."

"You needn't be."

"Yes, I am. You see, Jim, I've been a little blind. I didn't know all this about Hugh." She seemed embarrassed at calling him by name but covered it nicely.

"No one did. You're not to blame."

Kittering called, "Let's go!" and reined in close to the girl. He said brusquely, "Keep your chin up, Ann," and led them out toward the hill slope.

Before he rode out of sight, Jim turned and lifted his hand to the girl. She waved back and only after the far shadows hid him did she give way to a sob that she couldn't keep back.

Kittering led them three miles into the hills before he called a halt along a timber-fringed fold of the hills. He said, "Let's talk this thing out before we go any farther."

Holden, whose curiosity over what had happened to Jim today was even stronger than Kittering's, seconded the idea. They built a fire that was screened from sight below by the trees. Kittering, restless, wary, sent Dawes and Beeson up to the crests of the flanging hill to keep a prowling lookout.

"Now," said Kittering, as they hugged the fire's welcome warmth. "Let's have it—all of it, Jim. In case you don't know, I've come out of a long sleep."

Spade Deshay was a stubborn man. The way station operator's wary assertion that a Pitchfork man had sent the wire calling Virgil Pierce to Sands was proof enough, coupled with the fight back in the hills this afternoon, to convince him that Jim Allard had earlier spoken several truths. But this quick reversal of his luck made Spade hard to convince.

It was therefore not surprising that, when Two Card asked, "Where to, boss?" as they left the way station, Spade should answer, "Town."

Two Card's head jerked around. He eyed Spade's handsome profile a long moment in unfeigned surprise. "Town"? he echoed.

Spade's head jerked in a nod.

"Why?" Two Card queried against his better judgment, for he knew his partner's temper at a time like this.

"You think I'm ridin' into this thing blind?" was Spade's acid rejoinder.

"If it was me, I'd ride out instead of in."

"No one's stopping you!"

But Two Card made no move to pull his pony aside from the trail they now rode to Sands. His loyalty, such as it was, belonged to Spade; he had sided the outlaw for better than ten years, and in that time they had lived frugally or bountifully, as circumstances dictated. Dangerously, too, at times. Although Two Card was getting old and shied away from the risks he had taken as a younger man, the same slow anger was in him that was in Spade. It was plain that they had been double-crossed in a deal they thought they'd made with Kittering. It was just as plain that Spade Deshay would hang on here, stubbornly, and settle that account with Hugh Allard.

Two Card said, "What happens after you get your look at Pierce?" He knew that Spade would have to lay eyes on the ex-marshal as a final proof of Jim Allard's claim. He didn't relish riding into a town to get such proof; but if Spade went, he went.

When Spade didn't break his surly silence, Two Card reminded him, "Friend Jim isn't in this just for the hell of it."

"He's not in it at all, after tonight."

Two Card had almost forgotten that brief glimpse they'd had of Jim roped on a pony and surrounded by Pitchfork men. Strangely enough, he now felt regret over Jim's almost certain fate. In the old days, he'd respected Jim in a rare way; and even for the differences that had made Jim and Spade eventual enemies, he still respected him.

"Then we throw in with Kittering?" he asked.

"We don't throw in with anyone," came Spade's curt statement. He left it unsaid that they'd thrown in against Hugh Allard. Kittering had nothing to do with this. Spade would take his own way of settling with Pitchfork's owner.

They were better than an hour covering the distance to Sands. Approaching the town, Two Card called Spade's attention to the faint glow showing against the black hills far to the north.

"Could be a fire at Pitchfork," he commented.

But Spade was not to be moved out of his dark silence. They swung out toward the railroad right of way at the outskirts of town. Following the rails, they walked their horses along the alley behind the long row of stores. Spade had visited Sands twice in the months they'd been in this country. He remembered it well, though, and stopped his pony in the shadow of a shed built beyond the tracks at the back of the general store. He swung aground, tied his reins to a ring set in the shed's wall for that purpose, then looked up at Two Card and muttered, "Comin'?"

Two Card tied his pony and followed Spade's undersized slim shape up a narrow alleyway between the store and the adjoining building. Halfway up the passageway toward the street, he overtook Spade and said in a hushed voice, "You pick your spots, don't you?"

Spade's stride broke. He stopped, looked up and took in a small barred window set in the adobe wall almost directly over his head. For the first time since Jim's arrival at the hideout that afternoon, a genuine smile touched his aquiline face. He drawled, "Don't I?" and went on. The building to their left was the jail.

They approached the walk unobtrusively, passing a darkened window of the jail's office. Spade came out of the alleyway's mouth and leaned lazily against the corner of the general store's wide porch. Two Card, feeling less sure of himself, put his back to the jail's front corner and watched Spade build a cigarette. He took the makin's Spade passed across to him and cautioned unnecessarily, low-voiced, "Careful with that match."

He was looking obliquely out across the street to the hotel veranda, seeing that Spade's glance had gone that way. From this distance they could see clearly the figures sitting tilted in chairs along the veranda rail. Virgil Pierce wasn't there. But if Pierce was in town, the hotel was the logical place for him to be seen sooner or later. Spade would wait to get his look at the man.

In the next half hour the traffic along the street was no more than usual for a weekday night. But they noticed one thing out of the ordinary. There were people on the hotel roof, at first only three men, then more. "They're watchin' that blaze," Two Card said finally, and Spade nodded.

Shortly after they noticed the men on the roof, Fred Blythe came along the walk and turned into his office. Sight of the star on his vest as he passed them made Two Card stiffen. But no move of Spade's betrayed the fact that he was aware of the sheriff. It was dark here and Blythe had no reason to be curious over two men loafing by the store. A light came on in the office and shone out through one of its two windows almost directly on them. The window faced the passageway and the store's porch.

When Two Card gave Spade an uneasy glance, Spade said, "Stay set."

From where he stood, Spade could look back over his

shoulder and in through the window. This was his first sight of Fred Blythe. He rightly judged that he was seeing an efficient law officer. He knew within half a minute that Blythe was worried over something. After the lamp went on, the sheriff came to the window and lifted the lower sash a few inches. He then went to his desk, pushed his Stetson onto the back of his head, took a folded telegram from his hip pocket and stood examining it with a look of frowning concentration. He read the message over several times, finally tossing it onto the desk.

He left his office within three minutes of entering, leaving the light on and crossing the street to the hotel. Presently Spade saw him among the watchers on the roof.

What happened almost immediately after that came swiftly. Four riders appeared out of the darkness up the street and swung in at the jail tie rail. Spade immediately recognized Hugh Allard and Trent Harms and the two Pitchfork men who had sided Mule Evans this afternoon in the ambush at the canyon mouth. He said in a hoarse whisper, "Back!" and he and Two Card melted into the shadows along the passageway as Pitchfork's men crossed the walk.

He heard someone hail, "Allard?" from the hotel roof and Hugh Allard called back, "Where's Blythe?" The sheriff himself answered, "Right here. Be down in a minute."

Then came the banging of the jail office's screen door. Spade edged forward along the passageway, hugging the wall of the store. He looked in through the dust-smeared window again. Hugh Allard had thrown a leg over the corner of the desk and was sitting with his back to the window. Harms was across the room in a chair. The other pair weren't there; they were probably waiting out front, Spade decided.

He saw Hugh Allard's idle glance go down to the desk, to the telegram Blythe had left there a few minutes ago. Allard's look became sharper. He picked up the telegram and read it. At that moment Blythe, who was crossing from the hotel, spoke to Allard's two men at the hitch rail out front. Spade missed the sheriff's words and the answer he received. But at the sound of the lawman's voice, Hugh Allard's head came up and jerked toward the door. He laid the telegram back on the desk, came to his feet quickly and moved across the room and was standing near Harms when Blythe entered.

Spade eased across the passageway, leaned against the jail wall beside the open window, and plainly heard Blythe say, "When did it happen, Hugh?"

Allard said, "Right at dark. The whole roof was caught

by the time we discovered it. That blaze was set, Fred! It didn't start by itself."

There was a brief but potent silence, broken finally by Blythe's pointed question: "How could a man get in there to set it? You had guards around the layout the other night when I rode in."

"Not today. I wasn't looking for trouble again so soon. The crew's up in the hills looking for those critters that strayed last night."

"And you think it was Kittering again?"

"Think! I know, damn it! Who else would it be?"

"Now take it easy, Hugh! Don't go jumpin' to conclusions."

"I came in to report this . . . for the record. What I do from now on's my own business. I'm going to fight fire with fire."

Again, a brief silence ran out. A voice unfamiliar to Spade, Trent Harms', spoke up, "Yeah, we're through sittin' out the seat of our pants, sheriff."

Blythe's voice sounded again, a little strained. What he said changed the subject. It meant nothing to Spade until later. "Hugh, we can't find that hotel register. You know anything about it?"

"Should I?"

"I don't know. I'm askin' you."

"No."

"What about Chalmers? Did you see him that day before he died?"

Spade could feel the tension in the stillness that followed. Hugh Allard's voice was sharp-edged as he answered, "You've got something in your craw, Fred. Get it out!"

"It's nothin'," Blythe said. "Only I thought since you're a director of the Sierra and Western you might have heard Chalmers was to be in town."

"I've never laid eyes on the man, never even heard his name mentioned before the day he died. Does that satisfy you?"

"Sure. Sure." The lawman's tone was mollifying.

"I'm giving you a last chance," Allard went on. "I'm swearing out a warrant on Kittering. Will you go out there with me, tonight, to serve it?"

"I don't reckon I have any choice, do I?"

"Not any."

"Then let's get goin'."

The office's door slammed again. Spade flattened to the wall as Blythe crossed the mouth of the passageway, calling,

"Be with you in five minutes, Hugh. I've got to tell Bailey where I'm goin'."

Before he turned back along the passageway, Spade took one last look into the office. The telegram was gone from the desk. Blythe must have pocketed it.

Spade stepped back to where Two Card was waiting. "We're headed for Kittering's," he drawled. "Fast."

"Back there you said you weren't."

"I've changed my mind."

"How about Pierce?" Two Card queried.

"To hell with Pierce!"

16

FRED BLYTHE had no illusions about the spot he was in. He had the warrant for Kittering in his pocket and, whether Kittering was guilty or not, the arrest was inevitable. Unless . . .

The question that was in the sheriff's mind concerned the telegram he'd received tonight. At first the information it contained amazed and confused him. He'd been trying to read what lay behind its implications as Spade looked in at the office window and saw the puzzled look on his face. Since then, he'd had time to digest the message's startling revelations and fit them to the happenings of the past few days. He was afraid of the answers he was getting.

He was riding alongside Hugh Allard, who methodically set the pace to an alternate mile-eating run and walk. Harms and Tellew and Daniels came along behind. If Blythe had ever wondered about the new type of crewmen Hugh was hiring, he thought he knew the answer now.

At first anger, then helplessness, had its way with him. There were things he should be asking Hugh—the things mentioned in that telegram. But now, alone with Hugh and his crew, was no time to put the questions. He'd have to wait until the odds were more even.

He was mulling the thing over in his mind, trying to see the thing clearly, when he happened to think that he'd left te telegram on his desk during his brief absence from the office. Hugh Allard and Harms had been in there, alone! Had Hugh seen the telegram?

Blythe was instantly wary. A slow tide of honest fear

flowed into him. If Hugh knew, then Blythe was in as bad a spot as Miles Kittering; worse, perhaps, for Kittering still had men fighting with him, while the sheriff was alone.

He tried not to show his alarm. Hugh seemed intent only on covering distance and that helped. Maybe Hugh hadn't seen the telegram lying there on the desk after all. Gradually, his fears left him. He began to feel the enormous advantage he had over Hugh. With what he knew he'd wind this thing up in a hurry. And it wouldn't be Kittering who was the county's prisoner in the end.

Then, when the hope that Hugh hadn't seen the wire after all was becoming a real conviction, the rancher abruptly pulled his gelding in to a walk, turned in the saddle so that he faced the lawman, and queried blandly, "What did you think of that wire, Fred?"

An instant's panic settled through Blythe. That passed quickly, its place taken by a philosophy he had acquired with advancing age; namely, that a cool head and sharp honesty could pull a man out of most any trouble.

He answered evenly, "It surprised me, Hugh."

Allard laughed, turned in the saddle and called, "Trent, you and the boys drop back a ways." He waited until the hoof rattle of the three ponies behind had receded to a comfortable distance. Then: "It surprised me, too. I didn't suppose you'd think to make inquiries."

"That's what's funny about it. I didn't. Someone else did."

"Who?" Hugh spoke sharply, in a way that let the sheriff know he was gravely concerned at this piece of news.

Blythe had more than once tonight tried to get that very answer for himself. He hadn't succeeded beyond a vague theory that perhaps Jim Allard might have been responsible for that all-important telegram; but he had dismissed this in the belief that Jim Allard had left the country.

All the same, he now said, "Jim Allard."

Surprisingly enough, Hugh looked relieved. Or the faint expression the sheriff could catch on Hugh's face in the feeble starlight passed as relief.

"That might be," Allard said. "In that case, I needn't let it bother me. Jim Allard's dead."

"Dead?"

Hugh nodded. He lifted a hand to indicate the brighter glow of the fire in the hills. "Up there. We decided he'd be as good an excuse as any. No one'll be able to identify him. I can say it was a Kittering man."

Fred Blythe for a moment lost grip on his nerve. Hugh

Allard was blandly admitting a murder and the firing of his own barn. The man was mad, his insanity tempered by a cool brutality well masked.

The sheriff had a thought then that struck him as forcibly as a blow. Hugh was admitting these things to him because he thought that Antelope County's sheriff no longer mattered. The logical assumption Blythe reached was that he faced the same fate as had been meted out to Jim Allard tonight.

Blythe was a man who didn't give up easily. He said, "Why are you tellin' me all this, Hugh?"

The rancher shrugged. His expression was one of real concern. "I hate it. Hate it like hell, Fred! You and I always got on pretty well. But you knew too much the minute you read that wire."

What he meant was that Blythe wouldn't be allowed to live, knowing what he did. The sheriff took the remark stoically. All he had to do was to remember that he'd always hated facing old age. After that he didn't care what happened. If he was cashing in tonight—and it looked like his number was up—then there was nothing he could about it. He still had his gun and the use of his arm and maybe he could use them to advantage. He was crowded to the point where this reckless move seemed quite logical. But before he tried it, he had to have his curiosity satisfied.

He said, "So that's how it is, eh? Mind tellin' me a few things, Hugh?"

"Not at all. What things?"

"Several. First, how'd you lay hands on Jim Allard?"

Hugh told him, impersonally, as though he were speaking of the affairs of another man. His manner once again brought home to Fred Blythe the fact that Hugh was insane— not in the way of the country-asylum inmates, who had to be put in strait jackets, but coolly, stripped of conscience and his moral fiber. Hugh spoke of Spade Deshay and Jim Allard's device of discovering the outlaw's connection with Pitchfork's owner.

"Then it's been you and not Kittering, all along?" Fred interrupted to ask.

The rancher nodded willingly. He told about the fight at the canyon mouth this afternoon. There was even a trace of pride in the way he told of Mule Evans—how he'd bought Mule's loyalty, how the man had served him. He seemed to gloat over the telling of his maneuvers to frame Kittering.

Their horses were standing now. From time to time Blythe would put a question. Invariably, Allard answered with a truthful account of what had happened. Blythe, in seeing the intricate puzzle shaped by the events of the past weeks put neatly together, almost forgot that he was a condemned man.

Finally they were silent. There was nothing more Blythe could ask. Allard moved his shoulders in a nervous gesture, seeming all at once impatient to get on. He had the manner of a man who has unburdened his mind and feels better for it.

Blythe said, "It's a pity you didn't take the other way, Hugh."

"How could I?" Allard asked sharply, intently. "I was thirty when I brought my wife here—Kittering's wife. That was eighteen years ago. Do you think a man can live with a thing like that for eighteen years and not . . ."

"Not lose his mind?" Blythe supplied the phrase for him.

Allard laughed, softly, without merriment. "I'm as sane as you are, Fred! You know that. It's just that I want to wipe away the past. Kittering represents my past. When he's gone I'll have some peace."

"And a satchelful of money."

"The money doesn't matter. I have enough now. It only sweetens the broth, Fred. I'll admit there's some satisfaction in having used my wits better than the others!"

Suddenly anger, loathing and fear crowded in on Fred Blythe. Here he sat, calmly discussing trickery, theft, arson, bribery and murder with a man who had coolly committed all these crimes. And he was a law officer!

He realized that now he had but one slender chance of living to see the outcome of this thing. His right hand strayed down from its grip on the saddle horn toward his holstered gun.

Hugh Allard must have read his thought. For suddenly the rancher's off spur gouged his gelding's flank sharply. The animal lunged in toward Blythe's pony. Allard's fist arched up, then down. The solid butt of his quirt slashed out and slammed hard at the sheriff's head. It caught Blythe above the temple as he lifted his gun clear of leather.

The lawman's spare frame went limp. His hand fisting the gun opened. The weapon fell to the dust of the trail. Then, slowly, like an unbalanced bag of grain, Blythe's body tilted over and sideways. He fell out of the saddle, struck the ground face downward and lay without moving. Allard's single blow had beaten him into unconsciousness.

Allard stared down at him a brief moment, a half smile taking his narrow face. Then he turned and called, "Trent, get up here!"

Trent and Tellew and Daniels came up out of the obscurity. They saw the riderless pony, then Blythe stretched out on the ground. A startled oath came from Harms.

Before they could speak, Allard said crisply, "Daniels, you've got a rope. Tie him on his saddle and take him up to the layout. Lock him in the same place we put Jim Allard. The crew ought to be back by now. Leave one man there to watch Blythe and bring the rest to town. We'll be waiting for you at the hotel." His glance went to the other two. "Trent, you and Tellew come with me. We're headed for Kittering's."

17

THE glow of the campfire in the hills three miles south of Pitchfork didn't die for two hours. In that long interval two shapes moved restlessly about it from time to time, Fats Holden's gaunt and lean one, Kittering's short and blocky.

Jim didn't move from where he sat. It was good to rest here nearly out of reach of the fire's warmth, letting the cold crisp night air take the fever from his body. His arms and shoulders smarted where they had been burned and his wrists were raw in places where the thongs had rubbed through the skin. But the whisky in him helped him forget the ever-present smarting pain. He felt good, thankful to be alive.

He did most of the talking, his words thickened slightly by his swollen and cut lower lip, where Harms had hit him. At first they let him talk, Holden occasionally interrupting to explain something in greater detail to Kittering. Jim spoke directly to Block K's owner, understanding that something had awakened the man from his lethargic inaction of the last critical days. He wanted Kittering to understand exactly what he faced now, the brutal killing avarice of Hugh Allard that had come so near to costing him his life tonight.

Kittering listened soberly, somewhat eagerly. As the talk went on he time and again stopped Jim in midsentence and made him go back and repeat certain things. Once it was to get it straight in his mind how Hugh Allard had used Mule Evans in dealing with Spade Deshay.

At this point, Fats Holden's look darkened and outright rage showed on his face. "I've been a fool!" he cut in. "Just a plain damned locoed fool! Why didn't I bear down on him when he started roamin' nights? I knew he was up to somethin'! Miles, this is my fault!"

The proof Jim gave them of Mule's betrayal hit Holden a good bit harder than it did Kittering. Block K's owner had too much else to take in tonight to let this one strand of a finely woven mesh of intrigue against him assume too large a proportion. It was different with Holden. Fats had all along known most of the things Jim was telling Kittering tonight. The news of Mule was different. He felt personally responsible for Mule. It put him in a bleak dark mood as Jim continued, briefly telling them about the firing of the barn.

When Jim had finished, Kittering said, "I wish now we'd brought Ann with us."

Holden said, "She's best off right where she is."

Mention of Ann prompted a question from Jim. Holden then told him of the girl's visit to Kittering tonight, adding caustically that it took a woman to open a man's eyes. If Kittering resented the remark, he gave no sign of it.

But he did change the subject, asking Jim, "One thing I don't get straight. Why are you buyin' into this trouble?"

Jim wondered if he could explain. He tried. Concisely, without bitterness, he told them what he was—an ex-outlaw, once again an outcast after receiving a pardon for a killing he'd been forced into. He mentioned his finances, which were meager. He told them of receiving Allard's summons, that it looked like a way of getting a new start. He'd broken pardon parole to come across here. But he had been nearly desperate, looking for work. Then had come Allard's offer, the shock of discovering that his unearned reputation was once more cheating him of a sound future.

"I hated Allard's gall. If he hadn't set that man out to bushwhack me I'd have come to you, warned you and probably ridden out of here." He purposely avoided mention of Billy Walls, not yet sure of how Kittering tied into Locheim's death. "As it turned out, I couldn't let that pass. Maybe I'm bullheaded. But when a man sets out to kill me I don't run."

"So you shot up my cabin to make me hire you." Kittering laughed softly, a laugh that was unamused. "Well, it worked. I can say now I'm thankful it did. You're hired, Jim. We need you . . . like hell!"

Afterward, Jim found it strange that Kittering hadn't once mentioned Judge Locheim's death. Although Kittering wanted to know about Chalmers, about the unfinished letter

Jim had found in the dead man's room, he was strangely silent on the subject of the inquest. Once Holden pointedly provided an opening by blandly stating that it was his opinion the judge had been murdered. Kittering's quiet comment was, 'Don't talk that sort of hogwash! Kurt never made an enemy," and the subject was changed.

As time went on, Holden's impatience grew more apparent. "You're awful damn' fiddle-footed tonight, Fats," Kittering remarked, noticing it.

The thin man turned abruptly from the fire, starting over to the cedar where the horses were tied. "I'm headed for town," he said. "We ought to know what Allard's up to."

"We'll go along," Kittering suggested.

Holden wheeled around and said with curt sharpness, "No. We're not steppin' into any traps tonight. Get back to the layout. Stay set until we know where we stand. I'll ease in there, pick up what I can, and be back in a couple hours."

Jim said. "That's sense, Kittering. Allard may want to toll you in there tonight. You can afford to wait till you're sure."

"Anything you say," Kittering drawled, and Holden went on to climb into the saddle and ride away into the darkness.

Presently, Kittering called Beeson and Dawes down out of the timber. He told Beeson, "Ed, your legs are shorter than Jim's. Swap him your mare for that buckskin." Ann's stirrups had been uncomfortably short for Jim, and Kittering had noticed it.

They left the dying coals of the fire and struck straight across the hills toward Block K, Jim forking Beeson's roan. The miles fell behind. Jim, his pain-wracked muscles easing to the movement of the saddle, found something ominous and awkward in this waiting. He felt that they should be doing something; what it was he couldn't decide. Instead, they were leisurely returning to a night of sleep. Of course, they would have to await Holden's word to know exactly how to move. But the delay made Jim nervous. He was strangely troubled but thought it due to the letdown succeeding a tumultuous day.

He and Kittering went on ahead of the other two. Once he asked Kittering. "Did you leave anyone at the layout?" and Kittering replied simply, "No one to leave." The rancher's words somehow drove home to Jim the feebleness of any effort they could make.

They numbered five men against Hugh Allard's crew of a dozen or more. In addition to his men, Allard would have the law behind him in this. Jim wondered about Blythe, whether going in to see him and telling him the true state of affairs would in the end net them anything. He decided it wouldn't; Blythe couldn't be expected to believe all that had happened, regardless of his knowing from the judge's murder that there were undercurrents to this thing he had no knowledge of.

It was less than a minute after Jim had spoken to Kittering that the far-off sound of guns came rolling up across the hills. "Hear that?" Kittering breathed instantly, and reined in. Jim did likewise, and the ponies behind came close and halted.

There was a long silence. "Thunder?" Kittering asked, and lifted his glance to look skyward. The sky was clear, cloudless, sprinkled with a bright blanket of myriad stars.

On the heel of his words, they heard it again, wind-drifted, muted by distance. The sound was unmistakable, the swift-timed, sporadic explosions of guns.

Kittering's spurs gouged his black's flanks. He shouted, "Come on!" and his mare lunged ahead. Jim had been only half aware of the rifle boot that nudged his right knee. Now his palm slapped the stock of the Winchester thrust in the boot; he turned quickly on Dawes and Beeson and called, "I'll stick with Miles!" and dug in his spurs.

Jim punished Beeson's pony in the next ten minutes. He had Kittering in sight several times, then lost him altogether. But by then he had the sound of the guns to guide him, louder now. They spoke from his right, to the west, and he rode hard through a scattered stand of pines toward the sound.

Abruptly, he was at the head of Block K's home pasture, looking down on the layout. Half a mile below sprawled the buildings around Kittering's cabin. They were lighted by the glow of a fire along the front side of the haystack beyond the barn. Cabin, well house and one other building were outlined plainly. Jim knew instantly that the dry haystack had been fired.

Warily, he swung right, keeping to the margin of the trees. Shortly, the ground was familiar as he came to the place where he'd entered the timber night before last to get his position to fire down on the cabin. He went on, hearing the brittle crack of a rifle down there. No shot answered.

He was puzzled by the guns. It was logical that Pitchfork men had set the blaze. But who was down there to meet this sure-timed thrust of Allard's? Holden had gone to town. Mule Evans was on his way out of the country if he had the brains Jim gave him credit for having. Then who was defending Block K? He gave up trying to get the answer finally.

He was close now. He came aground, looped the roan's reins over a pine's broken branch, and started on afoot. He was now to the north of the cabin, almost even with his line of fire of two nights ago. Looking down through the trees, he was in time to see the flash of a rifle at the window that flanked the door. This time a gun behind the wagon shed answered; it was a six-gun, its explosions lower-toned than the rifle's.

He had started down there when suddenly a shape moved between him and the blazing haystack twenty yards lower along the slope. He called, "Miles!" The man below whirled, straightened, and the flash of a gun lined out from his hip. He shot wildly, three times, before Jim swung Ed Beeson's Winchester into line and squeezed the trigger.

The instant the weapon pounded against his shoulder, Jim saw the man below jackknife backward. As he fell he tried to catch himself. His boot caught on an exposed root and he sprawled in an ungainly backward dive to the ground. He rolled over once and, arms outspread, lay still, face down. When Jim stood over him, reaching down to take the long-barreled .38 from his lifeless fingers, he recognized Tellew's narrow thin-nosed face. Tellew was dead.

Beyond him on the hill slope, a rifle sent an even-timed burst of fire down at the cabin. The gun down there gave no answer. But an instant's high-pitched scream drifted up from below. Jim hesitated between circling and coming on the rifleman from the rear or going below and in behind the wagon shed and surprising the man forted up there. He chose the latter, for the top of the haystack was now a solid sheet of flame and the added light would help him. He was halfway down the slope when Hugh Allard's voice called loudly from behind the wagon shed: "Trent! Let's ride!"

Tellew's and Jim's guns on the hill slope must have warned Pitchfork's owner that others than the ones in the cabin were against his men now. Jim had a brief glimpse of a pony striking out from behind the wagon shed. The rider was gone before he could lift his gun. He heard another rider on the slope west of him going away. The sound gradually died out. In the silence that hung on afterward, all that could be heard was the steady low roar of the flames, on the increase now.

Jim looked down at the cabin. There was no sign of life

around it. He called again, louder, "Miles!" and moved out
from his position and behind a tree.

Far to his right he caught Kittering's answering hail.
He started in the direction of the voice. Abruptly someone
called from that cabin, "That you, Jim?"

Jim was several moments placing the voice as Spade
Deshay's. As he did, Spade called again, "I'm comin' out!
Two Card's with me."

In the strong light coming from beyond the barn, Jim
saw the cabin's door open. Spade and Two Card stepped
into sight. Spade lifted a hand in Jim's direction and waved
him in, calling, "Down here! Kittering's down here." He
pointed to the neck of timber that jutted out from the foot
of the hill behind the cabin to the west. He and Two Card
started in that direction.

Jim kept to the trees until he was out of range of the
light cast by the blazing stack, not sure that a Pitchfork
man hadn't stayed behind. Then he cut across the narrow
open indentation at the outer edge of the yard. A match's
faint glow flared alive ahead of a patch of brush forty feet
ahead of him. He went over there.

Miles Kittering knelt beside Ed Beeson. Spade and Two
Card and Johnny Dawes stood looking on. As Jim approached, Two Card's hand went up and he took off his
hat, solemnly. Now Jim could hear Miles Kittering's low-
breathed cursing. He heard Miles say, "I'll pay this back!
By God, I will!"

Jim stood silently by as Kittering lifted his head, seemingly aware of them for the first time. His look singled out
Jim. There were tears in his eyes. His bearded face was set
doggedly in a hard stare.

"He never did anything to deserve this!" His voice grated,
brokenly. "He . . ." It was impossible for him to go on.

Johnny Dawes said quietly, "We circled to catch anyone
comin' out the trail. Ed wanted to make a try for the cabin,
to see who was in there. I tried to argue him out of it but
he went on. Someone caught him from the slope up there."

"Harms," Spade said dully. "I tried to get a shot at him
before he got away."

Jim said, "Allard was behind the shed over there. One
of his men is up on the hill."

Kittering gave no sign that he'd heard. He looked down
at Ed Beeson, then slowly removed his coat and spread it
over Ed's face. He stood up and glanced toward the sky-
lancing flames beyond the barn's low roof. He breathed, "Let
it burn! Let the whole layout burn to the ground! All I want

is . . ." He went no further, leaving them to guess that he had Hugh Allard and Harms on his mind.

Jim said, "This is Deshay, Kittering. And Two Card Bates."

Kittering's glance came around to meet the outlaws. He said, "Thanks for the help."

"I couldn't help drawin' a hand when I heard they were headed this way. Anyone see the sheriff?" Spade asked.

"Was Blythe in on it?" Kittering was suddenly jerked from his stupor.

"He started out here with 'em. Allard was bringing him out to serve a warrant on you for firin' his place tonight. I came on ahead to tip you off."

Jim said, "What happened when they got here?"

"That's what I can't figure. There was only three men showed up. They didn't sing out when they rode in. Two of em' started for the barn, and the other circled and climbed the hill. I didn't know what to do except to open up on 'em. It was too dark to see my sights. All I did was give it away that the layout wasn't empty."

"It must've been Tellew and Allard that touched off the blaze," Jim said. "That would put Harms up the hill, where you saw him. But what happened to Blythe?"

"And there was another jasper of Allard's started out from town with 'em," Spade added.

Kittering began angrily, "If Blythe let Allard do this—"

"He didn't," Jim cut in. "Blythe never got here. What Spade says proves that. It's up to us to find out why."

Kittering motioned toward the body at his feet. "We'll take care of Ed first. He always liked that knoll back of the barn, used to go up there and just sit and be alone. Why in the name o' God did it have to be him?" He turned away, his emotion naked on his face. "I'll get some shovels."

18

FATS HOLDEN struck the Pitchfork-Sands trail thirty minutes after he had left Kittering and Jim at the fire in the hills. His gelding, feeling loose reins, went on at a slow walk. In this preoccupation, Fats didn't notice the animal's slow pace or the faint thunder of the guns that rolled down from high over the rim. Once he did hear them, very faintly.

But he was so engrossed in his dark thoughts that he casually accepted the sound as that of a localized storm on the far side of the peaks.

The thing that was bothering Kittering's gaunt-framed ramrod was his reason for setting out for Sands tonight. During the time Jim Allard had sat talking there by the fire, explaining things to Kittering, Fats couldn't shake the idea that Mule Evans was almost wholly responsible for Kittering's present circumstances. Finally, the bitterness and cold rage strong in him, he had made his decision; tonight he was going to hunt Mule down and kill him.

Now that he was on his way, he grew confused. Mule had certainly betrayed Kittering; that was obvious. But when Fats faced his own motives for wanting Mule dead, his conscience ran into several stumbling blocks. And, being as honest with himself as he was with others, the tall man had to singly batter down these obstacles that rose up in his mind.

First and foremost was the haunting picture of Mary Quinn, the conviction that she cared for Mule. Fats had shied away from Mary for this one reason—that she seemed to favor Mule above all others. He was jealous, he told himself; and jealousy was no valid reason for setting out to kill a man. He didn't like Mule personally; there again was a poor reason for taking a man's life.

He hadn't fought it out and arrived at any clear decision by the time Sands' lights winked out against the dark mantle of night that lay across the flats. The town in sight, he came close to turning back. But a stubbornness took him on. He halfway decided to forget Mule. He could go on in, pick up the rumors afloat and take them back to Kittering as he'd said he'd do. It wouldn't hurt to find out what Allard was up to.

As Spade Deshay had done earlier that night, Fats swung wide of the trail at the town's outskirts and took to an alley— the one opposite that which Spade had taken. His far inspection of the street's length had shown him deserted walks and near-empty hitch rails. Evidently the excitement over Pitchfork's fire and Allard's almost certain visit to town had died out.

He came down out of the saddle alongside the feed-barn corral, looping the reins over one of the poles. He walked on in through the corral and into the barn. Up front he could see young Mark Dorn sitting back-tilted in a caboose chair at one side of the big double doors. A lighted lantern stood beside Mark's chair.

Mark heard him coming and turned. Fats drawled, "Don't get up, kid."

He took his place opposite Mark near the door, leaning against the thin partition of the harness-room office. He took out tobacco and rolled a smoke while the boy, curious, watched him in silence. He looked up and down the street and obliquely across to the lighted window of Mary Quinn's restaurant. Sight of that window put a strange helpless regret in him. He said, "Kind of quiet, eh?"

"You ain't heard, then?" the boy queried in a low, awed voice.

"Heard what?"

"They've gone out to arrest Kittering for startin' that fire! Allard and the sheriff."

A momentary tension went along Fats' frame, then left as suddenly as it had come. He'd been halfway expecting this; still it was a surprise. He asked, "How long ago?"

"Couple hours." The look in the youth's eyes was one of deep concern. He admired this quiet tall Block K rider as much as any man he knew. He felt the need for adding something, and said, "I sure hope they don't get him."

"They won't," was Fats' reassuring answer. He wished he could believe they wouldn't.

Neither of them spoke for several minutes. The boy sensed Fats' unwillingness to talk. He was full of questions about the fire tonight; but, approaching manhood, he had lately tried to acquire the habit of man's reticence of speech.

Fats squatted on his heels so that he could have a full view of the street. Presently he asked, "Seen Mule tonight?"

Mark nodded, jerking a thumb back over his shoulder. "His jughead's back there. Been there since right after dark."

"Where is he?"

"Across there at the Elite."

Fats should have known. Mule was seeing Mary. He didn't want to appear too curious but couldn't help asking, "The whole time?"

"Ever since supper." Seeing the hurt in Fats' eyes, the boy was eager to please, and added, "Want me to go over and get him?"

"No. Let it go."

There was another silence, this time a briefer one. Mark ended it by saying, "Remember that job you promised me last year . . . after I'd grown up, you said?"

Fats nodded.

"Well . . ." The boy hesitated. "I'm taller'n I was and weigh a good bit more. Any chance of hirin' on?"

Fats softened out of his dark mood. Mark Dorn knew the trouble Kittering was in. This was his way of showing how he felt about it. "Later, maybe," Fats told him. "There ain't work enough out there now for the five of us as it is."

They listened to the far-off moan of a train's whistle. Mark got out his chair and took the lantern and went into the office to look at the alarm clock there. When he came out he said, "Twenty minutes late." He referred to the train, the midnight local.

Across the street, the slamming of the Elite's screen door brought Fats' head around. He saw Mule come out across the walk. Mary stood at the window watching him leave. Mule lifted a hand and waved to the girl, but she didn't wave back. Fats couldn't understand that. When he was sure that Mule was headed for the barn, he told Mark, "Don't mention me bein' here," and walked back into the deep shadows along the stalls.

Half a minute later, Mule was walking into the head of the center runway. Mark picked up his lantern. "You can wait here if you want. I'll saddle for you."

"Don't bother," Mule said. "I'm takin' the train out in a few minutes. Want to buy that saddle, kid?"

Fats caught Mark Dorn's quick puzzled frown. "Leaving for good?" the boy asked.

Mule laughed dryly. "You tell 'em I am! I'm through with this damned tank town! Give me twenty bucks and the saddle's yours. You can hold that crow-bait horse for Holden or Kittering the next time they're in." His tone was scornful, surly.

"I ain't got twenty dollars, Evans."

"You got it in the cash drawer, ain't you?"

Mark said, "Sure. But it's not mine. I couldn't pay Tate Olson back."

"Hell, I need money!" Mule flared. On sudden impulse, he wheeled toward the office.

"Where you goin'?" the boy called.

"After the money. You said it was here."

"You can't do that!"

Mule ignored him, disappeared in the office and the clink of coins sounded in there. Fats stepped out from behind the front stall, wiping his damp palms on the seat of his pants. Anger was in him—anger so strong that his legs felt weak and his arms trembled and he had to keep his teeth tight-clenched to stop their chattering.

Mule reappeared in the doorway to face the thoroughly frightened boy. He had a handful of paper money and silver dollars and stood there in the doorway counting them, letting each coin clink from one hand into the palm of the other. From down the street came the sound of several riders coming in past the stores.

Mule counted: ". . . twenty-eight, nine; thirty; thirty-one, two, three. Thirty-three! I reckon you've bought yourself a new hull, kid."

"But you said twenty!" Mark protested in a hushed frightened voice.

"The price has gone up."

In the brief silence that followed, Fats could no longer hear the horses on the street. He judged, unconsciously, that they had stopped down the street somewhere near the jail. Then the sight of Mule Evans standing there viciously out-staring Mark Dorn, daring him to do anything, snapped the last thread that held Fats to his caution.

He took a stride in toward Mule, drawling flatly, "Put the money back, Mule!"

What happened then came so swiftly that it caught Fats flat-footed. At the sound of his voice, Mule whirled. The silver dollars flashed against the lantern light as they fell from his hand. His two hands came alive slashing down at his thighs. Before Fats could think to reach for his own gun, both of Mule's had leaped from leather and were arcing up at him.

Fats made an awkward sideward lunge, snatching out his heavy .45. The gun in Mule's right hand exploded, stabbing a foot-long lance of powder flame. Fats felt the breath of that bullet strike against his left cheek. He hurried his own draw. Mule fired again, two shots so quick-spaced that they made one prolonged roar of sound. Neither bullet touched Fats. Suddenly he realized he had one small advantage. His shape was indistinct in the shadows, while Mule's was clearly outlined by the lantern's light.

His nervousness left him. He was looking along the sights of his gun, laying the notch on Mule's flat chest. As Mule's gun settled into sure line again, Fats squeezed the trigger. The weapon's solid pound traveled up his arm. Mule's frail body stiffened. His hands clawed open, the guns falling, and his arms crossed on his chest. Head back, stiffly, he fell backward. The thud of his body made an audible sound on the heel of the gun's explosion.

Fats lowered his Colt slowly. Mark Dorn, at last moving out of his paralysis of fear, turned at the sound of boots echoing along the walk down the street. He cried, "They're comin'! . . . Allard and Harms and Bailey!"

Fats turned and ran toward the barn's rear door. He jumped the two bottom poles of the corral gate, jerked loose the pony's reins and threw himself into the saddle. He wheeled the pony away from the corral. As he dug in his spurs, a rifle's sharp explosion sounded at the head of the passageway between feed barn and the adjoining building. Fats felt the sudden convulsive heave of the gelding's muscles, felt the buckling of the animal's front legs. Then he was falling, kicking his boots from stirrups. He was a fraction of a second tardy. The gelding went over on his side, hoofs thrashing. Fats' right leg was pinned to the ground.

He gave an involuntary cry of pain. Then a lantern's waving light showed in the barn door's high rectangle. Two men ran into the corral and, guided by the gelding's kicking, over to where Fats lay. It was Trent Harms who carried the lantern. Sid Bailey, Blythe's deputy, cradled a Winchester under his arm. When he saw what had happened, he whipped the gun to his shoulder and fired, once. The gelding stopped thrashing.

The deputy lowered the gun so that it covered Fats. He said, "Toss your iron across here, Holden." When Fats' .45 landed in the dust at his feet, he stepped in quickly and he and Harms heaved the animal's dead weight until Fats could crawl free. He reached down and helped Kittering's foreman to his feet.

Harms said, "Well, this is a start anyway. By mornin' we ought to have the whole bunch rounded up."

Bailey gave Pitchfork's foreman a frowning silencing look, then asked Fats, "What happened up there?"

From the doorway of the barn, Mark Dorn answered, "Mule took money from the cash drawer. When Holden tried to stop him he pulled his gun. Fats had to shoot him to keep from gettin' killed, Bailey. That's the honest to God's truth!"

"You're holdin' him anyway." Harms put in. He turned, called, "Kid, go get Allard!"

Twenty minutes later the door of a cell in Sands' jail was swinging shut on Fats Holden. Bailey locked the door. He looked in at Fats with a worried expression on his face and said in a voice that couldn't be overheard in the office, where Harms and Hugh Allard and young Mark Dorn were waiting, "I'm sorry as hell to have to do this, Fats. But you see how it is. Allard claims Kittering fired on him and the sheriff when they rode in to your place. They milled around a bit, burned some powder, and when it was all over they couldn't find Blythe. They had to come back without him. Now Allard claims Kittering either killed Blythe or is holdin' him by force."

"That's not the way Miles fights," Fats drawled.

The harassed deputy shrugged his shoulders. "Hell, you don't need to tell me! But I need this job and Allard's callin' the deal right now. He says to keep you here until Blythe turns up." He picked up his lantern and turned toward the door. "You'll eat good anyway. Mary Quinn dishes up a first-rate meal."

Mark Dorn had to repeat everything that had happened from the moment Fats had appeared in the feed barn until Mule lay dead on the runway floor. It was Bailey who first put the questions to him. Allard and Harms merely listened until Allard interrupted with, "Then Fats came here purposely to get Mule?"

"I didn't say that!" Mark protested, not able to overcome his awe at being in Allard's presence. Hugh Allard had always been unapproachable, aloof, cold. Now, to feel the weight of the man's flinty dark eyes on him, the boy could only stubbornly side with Fats and hope he didn't put his foot in it again, as he'd just now done.

"But you said he asked about Mule," Allard insisted.

Mark had no reply to that and held his silence.

Allard said irritably, "You see, Bailey. There was something behind all this. I had damned little respect for Evans. But he was murdered! I'll personally swear out a warrant to keep Holden here until we get to the bottom of it. He'll be in jail sooner or later anyway. Unless I'm wrong you'll never find Fred Blythe alive. If he isn't dead by now he soon will be. Kittering's gone mad—mad as a locoed steer! Get a posse together and let's go back out there. Either that, or I'll go round up my crew and settle it my own way!" He turned to the door. "You'll find me at the hotel when you're ready to start. Come on, Harms."

On the walk, he caught Harms by the coat sleeve and pulled him into the narrow passageway between the jail and the general store. He said, "Watch the kid, Trent."

In another minute, Mark Dorn left the sheriff's office and passed the head of the passageway toward the feed barn. "What about him?" Harms asked.

"Wait. You'll see. Keep an eye on the alley."

In less than three minutes the sound of a horse walking along the alley to the rear shuttled up to them. Allard led the way to the back of the passageway and was standing in its deep shadow as Mark Dorn passed.

When the boy had gone out of hearing, Allard said, "We won't need to ride out there now."

"I don't get this," Harms growled irritably, after puzzling a moment over Allard's words.

"You saw how that kid acted in the office, didn't you? Stickin' up for Holden?"

"What of it?"

"He's on the way to Kittering's to let them know Holden's in jail. They'll be in. When they come, they'll make for the jail. Daniels ought to have the crew in by then. We'll be waiting for them. If we fort up on the roofs, we ought to get every man."

He turned and led the way back to the head of the passageway. Crossing the street, he felt a great deal better than the scowl on his face indicated. He had that habit, long trained, of schooling his face to assume whatever expression he wanted, regardless of what he was thinking. Now, looking at him, even Harms wouldn't have expected that he was extremely satisfied over tonight's turn of events. Jim Allard was out of the way, Allard was thinking, Holden no longer counted and he'd made Block K unsafe for Kittering.

And Fred Blythe's outright honesty no longer stood between him and the accomplishing of his aims. If he had any worry, it was over the contents of the telegram that had been lying on Blythe's desk tonight. He'd have to think of a way of explaining away its contents, once things were settled with Kittering. It all depended, of course, on whether anyone had ever seen the telegram. He didn't think they had.

At the foot of the Prairie House steps, he told Harms, "Go tell Bailey I've changed my mind about the posse. You can have a drink, too, if you want. Then get back here. I'll be up in my room."

Harms walked across the dim rectangle of light shining down out of the lobby doors and headed for the Melodian, where Bailey was recruiting men for the posse. Allard started up the steps to the veranda, seeing the red glowing end of a cigar winking out of the darkness along the far end of the rail. Except for this one late lounger, the veranda was deserted.

He was halfway to the lobby door when the man smoking the cigar spoke to him: "Allard?"

Hugh turned and scanned the obscure shadows. "I'm Allard."

A tall gray-suited shape moved toward him out of the shadows. The man said, "I'm Virgil Pierce," and stood two strides away, his gray eyes looking down at the rancher. He had a lean hawkish face that a neatly trimmed gray Vandyke made distinguished-looking.

Allard hesitated a moment, said finally, "Should that mean anything to me?"

The expression in the eyes changed, became puzzled. "Think a minute, Allard. Pierce is the name. You sent for me."

"You've got the wrong man." Allard was polite enough but faintly irritated.

Momentary confusion touched the gray eyes. Pierce said, "How about the reward you offered on Jim Allard?"

The rancher's interest immediately quickened. "Reward?"

Pierce nodded. He reached up to an inside pocket of his coat and brought out a telegram, handing it across. Allard stepped over into the light coming through the narrow glass slide panels alongside the entrance and read it. It was the message Jim had sent Pierce. A brief smile played over Allard's face. He handed the telegram back. "I remember you now," he said. "Glad to make your acquaintance. But I didn't send that wire. You've come up here on a wild-goose chase. Jim Allard's dead!"

Pierce's face hardened in nicely concealed surprise. "Then who did send it?"

"You've got me." Allard shrugged. "Pity I didn't think of it myself. Maybe it was the sheriff."

"It says here not to see the sheriff."

Allard nodded soberly, dismissing the idea that Fred Blythe had called in the bounty hunter. Blythe's tactics were direct, not this subtle.

"Then I'm to understand there's no reward?" Anger was beginning to edge the ex-marshal's words.

"That's correct. I could hardly offer a reward on a dead man . . . even if I had wanted him out of the way." There seemed nothing more to say, so Allard added pleasantly, "Good night," and went in through the door.

A dark look of irritation crossed Virgil Pierce's face. He realized he'd somehow been made the butt of a joke. He wasn't the man to tolerate such horseplay, nor had Hugh Allard's manner entirely suited him. Allard didn't seem to realize that he'd wasted good time and money coming here to Sands. Nor had Allard apologized for the inconvenience the false summons had cost him.

Since his arrival this morning, Pierce had been wary about showing himself around town. He'd asked a few questions and strictly observed the unusual goings-on tonight along the street, reading his own meaning into them. Five minutes ago he had been idly thinking of what he could do with the two thousand dollars on Jim Allard's head. Now he had the feeling that he'd actually had the money and lost it.

Standing there, a neatly groomed man close to old age, he looked back over the years and could find no parallel to this letdown. People didn't make a habit of joking with Virgil Pierce.

He looked down the street toward the lighted walk under the awning of the Melodian. Three minutes ago he'd seen a man part company with Allard at the foot of the hotel steps. He'd had only a brief glimpse of him in the faint wash of light coming down out of the lobby door. But the man's face had struck Pierce as being vaguely familiar. Faces had that way with him, for his keen memory of reward dodgers had imprinted in his mind's eye many of them. And many times his inability to forget the face of a wanted man had served him well. It was this faculty of his that was mainly responsible for his having collected more rewards on wanted men than any other law officer in Arizona.

Feeling irritable and aware that he'd somehow been tricked in coming here, he sauntered down the steps and along the walk toward the saloon, where the posse was now breaking up. It wouldn't hurt to have another look at that face.

19

THEY buried Ed Beeson beneath a tall lone cedar that stood on a knoll a hundred yards behind the barn. Johnny Dawes got some tools from the wagon shed, some lumber from the barn, and he and Jim hammered together a crude box while Kittering and Spade and Two Card took turns with the shovel on the knoll in the light of the haystack's dying blaze. They worked better than two hours, all but Kittering stopping occasionally to watch the fire eat its way through the mound of dry hay.

"Lucky it wasn't the barn," Johnny remarked to Jim, leaving it unsaid that, but for Spade and Two Card's guns, the Pitchfork men would have fired the whole layout.

Kittering seemed less interested in the fire than any of them. He was strangely intent on the job at hand. It was as though by meticulously smoothing the steep walls of the grave he could in some way make up for having let Ed Beeson get in the way of a bullet tonight. He did the work of two men, relinquishing the shovel to Spade or Two Card only when he became too exhausted to stand on his feet.

The grave dug, he went to the cabin while Jim and Dawes carried the coffin up from the wagon shed. He came back up the knoll with a Bible in his hand. He looked on while they lifted Ed's body into the coffin. Then, as Jim picked up the hammer and a handful of nails, to put on the lid, he said tersely, "Let me finish it."

They left him up there. They stood beyond the cabin for a while watching the slowly crumbling ruin of a summer's hay crop. Beyond, they could hear the even-spaced hammer beats as Kittering nailed tight the lid on the coffin. Then there was a silence up there.

Spade said, "Hit him hard, didn't it?"

"He's had a lot to take today," Jim told him.

Two Card Bates glanced at Jim, his scarred wrists and the scorched holes on his shirt. "So've you, from your looks."

Jim began to tell them what had happened at Pitchfork. Halfway, finished, he stopped, listening. When they caught the sound he had heard, the far-off muffled pound of a running pony, Spade turned away and started for the trees on the hill slope, saying quickly, "This one don't get away!"

Two Card followed him. Johnny Dawes ran toward the knoll where Kittering was filling in the grave. Jim went to the cabin, lit a match and took a rifle down from a rack beside the door. As an afterhought he belted on a pair of .38's he found hanging there. He went out of the kitchen and into the bunkroom, opening a window that commanded the trail's climb up out of the pasture toward the yard. He levered a shell into the rifle's chamber, rested the weapon on the sill and waited.

Now he could plainly hear the steady cautionless approach of the rider. He thought of Holden, and hurried back through the room and out the door and called to the others, "Wait'll we see who it is!"

He stepped back into the doorway's shadow, scanning the darkness. Abruptly, a running horse appeared out of the obscurity, a small figure bent low in the saddle. The pony wasn't Holden's. It came well into the light before the rider straightened and tightened on the reins. The rider wasn't Holden. Jim recognized the boy he'd seen in the stable the other night and stepped out from the doorway into sight.

Mark saw him and put his horse on across the yard. Then, close, he recognized Jim and stopped. He glanced toward the fire and asked, warily, "Where's Kittering?"

"Up the hill," Jim said. "You can tell me about it, whatever it is."

Mark Dorn was remembering Holden's visit to the stable the morning after Jim's escape from the sheriff. He didn't know how Fats felt about this stranger, who stood accused of murder. But there was nothing he could do now but blurt out the news he'd carried from town: "They've got Fats! In jail. Him and Mule shot it out and they're arrested Fats. He was . . ."

"Who arrested him?"

"Bailey . . . and Allard. Allard's holdin' him until Kittering turns the sheriff loose. They've got up a posse and are on their way out here now!"

"The sheriff?" Jim saw it then—saw it in its entirety, this last play of Hugh Allard's that would tip the balance all the way against Miles Kittering. He turned, shouted, "Miles, get down here!" and saw Spade and Two Card drifting in toward him from the near margin of the trees.

When they got the whole story, Jim and the two outlaws and Dawes waited for Miles Kittering to speak. The boy was the only one who didn't see what lay behind his news—the fact that Allard was forcibly holding the sheriff and throwing the blame on Kittering. For, as Spade put it, "Blythe started out here with 'em. I'll swear it."

Kittering looked at Mark Dorn. "Thanks, kid," he said. Then his glance came around to Jim. What Jim saw in his eyes was stunned helplessness before this new complication. He asked, "What'll we do now?"

"If they're on the way out here, it oughtn't to be hard to bust Fats out of jail, had it?" Jim said.

"No," Kittering agreed, readily enough. "Let's be doin' it then!"

His deep-toned voice spoke the words that let them know he was over his temporary indecision. Jim had the feeling that this was the turning point, that Kittering's luck was due for a change.

They saddled fresh horses at the corral. Johnny Dawes went to the cabin and came back with two boxes of shells for the rifles. At the corral, Spade saw Jim inspecting the claybank's legs and said, "He's sound as a dollar. That fall didn't even bother him." Jim had already decided not to take the claybank. The stallion had done his share of work today.

The pace Kittering set was a stiff one. They stayed wide of the trail across the pasture and finally left it where it right-angled in through the timber toward Pitchfork's. Kittering was taking a short cut to town. Jim saw that Mark Dorn had drawn a scrubby small pony that wasn't standing the fast going very well. He dropped back to tell the boy, "We'll go on ahead. Stay off the trails and get back to the barn and keep out of sight when you hit town. We'll see you later."

Only one light winked out from Sands as they came in along the flats. The town had turned in for the night. They had struck deep through the badlands once beyond Block K's west fence and the going had winded their animals. Somewhere back there they were sure they'd passed Allard's posse on the way to the layout. Now Kittering, in the lead, pulled his mare in to a walk. As Jim drew in alongside him, he cast a glance upward at the wheeling stars. "We'll have to work fast," he told Kittering, for it was close to three o'clock and would be dawn in another hour and a half. Daybreak should see them in the hills, out of reach of any pursuit.

On this fast hard ride from Block K, his mind had worked apart from the matter immediately at hand. He was thinking that Allard had struck boldly tonight, almost too boldly. His attempt at Jim's life, hiding it in the burning of his own barn, was a logical maneuver. It seemed logical to Jim, knowing as he did the brutal yet smooth working of the man's mind. The raid on Kittering's place had also been logical, since Allard had framed evidence that would give him the right to fight Kittering openly. But Fred Blythe's disappearance was a different thing. Allard was forcing his hand; either that, or he was being made to force it by some circumstance Jim didn't know about.

When they pulled in to breathe their ponies half a mile out from the town, Jim rode in alongside Spade and asked, "You sure you told us everything? Blythe started out with Allard?"

Spade merely nodded and made no reply. It was Two Card who said, "Hell, we were standing right by his office window. It was open. We could even look in and see 'em."

"What happened in the office?" Jim asked.

"Blythe came in alone the first time," Spade told him. "He looked proddy over something. Telegram, I guess. He stood there readin' it and—"

Something clicked in Jim's mind. "A telegram!" he cut in. "Why didn't you say so?"

"He blew his nose, too," Spade said acidly. "I could have mentioned that."

"Go on," Jim drawled, his mouth shaping a wide grin. "What else?"

"Blythe left and went over to the hotel. Then Allard and his crew came in. They hailed the sheriff across. Allard and another man waited for him in the office. Allard sat on the desk and saw the telegram. Then, just before Blythe came in, he moved over across the room. He—"

"Allard read the telegram?"

Spade said, "Sure. That's what I said."

"Do you see it now, Kittering?" Jim asked.

Block K's owner was remembering what Jim had told him earlier that night as they talked by the fire up in the hills—of the two telegrams he'd sent from the way station below Sands yesterday afternoon. Virgil Pierce had come in answer to one of them. Now Kittering understood that Blythe had the answer to the other. He nodded in reply to Jim's question.

Jim said, "I'm going to the station to get a copy of it."

"Too late," Kittering told him. "It closes at midnight."

"We're breakin' into one place tonight. Might as well make it two," Jim reminded him. "I'll meet you in the alley behind the jail." He lifted his gelding into motion and cut out away from the trail toward the line of the railroad.

20

ANN didn't hear the guns sounding across from Block K. She lingered there by the cook shack, watching the awesome conflagration as the fire ate its way through the walls of the barn. They finally toppled inward, sending a geyser of flame and sparks plummeting two hundred feet into the sky. Then, in a prolonged fierce consuming of the tinder-dry wreckage, the fire burned itself out until nothing was left but a charred and glowing mass of broken timbers caved in over the high rock foundations. She shuddered at the thought that, but for a stroke of freakish luck, Jim Allard would be in there now, dead, murdered.

She was shocked at the implications to Jim's being left in the barn. At first, she wouldn't let herself believe that the obvious was true, that Hugh Allard had taken this way of ridding himself of an enemy. But in the end she knew that it was true, and that she faced the proof of her stepfather's guilt. He was more than a murderer. He was dragging down in the ruin of a range war a country that had been peaceful and prosperous. He had nursed an old hate—the knowledge of his wife's love for Miles Kittering—and his vengeance was sweeping away everything before it.

Weariness settled in over her tension of the past half hour like the dying of the blaze at the barn. A few minutes ago she had stood in a reflected light as bright as daylight. Now that the fire had burned out, the cook shanty was once more in the shadows.

She turned and was about to go across to the trees toward the house when she heard the rhythmic oncoming sound of a pair of horses approaching the layout in the direction of the corrals.

Curiosity and a dulled sense of alarm made her turn in time to see Daniels and a lead horse come into the faint outer margin of light. The crewman, one of those she knew Hugh had recently hired, got out of the saddle at the hitching rack by the big corral and unroped the burden from the saddle of the other animal. She was reminded of Eaton's roan bringing him to that almost exact spot two afternoons ago. Then she suddenly made out that shape as a man's body. Stark fear sent her back to the cook shack wall, where she was hidden in the deep shadows of a tamarisk tree. Had she gone on across the yard, Daniels would surely have seen her.

Her fear mounted to the verge of terror as Daniels slung the body over his shoulder and came on toward the cook shack, staggering a little under his load. Ann pressed her clenched hand to her mouth and her knees went so weak that she had to lean back against the tree for support.

Then, gradually, her fear left her. Daniels passed within thirty feet of her and went on at his plodding stride toward the root cellar dug in the side of the hill a hundred feet away. As her breath went out of her in a swift rush, she came abruptly tense again. Daniels had turned now so that the fire's faint light fell on the face of the man he was carrying. That man was Fred Blythe.

She watched, her senses numbed to a slow agony of fore-boding, as Daniels tried the padlock on the root-cellar door. He found it locked and coolly drew his gun and shot the padlock open. Once he had disappeared inside the door, she turned and ran. She didn't dare to even breathe again until she was deep in under the obscurity of the cottonwoods by the house. Even then she was afraid to look back.

In her room she threw herself on the bed, wanting to cry. But the tears wouldn't come. Her mind had taken too much tonight to give way to emotion. She felt dried up inside, as though the swift happenings of these past hours had swept away all that was worth living for, all that she had called her life.

Lying there, looking back on it, she felt real bitterness for the first time. Her life at Pitchfork was gone, ended as surely as though it had never existed. The things she had known since early girlhood—this spacious house, her room, the pleasant ritual of everyday existence—were completely shattered. Out of the broken pieces she could patch together only one thing that was completely whole. That thing was her respect and love for Miles Kittering. She had never dreamed of loving the man. But now she knew that she did—that she loved him for the restraint he'd used when her mother was alive, for the tireless patience he had shown in being around his child and not trying to take her from the man who had wrecked his life. She respected him for his weakness, the thing he had been powerless to fight—this intrigue against him that he couldn't bring into the open so long as she, Ann, stayed with Hugh Allard.

Strangely enough, she hadn't thought of Trent Harms until this moment in his proper relation to her stepfather. She knew now that she hadn't wanted to think about him, that she had consciously delayed facing the facts where he was concerned. She and Trent had lately drifted into a mild undeclared courtship. At Pitchfork, Hugh had drawn a sharp line between house and crew quarters, and Trent was the only man who could, at will, cross that line any time he chose. She had been thrown into constant contact with him and, hungering for the companionship of a man close to her age, they had become friendly. But now Trent was proven to have equal shares with Hugh when it came to attaching the guilt for today's doings. Realizing that, a self-loathing came quickly as another force to batter down her pride; it didn't make her feel any better to repeat over and over again that she'd had no real affection for him, for the fact remained that he had been the only man on the horizon of her consciousness when it came to looking far ahead into her future.

That feeling of utter helplessness before the crumbling of these strong ties to Pitchfork left her slowly. As it faded, another took its place. Her pride was humbled. But it wasn't broken. Until today she had turned her back on her real father, favoring the man of her mother's choice. Now she owed whatever was in her to give to Miles Kittering. He was in trouble, grave trouble. Her place was with him.

She abruptly sat up straight on the bed, her heartsickness

forgotten as she remembered Fred Blythe. For the moment she'd forgotten him in the face of her own troubles. Here she was, wasting precious time when Blythe might be needing her. He was hurt, or Daniels wouldn't have carried him. He was a prisoner, or Daniels would have brought him straight to the house. She remembered a time, long ago, when the sheriff before Blythe had stopped overnight at the ranch with a posse while returning to Sands with an Indian who had murdered his squaw and been captured back in the hills. They had locked the Indian in the root cellar. Another time the cellar had served to confine a drunken 'puncher who had run amuck in the bunkhouse with a gun; he stayed there for two days, until he sobered up. Ever since she had thought of the cellar as a sort of jail, and once Hugh had disciplined her by threatening to lock her up there.

She left her room and went out across the patio and through the trees, walking soundlessly. She came to the edge of the wide rectangle of the crew's quarters and was surprised at seeing activity around the bunkhouse, which was lighted. Men moved around it, in and out its door. The crew was back.

Looking beyond the cook shanty, she saw a man sitting on an upended keg by the root-cellar door. A rifle leaned against the frame of the door close by.

She hadn't looked for this added complication, the presence of these others. As she hesitated there, trying to think of a way of getting in to see Blythe, a man started across toward her from the bunkhouse. She recognized Shorty Adams, the oldest member of the crew both in years and in length of service.

When she saw that Shorty was headed for the house, she went quickly back through the trees and into the patio. She was standing there, in the light of the open door to the living room, when he came through the patio gate.

She said in a tone that surprised her for its evenness, "Did you want to see me, Shorty?"

His hat came off respectfully. He came beyond the low-hanging branches of the willow, saying, "I did, ma'am. It's so late I didn't know if you'd be up. Your father sent word that he's in town and won't be back until sometime tomorrow. He says you're not to worry."

"There's something wrong, Shorty. What is it?"

Shorty fingered the brim of his hat nervously, saying at length, "I wish I knew."

"Who set fire to the barn?"

He shook his head. "We don't know yet. Hugh sent for

us to come in to town. Maybe we'll find out then. I can't think why else he wants us."

"You mean . . . there's to be a fight?"

Shorty was plainly worried. But, remembering his duty, he shrugged his shoulders, put on a smile and drawled, "It won't come to that." He stood there a moment longer, obviously ill at ease—a plain cow-poke bewildered over the fast run of events. Then, turning away: "I've got to be goin'."

Ann asked quickly, "Do you think it was Kittering?"

"Daniels claims it was," came his reluctant answer.

She thought for a moment of asking him about Fred Blythe, of confiding in him. But then she remembered that there was no one here she could trust any longer. Shorty might be one of Hugh's trusted helpers, his frankness intended to deceive her. Certainly she'd had faith in Trent Harms, and he had betrayed her trust in him.

She said levelly, "I wouldn't worry about it, Shorty," and he left the patio without another word.

Once he was gone, she ran across to Hugh's office. She found a .38 Colt, loaded, in a drawer of his desk. She walked back through the cottonwoods again and from there watched the bunkhouse light go out and nine men file away from the corral along the path that led to the town trail. Once the sound of their going had faded in the still air, the silence pressed in on her. She looked off toward the root cellar. It was too far away to see anything clearly now. The barn was no longer a torch to light up the rectangle of yard between these outbuildings.

She started across toward the cook shanty and presently could see the root cellar and the man who still stood guard there. It wasn't Daniels but a newly hired crewman she had heard called Llano. He was another of this shifty-eyed lot that she now knew had been hired for their ability to use guns rather than for that of working cattle.

She was halfway across to him when she suddenly realized that she was carrying the gun openly, in her hand at her side. She reached around and held it behind her and went on. An instant later Llano saw her and was coming erect, reaching for his Winchester.

She ignored his gesture and came on without hesitating. When she was close enough to be recognized, she saw him relax and lean the rifle back against the cellar doorway again. She noticed that he wasn't wearing a side arm. The rifle was his only weapon. He called, "That you, Miss Allard?" He had a Texan's drawl, smooth, polite.

She said, "I heard the men ride out. Where are they going?"

She was close now, within three strides of him, and she stopped there.

"To town. Your father had 'em sent in."

"Why?"

He shrugged his shoulders. "No tellin'. Maybe he's corralin' Kittering tonight."

She asked abruptly, "What are you doing here?"

His confusion was plain even in this faint light. "Me? . . . Nothin'. . . . They wanted to leave someone on the place." He was nervous and resorted to the timetested device of building a smoke to rid him of his nervousness.

She agreed readily: "Yes, I suppose that's a good idea," and stood watching until both his hands were busy with his cigarette. Then, slowly, she drew the gun from behind her.

She said, "Llano!"

The tense huskiness of her voice brought his head up quickly. He saw the gun in her hand. His fingers opened and the tobacco sifted out of the paper.

She said, "Put your hands up!" Now her voice wasn't so steady.

His hands raised halfway to his shoulders. Then he lowered them again, his face going inscrutable as he drawled, "What're you up to?"

She had forgotten to cock the gun. She did it now, its click plainly audible in the stillness. "Step away from that door!"

He didn't move. His glance narrowed and now his lean face took on a hardness that put a real fear in her. He drawled, "Put that thing down."

"I mean it, Llano! I'll shoot if you don't move away from there!"

He drawled, "Now will you!" and his right hand slashed out for the rifle.

His move startled her. She had one wild moment of indecision. Then her fingers pressed the .38's trigger. The explosion nearly tore the gun from her grasp. She heard Llano's grunt of pain and saw his left leg go out from under him. He fell, sideways, away from the rifle, and rolled over and sat up with both hands clutching his thigh at a point close to his knee. He said, "You damned little hell-cat!" and swore under his breath. Then he made an awkward lunge for the rifle again.

She ran in and snatched it away. His fingers grazed its stock, then made a sweeping futile effort to reach one of her boots. She stepped quickly back, holding the rifle cradled under her left arm as she pointed the .38 at him again. A flood of weakness hit her.

She said in a voice that trembled, "Get back, Llano! Crawl away from there, or I'll do it again!"

Without waiting for him to move, she stepped in close to the door. The broken padlock hung from a nail on the frame. Nothing but a stout peg held the hasp shut. She lifted the peg out, pushed the door open and called, "Fred!"

She heard Blythe answer in a muffled choking cry. She wheeled on Llano again. He was sitting with his back to the mounded earth buttress of the cell's wall ten feet away. His pale eyes were hateful in the stare they fixed on her. Pain was written on his face. Both his hands clasped his leg tightly. She said, "Llano, stay away from here!" and backed down the steps and into the cellar.

Blythe's legs tripped her and she fell to her knees. Her hands ran over him, feeling the stout ropes that 'bound his arms and legs. There was a gag in his mouth. She pulled it down and he said thickly, "Good girl! That took guts!"

She worked at the ropes by feel alone, for the darkness in here was complete, oppressive. As her fingers strained against the stubborn knots, her glance was fixed frantically on the vague outline of the door where starlight broke the surrounding mantle of blackness. Soon she had the ropes about the sheriff's arms loosened. After that he helped her.

At first Fred Blythe was too weak to stand alone. He said impatiently, "Give me a minute," and leaned over to rub the circulation back into his legs.

Her breath sounded in a long sigh of relief as she gave him Hugh's gun, saying, "How did this happen, Fred?"

"It's a long story and it'll keep." He started for the door.

Outside, he spoke briefly to Llano. "In there!" he said, indicating the cellar door; and there was an ominous quality to his words that made Llano move immediately. He crawled in through the door and Blythe swung it shut on him, pegging the hasp.

"Fred, it's tonight . . . in town! Hugh sent out for the crew. They've gone."

"Then maybe we ought to do the same," was his calm rejoinder. His hand went up gingerly to feel of his scalp. He added, dryly, "Hugh's goin' to love it when he lays eyes on me!"

The last gaunt promontory of the badlands lay behind and they had taken the branching in the trails onto the flats four miles out from Sands, when Shorty Adams drew up behind Daniels and said, "I want to know more about this! what the hell're we headed into?"

Shorty wouldn't have been so emphatic about it without the backing of five other older members of the Pitchfork crew. But he knew they were with him and had been hanging back, letting Daniels and Matt Briggs and Utah Lucas take the lead. These three—Daniels and his partners—had for weeks now made up a disturbing element in the bunkhouse, a foreign one. They hadn't done much work and never traveled without their guns. Shorty and the others thought they knew the reasons for Allard's hiring the new men, the main one being the trouble with Kittering. They didn't blame Allard for wanting to protect himself. But Shorty and the others had spent a long hard day in the saddle and there was something ominous about the goings-on at Pitchfork tonight. There had been the fire, which Daniels claimed had been set by Kittering's men. When asked for proof, Daniels couldn't give it. Then there was the matter of the guarded root cellar. Shorty himself had asked Daniels about that and been told curtly to mind his own business, that he, Daniels, was acting under Allard's orders.

The other old hands had heard the interchange of words between Shorty and the new crew member. Just now they were as anxious as Shorty to get things straight in their minds. Some of them were pretty friendly with Kittering and Fats Holden. And Shorty, at least, had no intention of drawing a gun against Block K until he had this thing straight in his mind.

When Shorty had spoken, Daniels reined his gelding to a halt and turned slowly around. Beside him, Utah Lucas said bitingly, "What's the matter, Shorty, losin' your guts?"

"Guts don't enter into it!" Shorty blazed. "I want a straight answer. We been out o' this all day. What's up?"

"You heard me say Kittering fired the barn," Daniels drawled.

"Sure, Kittering does everything that goes wrong around here! But what the hell makes you so sure he did it?"

"Allard said so."

A man alongside Shorty drawled, "The boss makes mistakes sometimes. Last year me and Fats Holden went out after antelope together. He's a hell of a good shot. I want to know why I'm fightin' him before I let him look at me over his sights."

Daniels' lips curled into a derisive grin. "Yellow, huh! The whole damn' bunch of you!"

"Shuck them irons and I'll soap your mouth out for that!"
Shorty drawled.

The edgy temper of these men struck Daniels so forcibly
that he abruptly changed his tactics. "See here," he said
mildly, 'this talk ain't goin' to help us any. We're all proddy.
You've known all along this was comin'. Tonight Kittering's
made his play. Don't ask me how Allard knew it was him.
He just did. Now that the showdown's come, you all backin'
out?"

Shorty said uneasily, stubbornly, "I am . . . until I know
more about it."

"Then to hell with you!" Daniels' ability to reason calmly
was short-lived. He swung his pony around, said, "Come on,
let 'em be!" and went on down the trail. Utah and Matt
Briggs followed him.

A ten-second silence followed the departure of the three
new crewmen. Shorty ended it by drawling, "I don't know
about you gents; but I was hired to punch cattle, not to get
a bellyful of lead. If Allard don't like that, there's plenty
other places to find work."

"Same here," said another.

It was Shorty who first turned his horse back up the trail
toward Pitchfork. The rest followed him.

21

VIRGIL PIERCE had had his look at Harms in the Melodian
and gone from there to the sheriff's office, where Bailey
lingered wondering whether he ought to lock up and go home
to bed or stay up on the chance that his day's work wasn't
yet finished.

Pierce introduced himself and was asked to take a chair.
They passed a few pleasantries, and finally Bailey said, "Anything I can do for you?"

Pierce frowned. "I was wonderin' if you keep a file of
reward notices."

"How far back?" Bailey tried not to look surprised.

"Ten years maybe."

"We ought to have 'em. I can never get Fred to throw
anything away." The deputy got up out of his chair at the

desk, kneeling before the room's only filing cabinet. He pulled open the bottom drawer. "Help yourself."

Pierce moved his chair across and leaned over the drawer, sorting through its contents. Bailey brought the lamp over and set it on the floor beside the case.

Presently, the ex-marshal took out a reward notice with a picture on it. He held it near the light, examining it closely. But when Bailey leaned over in his chair at the desk to have a look, Pierce put the notice back again, closed the drawer and said, "No luck."

He left shortly afterward, and when he had taken his chair along the rail on the hotel veranda he saw Bailey going the opposite way along the walk; the light in the sheriff's office was out. He took a cigar from the case in his inner coat pocket, clipped the end off with a knife and lit his smoke. As he dragged deeply on the weed, he betrayed nothing of his inner excitement. Across there a few minutes ago he had seen a good likeness of Trent Harms' face staring at him out of the reward dodger. Across the face of the sheet, in bold print, had been the legend WANTED FOR MURDER: ONE THOUSAND DOLLARS REWARD: DEAD OR ALIVE. He wondered, idly, how it would turn out, whether he'd take Harms dead or alive.

In the next three quarters of an hour, several things happened that took his interest. They began with the appearance of three riders coming in off the north trail and turning in at the tie rail directly in front of the hotel. They climbed the steps and went into the lobby. Pierce heard them mount the stairs. He got up out of his chair and sauntered down the steps and had a look at the horses. They were branded Pitchfork, which, he had learned, was Hugh Allard's outfit. Since he hadn't seen Allard leave the hotel, he assumed that his men had gone up to his room. He resumed his chair on the porch, the last trace of sleepiness gone from him. Unless his long-trained sense of observation was failing him, something was happening here tonight in this gathering of Pitchfork's forces. Allard might be spending the night in the hotel himself, but it was a cinch his men weren't.

When he heard men coming down the stairs, he carefully shielded the glowing end of his cigar in his cupped hand. Five men came out of the door—the three who had ridden in, together with Allard and Harms.

They stopped grouped at the head of the steps. He saw Allard studying the shadows. It was too dark for Pierce to be seen. Allard seemed satisfied that they were alone, for presently he said, "Trent, you and Matt get over onto Slater's roof." Slater's, Pierce had noted earlier, was the general store. "Daniels, you and Utah take the roof of the saddleshop. I'll leave it to you, Harms, when to open up And, by God, make sure this time! I don't want any slip-ups."

One of his men asked querulously, "I don't see how you can be sure they'll turn up."

"They will, take my word for it," Allard answered. "All right, get over there!"

He stood leaning against a roof pillar, watching his men go across the street. Pierce was watching them, too. They disappeared into a passageway between two stores across there. Pierce's glance went up to the roofs of the stores flanking the jail. Five minutes later he was rewarded by seeing a shadowy figure move along the front of Slater's. Allard, saw, too, and lifted his hand and waved. Then, abruptly, Allard turned and disappeared inside the lobby door. Pierce heard him climb the stairs. Then, half a minute later, he heard one of the hotel's upstairs windows facing the street grate open. That would be Allard, watching his men.

Pierce was a little confused by what was developing. Earlier tonight there had been a shooting. Two of Kittering's men, so the story ran, working off a grudge over a girl. Holden, Kittering's foreman, was in jail across there. Why would Allard's men be attempting to break Holden out of jail? No, that wasn't it. There must be some other answer to Allard's placing of his men.

Then, with an abruptness that made him jump, came the sudden explosion of a gun behind the jail.

The station was dark as Jim walked the gelding in to the freight platform. He tied the animal, then went around to the front of the station. He tried the three windows of the office bay facing the tracks. They were locked. He broke one upper pane with the butt of a gun and reached in and opened the lock and threw up the sash and climbed in. He found a lamp on the shelf by the ticket window and lit it, turning it low and setting it on the floor alongside the small cubbyhole's one deal file case.

The top drawer was the file for the telegrams. He looked through a dozen forms before he found the dates on them to be a week old. Then he saw a spindle holding a sheaf of telegrams on the desk by the windows where the telegraph key was. The top sheet on the spindle was the one he wanted.

By the meager light of the lamp, he read:

SHERIFF ANTELOPE COUNTY
SANDS ARIZONA
    ALVIN CHALMERS SENT SANDS TO DISCUSS RIGHT OF
WAY OPTIONS WITH HUGH ALLARD STOP INSIST THAT YOU
KEEP THIS MATTER CONFIDENTIAL UNTIL OPTIONS TAKEN
STOP CHALMERS NEVER RESIDENT OF NEW MEXICO STOP
WIFE INSISTS THAT HE NEVER KNEW SENATOR ROLF OR A
JAMES ALLARD STOP SHE REQUESTS BODY BE SHIPPED TO
HER AT DENVER STOP UNLESS MAN WHO KILLED CHAL-
MERS APPREHENDED IMMEDIATELY WE WILL PUT OUR
OWN DETECTIVES ON CASE

                        SIGNED A R WILFORD
                      PRES SIERRA AND WESTERN RY

Five minutes later Jim was handing the telegram to Miles
Kittering, saying, "There's your answer. I wasn't expecting
it to be so plain."

Kittering read the message by the light of a match. They
were standing behind the woodshed where Spade and Two
Card had left their horses earlier that night. The jail's squatting shadow lay twenty yards in and to their left, beyond
the line of the rails.

Kittering gave Jim a frowning quizzical look. "What's
plain about it?"

"It's right there. Allard's reason for wanting your place.
I saw it the first day I set eyes on this country."

"Saw what?" Johnny Dawes put in.

Spade and Two Card were listening impatiently, making
little sense of this interchange of words.

Jim asked, "Spade, where'd you sell the beef you drove
out of Pitchfork?"

Spade said warily, "Why?"

"You took it through a pass to the east slope, didn't you?"

"What if I did?"

"There's a pass up there. One that's lower than any you
can see from here."

"What's this leadin' up to?"

"This," Jim said. "On my way in here, crossing the peaks,
I noticed that the railway makes a big swing to the south
around the foot of the hills, sort of like a big horseshoe.
There's a lot of waste there—waste of time and money. It
struck me they might have found a way straight across the
hills if they'd looked hard enough."

"I've thought o' that," Dawes commented. "It's two hundred
miles around, the way the rails go."

"Spade, there's a low pass up there. I think you know

about it. All I want is a yes or no. Have you found a short cut across the peaks?"

Jim's breath was coming shallowly as he waited for the outlaw's answer.

Spade said finally, "Yeah. It's the canyon where you found the hideout, deeper'n all get-out, and there's an off-shoot above the canyon that's plenty hard to find. I made a deal with a small outfit over near Cody to take my stuff."

"And that offshoot runs on a line above Kittering's place, doesn't it?" It was a strain on Jim to make his words sound casual; he knew Spade, knew the outlaw might shy away from admitting much of anything in connection with his rustling activities.

But Spade's answer came willingly enough. "Guess it won't cost me nothin' now to admit it. Yeah, you can look down and see Kittering's east fence three, four miles away."

Jim let out his breath in a gusty sigh. "There you've got it, Miles."

"Got what?"

"Hell, Miles. It's plain enough," Johnny Dawes said.

"Allard's reason for wanting your place," Jim went on. "He's a director of the Sierra and Western. Naturally, they'd come to him to help buy a right of way through this country. You heard what Spade said. There's a canyon up there, one lower than any of the passes. Allard knows about it, so did Chalmers. Allard's been trying to crowd you out to get his hands on all that land. But you didn't crowd fast enough. Chalmers came in, probably wanted to see you about buying a right of way through your land. Allard tried to bribe him first, as his letter said. When that didn't work . . ." Jim hunched his shoulders, his implication plain.

Kittering said in a hoarse, tense voice, "You mean Allard killed Chalmers?"

"Or had him killed. He had to have more time."

The full force of this new indictment against Hugh Allard hit Kittering and the others like a blow. Kittering said gravely, including all four—Jim, Spade, Two Card and Dawes—"Here's something I want straight before this goes any further. I settle with Hugh Allard! No one else! You get it?"

Spade said, "Sure." Jim and the others nodded.

Kittering turned slowly to face the jail. "Let's get this thing done!"

22

KITTERING didn't at once move out from the woodshed as he finished his brusque suggestion. He seemed to be hesitating while his mind took in the full import of the telegram, of all that had happened tonight and of all that Jim had so shrewdly guessed. He stood there, his shadow bulking solidly in the faint starlight. It was as though now, for the first time, he knew the full enormity of Hugh Allard's guilt and was appalled by it. Far out on the flats a train's whistle called two long signals and he took out his watch and glanced down at it and then dropped it back in his pocket again. It was too dark to read the time, and his move had been purely automatic before his run of thought.

Shortly, Jim's low voice broke the tension. "How do we go about it, Kittering?"

"Split up, take to the alleys and go in through the office. I'll wait on the walk with Dawes while you three go in and blow off the locks. Why didn't we think to bring along a jughead for Fats?"

"He can double up with me," came Dawes' easy drawl.

"Then let's get on with it." Kittering was through waiting and stepped out around Two Card and led the way from behind the far corner of the shed.

Spade and Two Card followed Kittering, heading for the gradual embankment on the near side of the tracks and, beyond it, the narrow passageway going along the jail's far side.

"Stick with me, Johnny," Jim said, and started out toward the alleyway between Slater's store and the jail.

He moved warily, trying to make no sound as his boots trod the edge of the railway's gravel bed. The warning signals of an unknown danger were threading his nerves. Two days ago, while riding to Kittering's from Pitchfork, he'd had the same feeling without knowing what caused it. Tonight he blamed it on the long keyed-up hours he'd spent since dawn; a lot had happened since then and a lot had gone out of him.

Dawes, close beside him, said in a low voice, "We've got to watch Miles, Jim. When he's like this he takes chances, he's wild as—"

A gun's startling explosion cut in on his words. Jim, whose

glance had strayed across to Kittering, saw Two Card Bates fold at the waist and lurch off balance at the exact instant of the shot.

A split second afterward Kittering whirled, stumbled into Two Card, then gathered the outlaw in his arms as he was falling. He shouted, "Cover!" and lifted Two Card in his arms and started back for the woodshed at a run. Other guns cut loose from the roofs of the buildings flanking the jail. Spade, slower than Kittering, lunged sideways momentarily as a bullet either hit him or came close. Then he was following Kittering at a zig-zag run, arms crossed over his waist for his draw.

Jim's glance had instantly swept around from Kittering to Dawes and beyond. He sensed that they were too far from the shed to gain its shelter easily. At the same moment he saw a waist-high pile of square-cut ties twenty feet on down the tracks and pushed Dawes that way, saying, "Over there!" The next instant a bullet swept his Stetson from his head.

Johnny Dawes streaked for the cover of the tie pile with Jim three strides behind. Jim saw two slashes of powder flame point the darkness up there along the roofs. As Dawes dropped to the ground up ahead, Jim left his feet in a rolling dive, right hand stabbing to holster and palming up a gun. He tried one snapshot at the roof as he hit the ground and rolled in behind the ties. Dawes, already crouching at the far end, let out a sharp breath as a scream echoed into the night from the rooftops. He looked back at Jim over his shoulder, grinning. "Dead center! If the slug didn't get him, the fall did!"

A spasmodic burst of fire rattled down on the shed and the stack of ties. Over behind the shed a .45 answered twice. A thin-drawn silence held for several seconds, until Dawes, hugging the gravel and leveling his Colt methodically, shot once. He hunched back and rolled over. "Missed him, damn it!" He squinted his eyes as a chip flew off the corner of the nearest tie before the answering volley of the guns on the roof.

Lying there, waiting out this renewed burst of firing, Jim saw vague shadows bulging the line of the shed's rear wall and called, "All right, Kittering?"

The deep bass voice of Block K's owner came back solemnly: "They got Bates."

Out across the flats the train whistle sounded again, nearer now. Dawes said, "They've got us cornered! We can't even get to our horses!" They had tied them along the far wall of the shed, in a direct line of fire from the roofs.

Two more shots came from Slater's store, then one from the roof of the saddleshop on the far side of the jail. Kittering didn't answer that fire, and in the ensuing silence Jim heard the faint hum of the approaching train singing along the rails.

He turned to Dawes. "When that train pulls past, we move."

"Not a chance! It's a two-car passenger hitch. Won't give us time."

Jim lay there trying to think. They could take their chances on running back across the open ground beyond the woodshed. But that would be a risk and they wouldn't have their horses. As the rumble of the approaching train grew louder, his mind tried to search out another way. There didn't seem to be any. Allard's men—and there was no doubt but what those guns on the roofs were Pitchfork's—had nicely trapped them. Allard's crew wasn't at Block K, as they'd supposed, but here in town. Holden was in jail charged with murder. Allard's story that Kittering was holding Blythe must have spread through the town by now; it would be only a matter of time before more guns backed those already against Kittering, who would be hunted down as mercilessly as a mad dog run amuck.

Dawes breathed ominously, "Jim, we're in a hell of a spot!" He spoke as though telling Jim something he hadn't known before.

Now Jim could hear the pound of the locomotive's exhaust as it was thrown back by the first few buildings two hundred yards away, at the outskirts of town. The train's light suddenly swung straight down the tracks and illuminated the scene. Against it, he saw the shapes of Kittering and Spade Deshay behind the woodshed. Spade was kneeling beside Two Card lying on the ground.

Jim had had warning of Kittering's rash temper and called, "Don't make a run for it, Miles!" trying to shout above the roar of the train.

Then, suddenly, he had a thought that made him roll over to a crouch. He glanced along the row of the stores, seeing one far down that jutted out close to the tracks. He had the time to say briefly, "Stay set, Johnny!" before the locomotive drew abreast of him.

He came to his feet and ran in toward the fast-moving train. The first of the two passenger coaches swept past him, its brakes squealing as the engineer slowed for the station. But it was still going fast. Jim ran close alongside, now shielded from the men on the roofs. Without slowing his stride he reached out for the rear handrail of the end coach as it blurred past. He caught hold and was jerked off his feet. His arm stretched out, pulling his weight along; a sudden stab of pain went into his wrist. Then his momentum carried him inward and one knee struck the bottom step of the car's platform. He caught his hold and got his feet under him.

He swung quickly outward onto the ladder that climbed to the car's roof and went up it. Behind him came a sporadic exploding of guns, uneven, vicious. He hurried to swing himself to the roof of the car. Once there he stood in a crouch, seeing the overhanging roof of the store he had noticed from down there sweeping past him.

He thought he was too late, and nearly hesitated. Then he jumped and his long frame vaulted across the ten-foot space between car roof and that of the store.

His boots struck on the roof's edge and he threw his body sharply sideways in a roll and slammed hard into the wall of the next building. It sickened him a little to look back and see the narrow strip of tarred roof that had saved him from instant death. Then he put that from his mind as he came to his feet, hearing the guns far back along the tracks again.

He climbed from the roof and up across the peaked one of the adjoining building. The sound of the guns down there stopped suddenly, and he had one wild moment in which he thought that maybe Kittering and the others had tried to make a break for it and been shot down. Then a single sharp explosion told him that the fight wasn't over. He jumped across an eight-foot open passageway that separated two buildings. Then he was over another peaked roof and crossing the next flat one. He looked obliquely down and saw that the woodshed beyond the tracks lay only two buildings away. This next building—the one beyond with the gradual pitch to its roof—was Slater's store.

He edged upward along the shingled slope, his boots slipping a little. He looked toward the street and could see the second floor of the hotel. He caught the sound of subdued voices out on the walks. A window midway the length of the hotel was open. He could see faintly a man's head and shoulders leaning out of it and thought, grimly, that whoever had rented that room tonight was getting his money's worth.

Near the crest of the roof, he flattened his body and edged upward slowly. He reached down and drew his right gun from holster. He took the time to punch out the two empties and put in fresh loads. Beyond, he heard a gun speak three times. Then he pushed himself upward so that he could look over the ridge.

Down across the far side, he saw two vague shapes crouched behind the false rear parapet. He tried to lay his sights on the nearest, but in the darkness he couldn't be sure of either the sights or his target. He shot by instinct, and hard on the heel of his gun's explosion saw his target come erect and heard Trent Harms' wild call.

"They're up here! Get down!"

Pitchfork's men had been caught by surprise. Not knowing how many guns were against him and only that he was exposed now, Harms' reaction was the natural one.

After calling to his men Harms turned and fanned his gun empty, four shots, that made a riot of swelling sound. He aimed at the roof's ridge. Jim winced as a bullet flicked a splinter from the ridge pole that gouged his face. Looking down there again, he was in time to see Harms turn and run—finally sliding off over the eaves gutter and dropping into the passageway alongside the jail. His companion, tardier, tried the same line of escape. But, instead of jumping at once, he turned and opened up with two guns on the vague line of the ridge. His shots were wide. Jim dropped his Colt into line and triggered once. Pitchfork's man grunted, vainly threw out his arms to regain his balance and fell stiffly backward and downward out of sight, the thud of his fall into the passageway plainly audible.

Beyond the jail, Jim heard men running across the saddle-shop roof toward the street. He stood up, called, "Come on, Kittering!" and started walking the ridge toward the street. Below he heard Harms running across the walk out of the passageway, and toward the saddleshop. The creaking board awning told him how the other Pitchfork men were leaving their roof. He could hear people running down the walks and concluded that the appearance of the Pitchfork men had flushed a few bystanders out of the way.

Suddenly, a gun flashed in the open window of the hotel's upper floor. A hard blow on Jim's left shoulder carried him off balance. He fell, letting his knees buckle under him, and was halfway down the roof slope before he could slow his roll. He lay belly-down and emptied his .38 through the open window across the street. Strangely enough, his shoulder didn't hurt; but a wetness along the thick muscle over his shoulder told him he was bleeding.

He forgot that as boots echoed up along the passageway immediately below. He called "Kittering!" and Johnny
Dawes' voice answered, "Down here, Jim!"

He worked down to the edge of the roof, swung out over
the gutter and dropped into the passageway.

Dawes said, close behind, "Nice work, Jim! Deshay and
Miles took the other side."

Jim went up the passageway, reloading, and came abreast
the wide porch of the store and even with the side window
of the sheriff's office. He lifted a boot and kicked out the
window's lower sash and stepped in through it as Kittering's
bulky shape wheeled in through the door off the walk.

Kittering said, "Who is it?"

Jim said flatly, "Cover the window, Kittering. We're going
in after Holden!"

As Jim turned toward the back of the office, to the spot
where he remembered the door, Kittering knocked out two
panes of the street window with the butt of his Colt. He knelt
there, glancing toward the hotel a moment. Then he raised
his gun and thumbed three slow-timed shots toward the hotel.
The gun's explosions were deafening in the confined space
of this small room. From outside, at the mouth of the alleyway at the far side of the jail, Jim heard another gun add
its din to Kittering's; he knew that this must be Spade and
gave Kittering the credit for having used the foresight to
leave the outlaw there to cover the street.

As the echo of Kittering's shots died out along the street's
wide canyon, Jim flicked a match alight and shielded its
flame in a cupped palm as he inspected the jail door. A big
sturdy padlock sealed the steel-face door. Jim said, "Back,
Johnny!" and fired two shots at the padlock. Lighting a
second match, he saw that his lead hadn't broken the lock.
So next he put the muzzle of his gun close to the shank
of the double hasp. He fired again. In the darkness he
reached out and found the heavy steel bent and twisted. He
shot once more, the sound of his gun blended with that of
Kittering's second burst, and this time the hasp broke off
from the door's face.

As he and Dawes strode down the short corridor between
the cells, Holden's voice said ominously, "That you, Harms?"

"Hell, no!" Johnny Dawes told him, striking a light.

Fats Holden's long face broke from severity into a wide
grin as the matchlight struck into his cell. "I'm damned!"
he breathed. "You didn't waste much time gettin' here!
What's up out there?"

"Later, Holden," Jim said quickly, his words punctuated by the exploding concussion of his single shot at the cell's lock. The plate of the lock broke under the bullet and Holden, sensing the urgency in Jim's tone, slammed his shoulder against the grilled door and broke the lock open.

As Holden stepped out, Jim handed him his second gun and belt and wheeled back into the office once more.

"Holden there?" Kittering asked as he heard them come into the office.

"Right here, Miles. How does it look?"

Kittering came away from the window as Jim put his query. From the alleyway close by, Spade's gun laid a flat sound along the street and was answered by several shots from the upper story of the hotel. Kittering said, "I'm goin' across there! Keep me covered!" and swung around toward the door onto the walk.

Jim reached out and took hold of his arm, pulling him back sharply. "And get killed?" he snapped. Then, "This way!" He pulled Kittering toward the side window of the office. "Johnny, stay here and keep those guns across the street busy!"

He and Kittering and Holden stepped out the window. When Jim turned to go back along the passageway, Kittering said in anger, "Hell, I'm not runnin' out!"

"No one's runnin'," Jim told him. "If you want your try at Allard, stay with me."

"But why go back there?" Kittering asked.

Jim ignored his question, not taking the time to explain as he ran back along the narrow passageway. He heard Kittering and Holden following and presently the three of them were standing in the mouth of another passageway four doors below the jail. Up the street, Johnny Dawes' and Spade's guns were lining a rattling fire across at the hotel. From this point they could see the street wasn't as deserted as it looked. Hushed voices came from the doorway of a store close by, and across the street a light glowed in the window of Mary Quinn's restaurant, its outwash vaguely showing other men standing across there in the shadows. Sands had been stirred from its deep before-dawn sleep. But these men watching the guns flare out down the street were making no attempt to join in the fight.

As they paused there, Kittering said, "Now what?" not querulously, for he was seeing the possibilities of this move of Jim's.

"Get onto the roofs across there if we can," Jim told him.

Fats said abruptly, "Mary Quain would let us use her upstairs window."

"Then come on!" Kittering led the way out across the walk.

Jim and Fats, close behind Block K's owner, carried their guns openly in their hands. Someone in the near store doorway whispered loudly, "It's Kittering!" the awed quality of his voice reassuring Jim that the townspeople had no wish to take sides in this fight now.

Jim and Fats were going in through the doorway of the restaurant when a man called out sharply two doors below, "Back, damn it! Want to get shot?"

"Bailey's down there, Miles," Fats told Kittering, recognizing that voice. "Didn't see us."

His voice echoed hollowly through the empty room of the restaurant. On the heel of his words, the curtains at the door to the kitchen parted and Mary Quinn stood there. Her blonde hair hung loosely about her shoulders and she wore a dark red wool robe gathered tightly by a knotted cord at her slim waist.

When she saw who it was her eyes widened and she breathed, "You, Fats!" in a hushed voice.

"We want to get out onto the roof through your upstairs window, Mary," Fats told her. She looked at him mutely a brief moment, alarm in her eyes, then nodded and held the curtain aside for them to pass through around the end of the counter.

A narrow stairway led up out of her kitchen. Kittering and Jim went ahead, Holden hanging back. Jim heard the girl say tensely, urgently, "Be careful, Fats!" and then Holden's step was mounting the stairs.

Mary Quinn's bedroom was dark, the rectangle of the curtained window the only relief in the blackness. Kittering opened the window and sat on the sill, swinging his legs through and dropping four feet to the roof of the neighboring building. A desultory pair of shots sounded along the street as Jim and Holden followed. Kittering said sharply, "What's the matter up there?" and went on, wasting no time now, going up a roof slope on hands and knees. The hotel's high outline was in sight in the far shadows, two buildings away.

"They may be thinkin' of this!" Holden called in a strident whisper, but if Kittering heard he gave no sign of it.

Shortly, they were on the flat roof adjoining the hotel— the roof Jim had jumped onto from his window two nights ago. There were four windows along this side. Jim said,

"Take the back one, Miles," seeing that the back one was open; Kittering swung off that way.

He stopped below the window. "Give me a boost," he said to Jim; it hadn't occurred to him but what he was to go in first.

"I've got a bum shoulder," Jim said. "Fats, you're the goat." This brief letdown had made him aware of a throbbing pain in his shoulder. But he could move it easily and knew that no bones were broken.

They stiffened and faced the street as a sudden violent slam of firing came sharply from out there. They heard Dawes' and Spade's guns now. Kittering smiled bleakly. "That's more like it!" He pushed Fats down and heaved himself up onto his foreman's back, reaching up and catching hold of the window sill.

"Don't forget me!" Fats said as Jim stepped up onto his shoulders. Kittering was already out of sight through the window overhead.

Jim had trouble pulling himself up. He found his left arm nearly useless, and only managed to keep from falling by a last upthrust of a boot that caught on the window ledge and braced him. He had to close his eyes and lean back against the wall, once inside the room. Gradually his reeling senses steadied themselves. His right fist clenched his hurt shoulder in a hard grip that finally numbed the pain. Then, one knee braced against the wall, he reached down from the window with his good arm and caught Fats' wrist and lifted. Fats got his hold on the sill and climbed on up, saying as he eased in through the window, "What's wrong with your shoulder?"

Before Jim had the time to answer, an explosion ripped its way along the hallway beyond the open door. Fats grated, "Why in hell didn't he wait for us!" and tramped loudly across the room to the door.

Jim caught up with him and laid a hand on his arm. "Easy!" he whispered. "I know my way around here. Let me go first!" He led the way soundlessly out into the hall, turning up along it toward the street.

Far up the corridor they heard steps cross a room and then a gun laid its shattering echoes along the hallway. In the following silence, hearing Holden's shallow breathing behind, Jim wondered where Kittering was and damned the man's impatience in not waiting. Now they wouldn't know whose guns they faced.

All at once a voice spoke up there, Trent Harms': "I don't like this, Hugh! Not a damn' bit! There's only two jaspers over there. Ought to be four, five if they busted Holden out!"

Answering him, Hugh Allard's voice said in sharp derision, "Spooked, Trent?"

23

AFTER that, the stillness grew so complete that Jim reached back and laid a hard hold on Fats Holden's shoulder, thinking that the sound of the thin man's breathing might give them away. The hallway, the whole building, seemed as deserted as it had three nights ago in the early-morning hours when he stood looking down at Chalmer's body in the chair by the washstand, waiting while the old clerk summoned the sheriff. Yet he knew that three, probably five, men besides himself and Holden were somewhere in this hallway or in these rooms. Harms' query and Allard's answer had shown a tension between the two men. Harms already sensed that something was wrong here; Allard probably sensed it too, but was coolly playing for a break.

Up there, somewhere, Miles Kittering had heard those two voices and was waiting for his chance. For the last ten seconds the guns at the jail had been silent. Spade, who hadn't been told what was happening, might be waiting for a target, saving his lead. Johnny Dawes was probably reloading. Jim longed for either of them to open up again. The utter stillness was almost too much to stand.

When it was broken, by the small sound of something slurring across the boards of the floor close at hand, the raw edges of Jim's nerves were frayed almost to the breaking point. His hold on Fats' shoulder tightened, warning the other to silence. In his right hand, the smooth cedar butt plates of the .38 were clammy with perspiration. He swiveled the gun up in line with the sound uncertainly, for he wasn't sure of its exact direction.

"Trent!"

Hugh Allard's muted call along the corridor brought Jim up rigid, then eased the tension out of him instantly.

"Trent! Get back here!"

This time Allard's call was louder, more intent.

Again, he got no answer. The flat echo of a lone shot came in off the street. There was no reply to it.

"Matt, where's Trent?" Allard called again.

"He ain't here," a voice shuttled down the cross passage at the head of the stairs from a room on the far corner.

"Ran out on us!" was Allard's curt statement, and Jim heard him moving across the room at the head of the passageway.

"What's wrong across there, boss?" Matt's voice called.

Allard didn't reply. But from the room where he had spoken welled a burst of sound as his gun sent four savage swiftly timed shots out across the street.

Suddenly Jim was aware again of that presence in front of him in the hallway. It was pitch-black here, but some strange intuition told him that a man was standing close to him.

He said softly, "Miles!" He heard the quick scrape of a boot. He dodged out from the wall.

A gun's close-confined concussion wiped out the stillness. In the flare of its foot-long stab of flame, lined at the wall where he had stood a split second ago, Jim saw Trent Harms' tight-drawn square face staring across at him. He whipped out with his Colt, slashing downward at Harms' head as that brief flash died out. His weapon traveled farther down than it should have and he knew he had missed his blow. Then it connected, glancing off Harms' shoulder. Harms' chopping slash on his wrist sent the .38 spinning from his hand. Remembering the other's weapon, Jim lunged in—his arms closing around Harms' thick upper body in a drive that carried them both off balance.

They fell into the partition across the hallway, and Jim heard Holden run on past and toward the stairway. Holden shouted, "Jim!" and a gunshot from the side hallway crowded out the echo of his call.

As more shots cut loose down there Jim let go his hold an instant, trying to reach for Harms' right hand that held the gun. But Harms was too quick for him and tore the arm away. Jim threw his body in a roll across the narrow corridor as Harms' gun exploded almost in his face. The scorching heat of the powder flash swept past his face. His back slammed against the far wall; he came to his feet and dived on Harms again.

This time he pinned Harms' right wrist to the floor. He tried to slug the foreman with his left; but the muscles of that arm seemed suddenly flabby and inaccurate. Harms hit him a blow at the base of the neck that took him off balance again. He fell onto his back but still held tight to the wrist. Then Harms was on him, slugging wildly with his free hand.

Jim turned his head, took a blow on the side of it, then lifted his legs in a sudden upthrust.

His boots came up over the Pitchfork man's shoulders and locked him in front of his face and, straightening his body, Jim pulled Harms backward. The drive of the ramrod's backward fall tore his wrist from Jim's grasp. Jim sat up, reaching out to fend off the blow he sensed was swinging down at him again. It hit his left arm, numbed it, but gave him its direction. He tried to throw himself across onto Harms, but his shoulder hit the wall hard; Harms had rolled out from under him.

He heard Harms getting to his feet and, boots braced against the wall, pushed out in the direction of the sound. His shoulder hit Harms' knees and swept the ramrod from his feet, back toward the head of the stairs. As Harms went down with a heavy thud, Jim heard the gun strike the boards and go skidding along the floor, far out of reach. Then both he and Harms were coming erect.

He gathered the whole weight of his body behind the first slamming drive of his right fist. He struck out wildly into that blackness. His fist brushed one of the ramrod's arms aside and glanced off his chest. Harms struck a hard blow that caught Jim in the pit of the stomach and drove the breath sharply out of him. Then they were standing close, feet-spraddled, slugging, gouging, Harms kicking out trying to use his spurs.

Jim threw his blows at Harms' head, time and again feeling the hard bony pattern of the man's face under his knuckles. He was hardly aware that guns were speaking again along the hallway. With each blow he drove in at Harms he took half a step forward, doggedly, his brain dulled to everything but the need for battering Harms off his feet. Suddenly, behind Harms, he saw the open well of the stairway faintly outlined by dim lamplight from the lobby below. He could see Harms' shape hunched over in a half-crouch, heavy shoulders rocking as he threw vicious hard punches.

Coolly now, striking to force Harms into the head of the stairs, he struck out time and again, feebly with his left, hard with his right. Once he connected to rock Harms' head sharply to one side. But the man stayed on his wide-spread feet, desperation seeming to give him a superhuman strength. Jim couldn't drag enough air into his lungs and his arms were going leaden on him. His punches were slow—so slow that he wondered why Harms didn't simply step out of the way. It never occurred to him that Harms didn't have the strength to move aside, that he was exhausted, too.

Finally, as Harms stood within a bare step of the last tread of the stairs, he seemed to sense his danger. He glanced back over his shoulder, then went to a lower crouch. He hunched his head down between his shoulders and stopped swinging with his arms, reaching out instead and lunging in at Jim.

Every ounce of energy in Jim's lean body was behind the blow his right arm struck that last time. The travel of his fist began at the level of his knees. It ended on the shelf of Harms' chin, lifting the ramrod's upper body erect and tilting his head far back.

The Pitchfork man fell out and backward, slowly, his whole body going loose. He hit the stairs with boots already wheeling up and over his head. His body doubled and he rolled on down the steps and over twice across the lobby floor until he lay face down, crumpled, fingers clawed into the carpet.

Jim stood looking down at him, fascinated, dragging a deep breath into his starved lungs. Never before had he consciously wanted to kill a man. But now he was hoping that that fall had killed Harms. It was a brutal and nerveless thought, he realized; still, he wanted it to end that way.

He started down there, slowly, holding to the stair railing to steady himself, wanting to make sure. Abruptly, a tall gray-clad figure moved out of the shadows at the foot of the stairs and knelt beside Harms.

Jim stopped. The man down there he recognized as Virgil Pierce, and his presence sent a flood of warning through him. He saw Pierce reach to his hip pocket and take out a pair of handcuffs and expertly flick them about the unconscious man's wrists. His move pronounced Harms still alive. But it confused Jim. Why was Pierce taking Harms a prisoner?

A quick flare of anger took him, then died. A killing urge had a moment ago robbed him of his reason. Now it returned in a wave of apprehension. The guns along the hallway were ominously silent now. Pierce had effectively removed Harms from the fight. It didn't matter what happened to Harms after this. He was out of it. But Pierce was down there, representing a new threat. Jim had no illusions on the man's cold-bloodedness, nor on what Pierce would do if he saw him.

He wheeled quickly up the stairs and went back along

the hall in search of his gun. His boot kicked an object on the floor and he stooped and his groping fingers touched the cold steel of a gun's frame. Its weight told him that it was his, not the .45 Harms had dropped.

For a moment he stood there, arm bracing him against the wall, listening. He should go prowling the hallways, looking for Kittering and Holden; the firing that had sounded up here as he and Harms fought at the stairhead had meaning now, as it didn't then. But now he had nothing to go on, the stillness as ominous as it had been when he and Fats first came into the hallway. He wanted to call out but couldn't risk it. Hugh Allard had been up there three minutes ago; he might still be there, waiting, ready.

He saw a flickering light come on in the doorway at the end of the corridor. A man's elongated shadow wavered against the wall beyond the door.

He thumbed back the hammer of the Colt and started walking soundlessly toward that open door. The acrid stench of powder smoke was strong along this narrow confined space. It seemed to steady his nerves to facing whoever had struck the match in that room up ahead. Whoever it was, a Pitchfork man or a Block K rider, he was going to see this thing finished.

When Fats Holden had felt Jim's grip on his shoulder suddenly ease off, he sensed, as Jim had, that they were not alone in the narrow corridor. He heard Jim whisper, "Miles!" Then, in quick succession, he felt Jim move away from him, a gun exploded deafeningly less than three feet ahead and he heard the hard slam of two bodies colliding.

In the confusion of the following brief seconds, Fats thought that Jim had gone toward the stairs. He ran that way along the hall, calling, "Jim!"

He reached the head of the stairs. Suddenly, to his left, a .45 laid a sharp burst of sound along the side corridor. A searing pain burned along the thin man's left thigh. His glance whipped down the passageway in time to see a man's outline against the faintly lighted window at the far end. In the split second he leveled his Colt, he knew that the shape was too slim, too high, to be Kittering's. He pressed the trigger, and thumbed the hammer back as the gun bucked. The action of the .38 was smooth. He shot twice more, until that shape melted down out of the window's rectangle. He heard a choked cough and knew his bullets had found a target.

As he lowered the Colt a single shot beat along the main

hallway to send him up the passageway toward the front of the building. That close-confined explosion told him that the gun up there hadn't been aimed out a window at the jail. He was remembering that Miles Kittering was up here somewhere, remembering, too, Hugh Allard's voice as he and Jim had stood down the hallway listening.

A flood of panic took him as he stumbled blindly streetward along the corridor. A brief ominous silence was ended by a prolonged deafening burst of shots that blended together in a continuous roar. They ended suddenly, and afterward Fats heard a scuffling sound behind him at the thump of a heavy body hitting the stairs and rolling down it.

He ignored what was happening behind and plunged through the door at the hallway end, thinking of Kittering. Faint light showed him the room's single window. His throat balled up as stark fear laid its hold on him. He wanted to call Kittering's name, couldn't summon the word. His trembling fingers groped in vest pocket for a match. He flicked his thumbnail over the match's sulphur tip and squinted against the sudden flare of light, tense, his gun ready. His glance took in the gray-blanketed iron bed, a varnished wardrobe at the far wall and the white gleam of a basin and pitcher on a low washstand.

Then, almost at his feet, he saw a shadow. He held the match out and looked down. He was staring into Hugh Allard's glassy-eyed narrow face. A nausea gripped him at the sight of the bloody red-stained shirt front.

He whirled as a dragging step came from the back corner of the room. There stood Miles Kittering, a .44 hanging from his right hand, his left pressed to his side. To one side of Kittering a cluster of bullet holes had scarred the bare board wall. Kittering didn't seem aware of Holden's presence as he stared unwinkingly across at the body on the floor.

The match burned out. Fats reached for another, realizing that a moment ago those shots had signaled the fact of Kittering exacting his vengeance. Allard's call to Trent Harms had told Kittering which room to enter. Holden had no way of knowing how they had fought it out, probably would never know. All that mattered was that Kittering was still on his feet and that Allard lay there with a bullet-riddled chest, dead.

The thin man was humble before a momentary feeling of thankfulness. Then he remembered Jim Allard.

He stepped over to the door, wiping a match alight along his flat thigh. Its sudden flare showed him Jim Allard standing in the doorway, a Colt leveled in his hand, his lean face tight with nerve strain.

Jim let his breath out in a long low whistle, nosing the .38 down as he drawled, "That's better!" His glance went beyond Holden to the body on the floor, then across to Kittering. And, briefly, a smile broke the flat planes of his face, then faded as he looked more closely at Kittering. He said, "Miles!" urgently, and stepped over there and put an arm around the rancher, who now swayed on his feet.

He had seen the blood smearing the hand Kittering held to his side. He said, "Sit down, Miles." Then, jerking a nod at Holden, who was lighting a lamp on the washstand, he added, "Better get a doctor!"

Kittering breathed, "I'm all right," but leaned back heavily against the wall. For the first time, he took his glance away from Allard's upturned face and stared around the room dazedly, as though not realizing where he was. Fats Holden turned out the door and his boots struck quickly back along the hallway.

Jim ripped Kittering's shirt open. An ugly deep wound had torn the flesh away along his lower ribs on his left side. But the bullet had glanced off a rib and not penetrated.

Now, from out on the street, came shouts and the quick-timed sound of riders swinging in toward the veranda. The screen door of the lobby slammed loudly and voices shuttled in through the open window. Stepping over there, Jim saw a knot of riders directly below. He recognized one voice as Fred Blythe's, then a call from the veranda as Virgil Pierce's.

He turned slowly from the window to face Kittering. "Well, it's over, Miles," he said.

Kittering nodded slowly. He stepped over to a chair and sat down heavily on it. He gave Jim a long steady look. 'I gave him a fair chance, Jim," he said. "He had the first try."

There was a strong admiration for this man in Jim. Kittering had fought a hard battle and had won. His life from now on would smooth out into straight channels, and his tomorrows would be certain, even happy, now that he and Ann were together.

Thinking this, Jim was reminded of his own future, of something even more urgent—the presence of Virgil Pierce down there with the man who had just ridden in along the street. He had a moment of indecision as those voices came up to him again. Then, reluctantly, he stepped over along-side Kittering's chair. He held out his hand.

"It's *adios,* Miles."

Kittering's puzzled glance lifted to meet his. "Where to?"

"Back home."

"Thought they wanted you back there."

"They do. But I'll make out all right. I can pull a few strings."

Kittering's firm grasp met Jim's. The rancher's face took on a deep scowl. "We'd like you to stay on," he said.

Jim shook his head and lied calmly, "Not a chance. Back there's home, Miles."

He heard men crossing the lobby downstairs and took his hand away. "Tell Fats not to take any wooden nickels," he said, and went out the door.

Passing the head of the stairs, he glanced down and saw Fred Blythe mounting the steps. Below the sheriff, passing the counter, came Ann Allard. Jim had that brief glimpse of her before he went on, quietly, and down the narrow back stairs at the end of the hall.

Sight of the girl hardened a growing bitterness within him. He was leaving Sands tonight, for good, without the answers he had sworn to get before pulling out. But those answers to Billy Walls' death, to the murder of Locheim and Chalmers, didn't count now. What did was that tonight he had seen the score against Hugh Allard written off; that was all that mattered.

Only now did he soberly weigh his reasons for leaving and his chances on remaining. Staying on, he told himself, would be a futile gesture even if it were possible. Holden and Kittering had needed him and he had thrown in with them for private reasons. Tonight had seen the last of their trouble. There would be a new beginning for them, a settling into the placid grooves of a well-ordered life. There would be no place for him, an outlaw, no matter how willing Kittering and Holden might be to make that place for him.

Ann represented the embodiment of all he was riding away from. Under other circumstances, with a clean back trail and a solid future before him, he knew that to be able to even speak a word with her now and then, would be his ultimate hope. But a past that was now crowding in on him crowded out that hope and left nothing in its place.

He came out into the narrow yard behind the hotel, went through the gate in the picket fence and sauntered up along the backs of the stores. He passed the lean-to kitchen at the back of Mary Quinn's restaurant and was reminded of the girl's intent words as she spoke to Fats Holden before they had gone out onto the roofs. He knew that tonight marked the beginning of a new and unlooked-for chapter in Holden's life, one the thin man possibly wasn't yet quite aware of.

He came obliquely onto the street by crossing a vacant lot. Before he went over to its far side, he glanced down toward the hotel. A crowd had gathered on the walk by the hitch rails. Here, beyond the stores, the walks were deserted.

Coming up on the woodshed behind the jail, he saw a man's low shape standing near the horses.

Spade Deshay called carefully, "I'd about given you up. Headed out?"

Jim said, "I'll stop at Kittering's for the claybank."

"How'd it wind up across there?" Spade asked. "I wanted to go over and have a look. But that bunch swarmed in and I couldn't. Dawes said he'd be back but he hasn't showed up yet."

"Kittering was hurt, not bad. Allard's dead."

Spade said, "That about takes care of everything, don't it?" He gave Jim a long inspecting glance. "Are we travelin' together?"

Jim moved his head in a brief negative. "It wouldn't work. Spade. Besides, I'm going back and try to square things."

Spade smiled narrowly, his face strikingly young and handsome in this moment. "You sure believe in stickin' your neck out, don't you? Well . . ." He shrugged and stepped up into the saddle. "We had fun while it lasted, didn't we?"

"I'm sorry about Two Card, Spade."

The outlaw glanced toward the back of the shed. He said in a low voice, "He'd have wanted to cash in that way. He was gettin' old, a little tired. Maybe it's a good thing."

He reined out from Jim, said, "Adios, amigo," and walked his horse away in the darkness.

Jim stood looking after him, a little irritated at the thought of the old enmity that had lain between them—the feeling that was now replaced by something he found close to genuine affection. But he didn't belong with Spade. In time their wills, both strong, would clash again and they would go their separate ways. It was better to leave it like this, each respecting the other, to break it off clearly.

An impatience filled him as the sound of Spade's pony faded down the line of the tracks. Spade was heading south. He jerked the gelding's reins free and swung up into leather. He didn't look over toward the street and the hotel as he left town, taking the trail north.

24

FATS HOLDEN left Swain four doors short of the hotel, telling him, "I'll be along in a minute, Doc." He turned off the walk and climbed the two steps to the door of Mary Quinn's restaurant and reached out to open it. It opened before his hand touched the knob. There stood Mary Quinn. She wore a light coat. She had dressed and was leaving.

When he stepped into the light, when she saw who it was, a startled relieved look crossed her face. Then, with a choked cry that was nearly a sob, she came impulsively into his arms, saying in a broken voice, "Don't ever leave me again! I thought you'd been killed!"

Within the tall man a new hope burst into life. He hadn't understood what she'd said before tonight; he understood even less what she was saying now.

He reached down and took her face in his hands, looking down into it. "Mary, I ought to tell you about Mule," he said haltingly, with direct honesty, voicing the thing that had been preying on his mind the whole evening.

"You don't have to, Fats. I know. He was here tonight. He . . . he asked me to marry him. He told me he had a ranch near Santa Fe and offered to take me there with him. I wouldn't believe it. He was angry. Then he accused me of being in love with you." Her glance took on a new tenderness. "Fats, why haven't you told me?"

"Told you what?"

"How you feel about me."

"Would it have made a difference?"

"Yes," she murmured.

The tall man could hardly believe his hearing. He was half embarrassed, half eager, totally lost when it came to love-making. So he almost welcomed the interruption that came at that moment. A man turned in from the walk, saw them and said, "How soon before I can get breakfast, Mary?"

"Right now, Harvey," the girl said, and gave Holden's hand a firm pressure, adding in a lower voice, "You'd better get down there and see about Kittering now. Come back soon."

Holden had the feeling that all the goodness in the world was coming to life with the dawn now snuffing out the brightness of the stars in the paling sky overhead. He was suddenly once more worried about Kittering and hurried his long stride on down to the hotel and up the veranda steps.

Sid Bailey had been stationed at the door to keep the crowd out. He moved aside for Holden to enter.

"How's Miles, Sid?"

"Not bad." The deputy nodded to the group in the far front corner of the lobby.

Kittering was across there, lying on a plush settee, his shirt off and Doc Swain bending over him applying a square bandage to his side with strips of sticking plaster. Kittering's bearded face was set in pain and a sultry anger and he was looking across to where Trent Harms sat handcuffed in a rocker, the full glare of an unshaded lamp shining into his bruised and battered face.

One of Harms' eyes was swollen, blue and shut, the other puffed and red. A long gash down his left cheek bled a line of crimson to the tip of his chin. The look in his one open eye was sullen, hard.

Ann stood at the head of the couch where her father lay, her face pale and tense and a little afraid. In front of Harms' chair stood Virgil Pierce, Fred Blythe and Tom Oldham, the lawyer. It was obvious that something had been said immediately before Holden had entered to bring the sober angry looks to the faces of these people, for Blythe stood staring down at his prisoner now with a baleful light in his eyes.

As Holden crossed the room, Blythe turned to give him a quick look; then the lawman wheeled on Harms again. "All right, tell us why you did it! Why did you kill Chalmers?"

"I didn't! Whoever said I did is lyin'!"

"Hugh told me it was you. He told me a lot of other things, too. Come clean now and it may save your neck!"

Harms sat there in a stubborn silence that dragged out for several moments. Finally the sheriff shrugged and turned to Virgil Pierce. "All right, you can have him, Pierce. But you can't have Jim Allard. I'm writing the Governor in Santa Fe tomorrow. I'll tell him how things stand here. I'm going to get Jim Allard a full pardon."

Pierce said mildly, "Go ahead. I don't want him. But I do want this man. Harms isn't your real handle, is it?" he queried sharply, looking down at the Pitchfork man. "Across in Goldfield you were known as Ed Trent."

Harms' sullen look lifted to the ex-marshal. "Go on," he said in surly tones. "Make it good!"

"Don't worry, I won't have to add anything to what's already known. That reward notice says you clubbed your partner to death with a stick of firewood, fought him for six ounces of gold dust. They have a law across there. You'll hang!"

When Harms made no attempt to either deny the statement or defend himself, Pierce shrugged and nodded to Blythe. "Go ahead with this other."

"Hugh had been in to see Chalmers earlier that night, hadn't he, Trent?" the sheriff asked.

Harms said, "Had he?"

"He offered Chalmers money to hold off on buying those options. Chalmers wouldn't take a bribe. So Hugh sent you back to take care of him. You crawled through the window to his room and shot him in the back. The next morning Mule Evans was sent in to plant that note in Jim Allard's shaving mug and steal the hotel register."

Harms' face had gone a sickly yellow, but he didn't speak. He sat hunched over to one side, for his fall down the stairway had cost him some broken ribs.

Blythe shrugged and turned away.

Holden said, "What's this about options, Fred? Did you get a wire from Denver?" He had already connected the sheriff's solution of Chalmers' death with the telegram Jim had sent yesterday from the way station below Sands. But he didn't yet know how the answer to that wire had explained Hugh Allard's actions.

Blythe nodded, smiling wryly. "I reckon your sidekick outguessed me there. I didn't think to wire for the information he did. This whole thing was built up around Hugh trying to get control of land to sell the railroad for a new pass across the peaks. Kittering's layout was a big part of it."

Holden whistled softly, seeing things he had only suspected before—things Jim had told him about. He said, "What else do you know?"

"Plenty. All there is. Hugh met Kurt Locheim on the trail that afternoon. Come to find out, Hugh knew Kurt was due at the ranch to see him so he went out to meet him. Packed a shotgun on his saddle just in case."

"In case of what?"

"Just what happened. The judge told Hugh he was giving the decision against him. Hugh tried to argue him out of it. Kurt wouldn't budge and Hugh lost his head. He cut him down. Then to cover the murder, he wedged the judge's boot through the stirrup so the stallion would drag him." Blythe's face had taken on a grim look. He added, "Hugh had the gall to tell me all this tonight, on the way to Kittering's, before he slugged me and had me put out of the way . . . so he thought. Ann managed to get me out of that spot." The look he gave the girl was grateful.

Ann said in a brittle voice, "There was more, too, Fred. You told me Hugh mentioned Billy Walls and Bob Elder."

Blythe nodded. "I'd forgotten that. Walls, it seems, was riding fence that day. When he heard Hugh's shotgun cut loose, he rode over to see what was wrong. Hugh saw him and thought Walls had witnessed the killing. So he hurried back home and sent Elder and Harms out to get Walls. They caught up with him as he was headed over the peaks. It seems Walls had spooked and was leaving the country as fast as he could." The lawman remembered something then and looked at Holden more sharply. "Where's Jim Allard?"

It was Kittering who answered his question. "Gone."

"Gone where?" Holden asked sharply.

Kittering winced as Doc Swain applied the dressing to his wound. "He said he was headed out. I tried to make him stay, but he wouldn't."

Fat's look went to Ann. He saw her face lose its color and a hurt look come into her hazel eyes. He read his meaning into that look, having seen her thoughts mirrored plainly on her face once before tonight—when they had helped Jim away from the blazing barn at Pitchfork.

He said, "We can't let him run out on us like this! Hell, they've got a reward on him back there!" He was feeling much the same as Ann at this moment—hurt to think that Jim would leave this way, giving no one time to even thank him.

Tom Oldham, whose presence here hadn't yet been explained, spoke up abruptly: "You'll have to go after him, Fred. There's this matter of Allard's will."

"What about Hugh's will?" Blythe asked.

The lawyer cleared his throat in his accustomed way before making an important statement. "Hugh named Jim Allard as one of his heirs in a new will he wrote up two weeks ago. I assume now that he had the papers drawn for a motive that was far from his real wish. But the fact remains, his new will is legal."

The startling announcement affected his listeners differently. Blythe's mouth dropped open in sheer amazement. Kittering appeared bewildered, Virgil Pierce puzzled. Holden, who wasn't as surprised as the rest, was watching Ann.

He saw a gladness break across her oval face and heard her breathe humbly, "Then he was telling the truth!" She felt Holden's glance on her and her eyes came around to meet his with an imploring look.

He went over to her and said, low enough so that only Miles Kittering heard him, "Jim wouldn't leave without his claybank. You could head him off if you get out there to Miles' place in a hurry."

Block K lay in the shadow of the peaks as Jim led the claybank, saddled, from the corral. The air was crisp, cold, and a heavy dew whitened the grass out across the upper meadow. Far out beyond the flats the sun's first full light was lifting the desert's purple haze from the even horizon. It was one of those fresh bracing mornings that bore a faint reminder of winter's slow approach.

The beauty of this new day was lost on Jim, for his mind was too crowded with memories of the dark hours just passed. He had tied his neckpiece around his shoulder after washing clean his wound at the well house. In two more weeks he wouldn't know that the shoulder had ever been torn by a bullet. Perhaps the scar would occasionally remind him of these brief full days in Sands and of what he had left behind him here, the unfulfilled promise of a better and an easier life, friends, a little happiness.

He climbed awkwardly into the saddle, favoring his bad arm. His glance traveled slowly over the layout—the cabin, the spot where Ed Beeson had died last night, the freshly mounded grave on the knoll, the burned haystack. Then he looked out across the pasture, trying to judge the best way of gaining the pass upward toward the peaks. And he saw the rider on the buckskin horse coming into the far end of the pasture.

He knew instantly who that rider was, and waited with a heavy feeling of dread. He had hoped that he could put Ann Allard from his mind; now to think that he must see her again, talk to her, deepened his bitterness.

The buckskin was badly blown as she reined in in front of him. Ann's face was radiant, smiling. He lifted his hand to the brim of his Stetson and the move brought his left shoulder into sight.

Her smile vanished quickly. She said, "Jim, you're hurt!"

"Nothin' I won't get over in a hurry," he answered.

Relief came into her eyes. She gave him a long smiling look then. "You're staying," she said. Her face took on a deeper color. She seemed strangely embarrassed at what she was having to say.

"Stayin'?" He shook his head. "No, it's not in the cards."

"It is, Jim! That will Hugh had written to show you is legal. You're part owner of Pitchfork."

He remembered that first visit he'd made Hugh Allard. He laughed softly, mockingly. "Hugh should be here to hear this!" Sober again, he added, "No, Ann. Pitchfork's yours. I wouldn't hold you to that kind of a bargain."

"But I'm asking to be held to it! I'm asking you to stay!"

What he saw in her eyes, the tenderness and warmth that was in them, made him drawl soberly, "You don't quite mean that."

"I do! Would I be here if I didn't?"

He reined the claybank across until his stirrup touched hers, a wild hope suddenly stirring in him.

"Ann. Look at me." He reached out and tilted her chin up and looked into her eyes.

Suddenly, because her eyes asked him to, he leaned over and kissed her on the lips. And her arms came out and held him there.

Peter Dawson is the *nom de plume* used by Jonathon Hurff Glidden. He was born in Kewanee, Illinois, and was graduated from the University of Illinois with a degree in English literature. He came first to write Western fiction because of prompting from his brother Frederick Dilley Glidden who wrote Western fiction under the pseudonym Luke Short. In his career as a western writer, he published sixteen Western novels and over 120 Western novelettes and short stories for the magazine market. From the beginning, he was a dedicated craftsman who revised and polished his fiction until it shone as a fine gem. His Peter Dawson novels are noted for their adept plotting, interesting and well developed characters, their authentically researched historical backgrounds, and his stylistic flair. His first novel *The Crimson Horseshoe* won the Dodd, Mead Prize as the best Western of the year 1941 and ran serially in Street Smith's *Western Story Magazine* prior to book publication. During the Second World War, Glidden served with the U.S. Strategic and Tactical Air Force in the United Kingdom. Later in 1950 he served for a time as Assistant to Chief of Station in Germany. After the war, his novels were frequently serialised in *The Saturday Evening Post*. He died while on a fishing trip in 1957. Peter Dawson titles such as *High Country, Gunsmoke Graze, and Royal Gorge are generally conceded to be among his masterpieces although he was an extremely consistent writer and virtually all his fiction has retained its classic stature among readers of all generations. His short story Long Gone* (1950) was adapted for the screen as *Face of a Fugitive* (Columbia, 1959) starring Fred MacMurray and James Coburn. One of Jon Glidden's finest techniques was his ability after the fashion of Dickens and Tolstory to tell his stories via a series of dramatic vignettes which focus on a wide assortment of different characters, all tending to develop their own lives, situations, and predicaments, while at the same time propelling the general plot of the story toward a suspenseful conclusion. He was no less gifted as a master of the short story and *Dark Riders of Doom* is the title for his first short story collection.